THE JUNIPER KEY

LOSERS CLUB MURDER MYSTERY BOOK FIVE

YVONNE VINCENT

Copyright © 2023 Yvonne Vincent
All rights reserved.

By Yvonne Vincent:

The Big Blue Jobbie
The Big Blue Jobbie #2
The Wee Hairy Anthology
Frock In Hell
Losers Club (Losers Club Book 1)
The Laird's Ladle (Losers Club Book 2)
The Angels' Share (Losers Club Book 3)
Sleighed! (Losers Club Book 4)

*Scotland will never be rich, be rich,
Till they find the keys of Bennachie;
They shall be found by a wife's ae son, wi' ae e'e,
Aneath a juniper tree.*

*Attributed to Thomas the Rhymer in the book Bennachie by Alex.
Inkson McConnochie, 1890.*

A Wee Word Before We Begin

Bennachie (pronounced Ben-a-hee) is a range of peaks in Aberdeenshire, although to many it is synonymous with the most well-known, Mither Tap. The name "Bennachie" is believed to derive from the Gaelic, Beinn na Ciche, which means hill of the breast, reflecting its breast-like shape, with the distinctive Mither Tap (Mother Top) forming the nipple.

Like any ancient landmark, Bennachie is steeped in history and legends, such as the boulder throwing giant, Jock O' Bennachie. It is said that Jock lies, held by an enchantment, somewhere beneath the mountain and that the key to release him will be found under a juniper tree by a one-eyed boy who is an only son.

Aberdeenshire abounds with standing stones, castles and cairns; rich pickings for anyone with imagination. Yet a few years ago, a wee spark was lit within me during a visit to the Garioch (pronounced gee-ree) Heritage Centre in Inverurie, where I learned of the Colony, a squatter community resident on common land on Bennachie from the early nineteenth century. The neighbouring landlords eventually took possession of the commonty, demanding rents, and the population declined. The last of the Colonists, George Esson, lived there until his death in 1939, and the remains of his and other Colonist crofts can still be explored today.

Learning about the lives of these people made me wonder – what if there were Colonists in the here and now? Who would they be? My story of road protesters is fiction, of course, but Transport Scotland really did propose to build a dual carriageway through the foot of Bennachie. The local community strenuously voiced their objections, and the proposal has since been dropped.

I wish I had known about the history when my parents dragged me up Bennachie every weekend (we were poor, and it was free). Had someone told me there was a sleeping giant nearby, I think I would have been more excited at the prospect of freezing my Mither Taps off and losing my wellies to hidden rocks in the heather.

My thanks go to Una at the Garioch Heritage Centre and to Heather MacEwen, who answered a thousand daft questions and gave me a peek into the inner workings of Inverurie Police Office. Plus, Anette, Fiona, Dawn, Louise and Dianne, who are my writing angels. Finally, I can't walk away without mentioning the readers of my Facebook blog, Growing Old Disgracefully, who enthusiastically joined a heated debate as to how you express the Mission Impossible theme tune in do-dos, diddlies and dum-dums. Marvellous nonsense.

As an aside, Juniper Investments does not relate to any real companies with similar names.

PROLOGUE

The power of the afternoon sun was waning as the young woman trudged upwards. It was sinking low behind the trees, shrouding the path in a cold gloom. She shivered and removed the jumper that she had tied around her waist at the beginning of the walk, when it had been unnaturally warm for a March day in Scotland. She was used to this, though, used to the capricious weather and the long walk back to the place she called home, for now at least.

She was almost there now, at the camp they called the Colony. One more steep bank and she'd be back with her tribe. Only, things were different from when she'd left that morning; her happy little world tainted by the words of that man. Trust no one, he'd said.

She hefted her backpack from her shoulder, the weight of its contents metaphorical as much as physical. Her secrets were in there, locked away from prying eyes behind passwords and firewalls. Trust no one, he'd said.

The jumper provided immediate solace from the cool nip that had burrowed into her bones. She hadn't noticed it at first, so focused was she on getting up the hill as quickly as possible. Youth and long strides had kept her body warm, leaving her mind free to obsess over the seed that the man had planted, the notion that even here, disconnected from the world, she was not safe. But now the early evening was almost upon her, creeping stealthily through the forest dragging behind it the eerie blanket of night that only the warm fireside of the camp above could dispel.

She had walked this lonely path a hundred times, yet she had never felt so afraid as she did in this moment. Trust no one, he'd said.

Her mind being preoccupied by more human fears, the faint rustle in the bushes passed her by. Weeks ago, it would have startled her, but now, inured to the foraging of the birds and animals with whom she shared these heather slopes, the young woman paid no heed to the crackle of branches and the whisper of leaves. They did not so much as gently brush her consciousness.

The shock of the blow seemed to come from nowhere and everywhere all at once.

Bang.

A lance of pure agony piercing her brain to the very core.

Spreading. Neck, jaw, eyes, ears. Hot and bursting.

Hands out.

Knees ripping and burning.

Slowly sinking, down, down, towards the blackness.

Grey.

Panting and dragging.

Jumper snagging and pulling, then down, down again.

Gasping.

Fear, visceral, primal.

'Don't move, bitch.' Who said that?

'Enjoy the ride.'

'No. No.' Who said that?

A tightening then a prick. No, stop.

Sleepy, so sleepy. Shh. Go to sleep.

Down, down, down. Forever down.

Trust no one, he said.

And then she was dead.

CHAPTER 1

VIK GAZETTE 6th MARCH

LOSERS WIN!

The members of a weight-loss group travel to the mainland today to attend the Police Scotland Bravery Awards, where they will be presented with the Chief Constable's Special Award for Outstanding Bravery.

Losers Club, the weight-loss and healthy lifestyle group founded by islander Penny Moon, has repeatedly made the headlines for its involvement in the capture of several murderers, but it was the group's takedown of a cult leader that caught the attention of the judging panel.

Local vet, Jim Space, who was injured in the capture of Thaddeus Height, a fugitive wanted by Police Scotland since the 1970s, told the Gazette, "Aye, well, aye." A profound statement from the man who also sustained a severe brain injury when he saved the life of Penny Moon a few months earlier.

An islander, who wishes to remain anonymous, said, "Aye, and mine he murdert Elsie the librarian as well. Yon bampot Height, I mean. Nae Jim Space. He's a fine loon, for a vet. There's nae a coo on the island that he hisna had a hand in. Aye, I mean the calving, nae their backsides. Onywye, dinna print my name in yer paper. I dinna want onybody ti ken it wis Randy Mair. I couldna cope wi' the celebrity."

Losers Club members, Penny Moon, Jim Space, Eileen Bates, Mrs Hubbard, Sandra Next Door, Sergeant Wilson and Fiona and Gordon from Braebank farm, are to be honoured next Friday night in a ceremony at Garioch House Hotel near Inverurie. To thank them for their efforts in retrieving his stolen diamond last Christmas, Laird Hamish Deer has arranged for the group to spend the week in the luxury hotel, calling it "A well-deserved five-star break for some ten-star people."

In the proud tradition of celebrating our achievements as an island community, the trophy will be on public display in the big cabinet at Vik Police Office, alongside PC Piecey's Cycling Proficiency certificate and the swimming badges posthumously awarded to Fred the Fisher, three months after he was lost at sea.

· · ·

BRINGING PRESSURE TO BEAR

A march through Port Vik is planned for tomorrow, to coincide with the arrival of Elaine Bear, Cabinet Secretary for Net Zero, Energy and Transport, who will be visiting the island to discuss a proposed offshore windfarm.

The windfarm is facing stiff opposition from islanders, who rely heavily on tourism and are concerned that the installation will affect the unspoilt character of Vik.

There will be a public meeting at 6pm in the church hall, where Mrs Bear will outline the plans and hear concerns.

Mary Hopper, self-appointed chief spokesperson for the Warrior Islanders, Vik's battle re-enactment group, is encouraging all islanders to join the march and make their voices heard.

"The Vik economy is built on tourism and fishing. This will displace our fishermen from the areas they have fished for centuries, and it will ruin our beautiful seaside views. More importantly, it will scare off the seagulls, who rely on stolen chips and ice cream for their survival. Really, if they're that desperate for wind power, they just need to feed my Len a few parsnips, and Aberdeen will be lit for a week. March with us to stop the windfarm."

The Scottish Government declined to respond to Mary's statement, but #feedlenparsnips is trending on Twitter, and the

Cabinet Secretary can expect some difficult questions tomorrow.

The Parish Council has asked for volunteers to help clear up after the meeting because the football club have the hall booked for five-a-side at 8pm.

Elaine Bear is tipped to be Scotland's new First Minister following the shock resignation last month of Andrea Forglen,

A FINE FANDANGO

Araminta Hubbard stunned onlookers at the Vik Ballroom Dancing Championships yesterday with her lively fandango.

Mrs Hubbard and her husband Douglas have been practising for weeks and, while the dance isn't traditionally seen in ballroom competitions, Mrs Hubbard's modified fandango straddled the divide. It was certainly enough to take the couple through to the finals, where they will come up against Ben McCulloch's cha-cha-cha. Let's hope they can pull it off.

CHAPTER 2

'Give it a wee shoogle, dearie.'

'Cordon bleu, I think we're at the max here, Mrs H.'

'Och, we can surely fit a few more in. It's my second biggest handbag!'

'I suppose we should be glad you didn't bring your biggest one. We'd have to hire some of them shepherds come check-out time.'

'What are you on about, Eileen? Which shepherds? German Shepherds?'

'No. The ones that help folk on Mount Everest.'

'Do you mean St. Bernards? The ones with the little barrels of brandy on their collars? I always thought the Swiss must be such nice people, bringing folk a wee nip up there in the mountains.'

'Buggre-moi, the Swiss send sainted shepherds up mountains to deliver booze? On top of making nice clocks and Toblerones? Is there nothing they can't do? Maybe I should move there.'

'You'd have to move to the German speaking part, dearie. Your French still needs some work.'

'Which bit is Mount Everest in?'

7

'Oh, I think that's in the Tibetan part.'

'Oi! Will I arrest you for thievery now, or shall we wait until after the awards ceremony?'

The two women froze at the sound of Sergeant Wilson's voice. Mrs Hubbard was midway through transferring a small bottle of conditioner from the housekeeping trolley to her handbag, which Eileen was struggling to hold due to the weight of the illicit goods within.

'Well, they shouldn't leave trollies full of free stuff just lying about the place, waiting for the unwary pilferer,' sniffed Mrs Hubbard, placing the conditioner back on the cart.

'What's the haul so far?' asked Sergeant Wilson.

Eileen took a moment to inspect the contents of Mrs Hubbard's second biggest handbag and surmised, 'About fourteen shampoos, eight conditioners, five rose-scented soaps and twelve teacakes.'

'Fuck's sake!' exclaimed the Sergeant. 'You put the teacakes in with the smelly stuff? That's just ignorant. Next time, bring two bags. Right, are we off to breakfast?'

Mrs Hubbard regarded the Sergeant doubtfully. Martisha Wilson was dressed in a faded pink dressing gown and a pair of battered carpet slippers with a hole above the left big toe. Her upper torso looked suspiciously well padded.

'Will you be wanting to get dressed first, dearie?' the older woman suggested.

In response, Sergeant Wilson scowled defiantly and declared, 'The leaflet in my room said to make myself at home.' Then she marched off in the direction of the dining room.

'Is she wearing her body armour under her housecoat?' Mrs Hubbard whispered to Eileen, eyeing the rather stout retreating back of the police officer.

'She's probably expecting to be accosted by a big sausage.'

Eileen turned at the sound of a short snort of laughter and smiled to see Jim standing behind them, fully dressed in jeans, dog-haired fleece and walking boots.

Jim gave her a salacious wink and said, 'If that woman ever wants to be on the receiving end of a big sausage, she'll have to stop sleeping in her stab vest. Do you reckon she wears it over or under her nightie?'

Laughing, the trio followed Sergeant Wilson to the dining room, where Penny, Sandra Next Door, Fiona and Gordon had installed themselves at a large, circular table and were practically mainlining a full Scottish breakfast.

'God, this is so good,' mumbled Penny through a mouthful of square sausage. 'I know I should be setting an example, but I could never resist a nice sausage.'

She ignored Jim's low chuckle. If they were to get through the next three days of fabulous breakfasts, he was going to have to grow past the sniggering every time someone said sausage. Yesterday, it had taken him ten minutes to calm down after she'd asked the waiter "is your sausage locally sourced?"

Now, his expression one of contrived innocence, Jim enquired, 'How many sausages have you had this morning?'

'Three,' she told him.

'And how many for breakfast?'

'Shut up.'

'This isn't helping me shift the baby weight,' Fiona chimed in, spearing a chunk of fried tomato and popping it in her mouth.

'Och, dearie, you're slimmer than you ever were,' said Mrs Hubbard, settling in next to Fiona and ladling three spoonfuls of sugar into a large bowl of porridge.

'I wasn't talking about me,' said Fiona, jerking her head in the direction of her husband. 'I had to use the emergency sewing kit in the bathroom last night after Gordon bent over to pick up the remote control off the floor. That's the third pair of dungarees this month.'

Hearing his name, Gordon looked up and winced as his wife deftly plucked a baked bean from his beard before continuing, 'It wouldn't be so bad if he wore underwear.

Honestly, I'm having nightmares about being winked at by a muckle ginger tabby.'

'Matching collar and cuffs, eh, Gordon?' said Sergeant Wilson, clapping a hand on his shoulder so hard that a baked bean shot out of his mouth and landed on Sandra Next Door's toast.

Sandra Next Door opened her mouth to object but was beaten to the punch by Eileen, who asked, 'Why are you going paratrooper?'

'Commando,' Gordon corrected her.

'I don't think they'll let you command anything with no pants on, dearie,' said Mrs Hubbard.

'It's an expression for not wearing underwear. Me and Fiona are going to try for another baby, and I thought I'd get a head start on...'

'Whipping the boys into shape? Tadpole production?' interjected Sergeant Wilson. 'By the time you two get round to having another one, it'll be like a pair of loose maracas down there.'

Penny said, 'Sometimes I feel like I know too much about what goes on in Gordon's dungarees. Can we discuss our plans? We have five nights in a posh hotel, courtesy of Laird Hamish being pals with the owner, and we still haven't agreed anything beyond attending the awards ceremony on Friday.'

'I looked up "things to do in Inverurie" on Trip Advisor,' said Sandra Next Door. 'Don't look at me like that. I can do internets. There's a lot of stones and Kemnay Library comes in at number seven, so I thought I might stay here instead and make sure they clean the room properly.'

'No way,' declared Penny. 'We're supposed to be a weight-loss and healthy lifestyle group, yet we've eaten about forty sausages between us. How about a nice walk up Bennachie?'

Mrs Hubbard frowned anxiously and said, 'I promised my Douglas I'd be careful. We have the island ballroom dancing championships next week, and I have to be in top shape if we're going to beat Mr and Mrs McCulloch. Marjorie got a new hip last year and she's been lording it over everyone that she can do the cha-cha-cha. I'm not so sure about Ben, though. He can only go left since the stroke. Och, listen to me, babbling on about dancing. I'll try Bennachie, but I might not make it all the way up the hill.'

'We'll stick to the easier paths, and you can go back to the car any time you like,' Penny offered, showing Mrs Hubbard the leaflet she had found in her room. 'How about we try the Colony Trail? I quite like the idea of a group of olden days people sticking it to The Man and living on common land. It would be quite interesting to see the remains of their crofts.'

'If you ask me, it's disgusting behaviour,' said Sandra Next Door. 'You can't just go around doing what you please. I bet they were filthy and ruined the place for everyone else.'

Penny privately thought that Sandra Next Door ought to take a long hard look at her own behaviour but confined her response to, 'I expect some of the locals had the same opinion. Although it says here that the Colonists did skilled work, so people must have employed them. It would have been a very hard life.'

'A rod they made for their own backs,' snapped Sandra Next Door. 'If folk did that on Vik, I'd be straight on the phone to the police.'

'And I'd tell you to borrow their rod and ram it up your jacksy,' said Sergeant Wilson, flashing her an evil grin.

'And I'd write to your Chief Inspector,' countered Sandra Next Door, unsure as to all the police ranks but deciding that Chief Inspector sounded reasonably high up.

Glaring at her nemesis, Sergeant Wilson sneered, 'Good luck with that. The bugger's in hospital. They say it's his heart, but I think it's complications from the spinectomy he had when he got promoted.'

'They make you have an operation when you get promoted?' Eileen gasped.

'Aye. Complete removal of the backbone. There's a lad

standing in for him…whatshisname…usually works in Tayside but they were that short of high heidyins, they had to scrape the bottom of the barrel.'

Sergeant Wilson clicked her fingers as she struggled to remember the man's name then beamed when it came to her.

'Acting Chief Inspector Dunderheid. He's the one who gave me a row for telling Stevie Mains that if I caught him poaching again, I'd use his bollocks as a bow tie. Actually, he's a not an unreasonable man. Completely accepted that I'd exercised admirable restraint in not nailing Stevie's todger to the police office noticeboard. Which I would have done if Easy hadn't taken the police hammer home to put up a sex swing or whatever it is he does in his spare time, the wee deviant.'

'Bugger me with a nine foot–' Jim started to say.

'You wouldn't want to say that in front of Easy,' said Sergeant Wilson, wagging an admonishing finger at him.

'I somehow doubt that PC Piecey has a dark side,' Penny sighed, feeling a little sorry for the hapless clod who, having been left in charge of policing Vik in Sergeant Wilson's absence, had probably already brought the island to its knees. 'Can we get back to the point please? Are we all happy to go for a wander up Bennachie to look at the Colony ruins?'

'As long as we can do Kemnay Library tomorrow,' said Eileen. Then, catching Penny's withering glance, she shrugged and added, 'It doesn't get to number seven on Trip Advisor for no reason.'

Penny's objection was forestalled by a blast of Ice Ice Baby from across the table. Fiona peered at her phone and was about to answer, when she thought better of it. All seven of her friends were nodding in time to the beat. She let the ringtone play out, as the group sang along.

The phone had long stopped ringing, but everyone continued, their rap slowly petering out until only one voice remained.

'If there was a problem dearie, yo I'll solve it, check out

the hook while my DJ revolves it,' boomed Mrs Hubbard, like Mrs Doubtfire from the Hood, delighted to show off her party trick of knowing all the words.

After the final chorus, Gordon asked, 'Who was on the phone?'

'Penny's mum,' said Fiona. 'Don't worry. It'll be another daft babysitting question. She called me when we were on the ferry to ask whether I thought Coronation Street would be a bad influence on a young mind. Apparently, Len had threatened to divorce her if she made him watch any more Tots TV. I told her Ellie-Minty's only a few months old, so they could watch Nightmare on Elm Street if they liked. Then Sandra Next Door grabbed the phone and threatened to report Mary to Social Services if she made the baby watch anything worse than Andy Pandy.'

'What's an Andy Pandy?' asked Gordon.

'No idea, but I suppose I better call back.'

'Put her on FaceTime,' said Penny, 'so we can all see Ellie-Minty.'

Fiona and Gordon, who had long since accepted that their baby also belonged to an extended "family" of islanders, smiled as everyone crowded around the phone.

'Hello. Zero seven seven zero zero nine zero–'

Penny yelled, 'Mum, you don't need to say the number when you answer. Nobody does that anymore.'

'She's right, Mary,' came Len's voice. 'Oh, look, is that Gordon's nostril.'

'I think it is,' said Mary. 'It's definitely ginger. Imagine going on holiday and not trimming your nose hair.'

Self-consciously, Fiona pulled away from the phone, allowing the others to come into view.

'Switch your camera on, parents,' said Penny.

'Give me a minute,' Mary replied.

After much debate over which button they should press, Mary and Len's faces eventually appeared on screen.

'Sorry,' said Len. 'I think it's all the internets on this

phone. Mary gets them mixed up and I have to keep her right. It's a good job one of us knows what we're doing.'

'Is Ellie-Minty awake?' asked Fiona. 'Did she sleep through the night?'

'She's been no bother, the wee angel,' said Mary, at the same time as Len said, 'Had us up every two hours, the greedy wee madam.'

'Och, Len, don't tell them that. Here, you can see for yourself.'

The screen wobbled as Mary walked through to the living room. Not realising that she could flip the camera, she pointed the phone at the sofa.

'Ooh, that's my mum,' said Eileen.

'How can you tell?' asked Sandra Next Door.

'She always wears knickers over her tights.'

'Mum, can you raise the camera a bit please?' asked Penny. 'We can practically see what Jeanie had for breakfast.'

Jeanie Campbell came into view. She was sitting on the sofa, holding the precious, sleeping bundle in her arms. Next to her sat Mrs Hubbard's husband, Douglas.

Scowling into the camera, he said, 'Is that you, good Mrs? How's your knee? There better not have been any sweetie juice last night. We need you match fit for the dancing.'

'Only lime juice,' Mrs Hubbard assured him, neglecting to mention the generous measures of tequila and triple sec within. Perhaps she should change the subject. 'Ellie-Minty looks beautiful.'

Douglas' scowl cleared and his moustache twitched as he smiled down on the sleeping baby.

'We're taking her to the bowling club,' he said. 'She's going to be my lucky mascot.'

Jeanie Campbell moved the baby away from him and snapped, 'No, we're going to Cuppachino. Minky Wallace gave Mary and I a free slice of cake last time we took Ellie-Minty to see her. You're our lucky charm, aren't you Ellie wellie woo?'

'That's why we called,' said Mary. 'Fiona, you said to only phone if it's important, and this definitely counts as important. Len and Douglas are for going to the bowling club and me and Jeanie say Cuppachino. Which do you think is best?'

'Ooh, ooh, I know what you should do,' shouted Eileen, waving her phone at the camera. 'Vik Riding Club. It's number three on Trip Advisor. Says it's run by Percy Piecey.'

'There you go!' said Sergeant Wilson triumphantly. 'Riding club. I told you he was a wee deviant in his spare time. Although that explains the vouchers he gave me for Christmas.'

'Horse riding?' Penny suggested.

Sergeant Wilson rubbed her hands together, grinning with malevolent glee. 'Horses, men, whatever. I'll need a fucking whip and some big boots to keep them in line. Eileen, what does Trip Advisor have to say about riding shops in Inverurie?'

'So, it's Bennachie via the riding shop?' asked Jim with a sigh.

He turned to Penny and pressed his hands together in supplication.

'Do you think we could put her in the boot? I can't take another bollocking for failing to run over an old lady.'

'That was ten easy points you missed!' harrumphed Sergeant Wilson. 'If you're going to be like that, I'll go with…'

She looked around for another candidate. Her gaze rested for a moment on Sandra Next Door, who narrowed her eyes and mouthed "go to hell," before she settled on Gordon.

'…Strap yourself in, boy, and prepare to give me the ride of your life.'

Gordon's anxious squeak was muffled by Sergeant Wilson's right breast, as she leaned past him and glared at Fiona's phone screen.

'Lugs up and listen, Mary. Fred and George are supposed to be on holiday. If you phone them again for no good reason, I'll have Easy arrest the lot of you for knowingly being fuckwits in a public place. Ellie-Minty might be only three months, but you're never too young for a criminal record.'

With that, she pressed the red button to disconnect the call and looked around at her companions.

'Well, are we going or what? Get a fucking shifty on.'

CHAPTER 3

Gordon was exhausted. The others were miles ahead of him, clambering over rocks and around trees like a herd of graceful mountain goats, whereas his abject failure to lose the baby weight had rendered him lumbering and ponderous…that was a good word…ponderous…what did it actually mean? At the moment, he was pondering the consequences of marching back downhill and waiting in the car. The only thing keeping him going upwards was the fear of another "Giddy the fuck up, Weasley" and a slap on the bottom from Sergeant Wilson's riding crop.

No sooner had the thought entered his mind, than Sergeant Wilson's cry came rolling down the hillside.

'Don't make me come back down there, Weasley, you big fannybiscuit. If I have to come and get you, I'll whip your backside all the way to Mither Tap!'

He could see her up ahead. There seemed to be some other people there, too. Quite a few of them. What was that all about? Fiona's ginger hair stood out in the crowd, and she appeared to be talking to a man with a placard, but it was too far away for Gordon to make out the wording. One last big push and he'd be able to find out, he told himself. Or he could sit on that boulder over there and wait for Fiona to come down and tell him. Assuming that Sergeant Wilson wasn't true to her word, of course.

Gordon could feel the seams of his dungarees straining as he lowered himself onto the rough rock. Careful there, he thought. Fiona might actually make him dig his own grave in the woods if he burst another pair of dungers. He felt the boulder move beneath him, unsteady in its mooring. Tentatively, he wriggled his bottom sideways, feeling for a comfy spot that wouldn't cut off the circulation to his legs. Ah, that was it. A touch precarious, but nothing poking where it shouldn't be.

The small start he gave when his phone rang, set the boulder rocking again. His position, hunched over his knees, made it very difficult to pull the device from an over-tight pocket, and he wondered which would stop first - the ringing or any sensation in his fingers. He leaned back and stretched his leg out, digging deep into the folds of material. With a triumphant whoop, Gordon freed the phone and pressed the green button; however, just as he did so, the boulder tilted alarmingly, pitching him backwards into a spiky thicket. Twigs snatched at his anorak and Gordon felt his dungarees breathe a sigh of relief as the sound of popping stitches accompanied the rustle and thud of his descent. His fall was broken by a patch of heather, and he lay panting, staring up at the ragged outline of a bush, dark against the unrelenting grey of the March sky.

'Gordon? Are you okay? What's happening? Gordon?'

The voice, distant and tinny, came from above.

'Is that you, God?' mumbled Gordon.

'Christ! Are you hurt?'

'I'm okay, Christ. I fell off a big stone and down the hill. But it was good of the big man to send his only son to check on me. I have to say, Jesus, you sound a bit like Jim.'

'I *am* Jim!'

Gordon looked to his right, where his arm was suspended among the tiny twigs of the bush, the phone still firmly clutched in his hand. He let his head roll back to its former position and smiled at the sky.

'For a minute there, I was so happy that Jesus was Scottish.'

'Hang on, pal. We're coming down to get you.'

'Alright,' said Gordon, unhooking his arm from the bush and trying to push himself up. 'I'm okay, though. If I just roll onto my left side...aargh!'

Gordon's scream came directly from the belly; a sound of pure fear that carried across the mountain and up to the party above. If this had been a movie, flocks of birds would have taken off in panic. But this was Scotland at the end of a long, hard winter. This was a whole different show altogether. One where creatures were determinedly scavenging, clinging on to a precarious existence in a shrinking wilderness. One where a buzzard circled slowly in the sky above Gordon, wondering whether the ginger tabby winking at him below warranted further investigation.

For his part, Gordon was on his hands and knees, a cool breeze up his backside, vomiting into the heather. The corpse lay beside him, cold and stiff, her glassy stare fixed on the bird overhead. Gordon held up the side of his anorak, partly to shield himself from the view of the dead woman and partly to prevent the wind spraying strings of bile onto her. Already, his beard was plastered with flecks of partially digested sausage and oatmeal, and one hard gust was all it took for the inner lining of the anorak to mould itself to his face. He peeled it away and noted, to his disgust, that a near perfect imprint of his face, formed of sweat and vomit, now darkened the material. The Shroud of Spew-rin, he thought wryly, and despite his distress, he made a mental note to tell Fiona that one later. He ran a hand around the back of his dungarees. Maybe he'd wait until after she'd finished yelling at him for having no trousers left.

'I mean, it's nae a bonnie sight,' said a familiar voice, 'but flashing your arse at lassies doesn't normally kill them. You might get away wi' culpable homicide, though.'

Sergeant Wilson's head, which had appeared around the edge of the bush, was soon followed by the rest of her until she stood, resplendent in jodhpurs, riding boots and Police Scotland body armour, gazing down at the miserable figure who had just finished decorating the heather.

The body, Sergeant Wilson noted, was that of a young woman, no older than mid-twenties. She was dressed in hiking boots, black jeans and a thick, green jumper, which had likely acted as camouflage and prevented her being spotted sooner. Beside her lay a small backpack, and it took all the Sergeant's willpower not to open it. Strangely, the body bore no visible signs of trauma, and had it not been for the slightly grey tinge to her skin, the girl would appear to have simply gone for a lie down in the heather.

Weasley, however, was very much alive and currently ruining her crime scene. Because there was little doubt in Sergeant Wilson's mind that this was a crime. Young lassies didn't drop dead for no reason behind bushes, halfway up a hill. George better not have got any of his breakfast on the body. Fuck me, she thought, how much porridge can one man hold? And he must have inhaled those sausages because he definitely hadn't bloody chewed them. Well, the bugger's at the dry heaving stage, so at least he's empty.

'Here,' she said, relenting and holding out a hand to help Gordon to his feet.

Allowing himself to be hauled upright, Gordon moaned, 'It wasn't me or my bum.'

'Of course it wasn't,' the Sergeant agreed. 'Otherwise, Fred would have taken one look and died of shock long before she married you. Sit yourself down over here, man. You're shaking.'

She guided Gordon around the bush and laid his anorak on the ground at the side of the path so that he could sit down without, in her words, "hoovering heather up your hole." He appreciated that she was trying to be kind, in her own unique way.

'Is Fiona coming?' he shouted as Sergeant Wilson disappeared around the side of the bush, on her way to inspect the scene.

'I'm here. We're all here,' came Fiona's voice from behind him. 'Are you okay, love?'

Sure enough, they were there. Fiona, Eileen, Penny, Jim, Mrs Hubbard and Sandra Next Door - all were peering down at him, looking puzzled.

'What was the screaming about?' asked Jim. 'We thought you were being murdered. Sergeant Wilson hoped you were being murdered. She was off down the hill faster than Sandra Next Door that time the window cleaners missed a bit.'

'Eight pounds and they forgot the bathroom window,' Sandra protested.

'Aye, well, now we know you can run faster than a Ford Transit.'

With an air of satisfaction, Sandra Next Door said, 'They didn't get very far, and I got my money back. All that lobbying the council to install speed bumps in the village was worth it.'

Eileen could see yet another argument brewing about whether the village needed speed bumps, so she dragged the conversation back on topic, telling Gordon, 'I'm quite glad you're not dead. Your ghost would be tethered to this place, and it's a long way for us to come and visit. I'd much rather you died on Vik.'

'Erm...thanks...I think,' said Gordon. 'The poor lassie behind that bush, though.'

'Och, Sergeant Wilson will be fine. She's probably just having a pee,' said Mrs Hubbard. 'I hope there's no nettles. I once squatted in nettles and you should have seen the state of my...oh, there I go again. Blethering on and giving everyone PMT.'

'TMI?' asked Penny.

'Which is the one where everybody is annoyed with you, dearie?'

'IDC,' said Fiona, crouching down and putting an arm around her husband's shoulders. 'What happened, Gordon?'

'I sat down on a big stone, rolled off, had a conversation with Scottish Jesus and came face to face with a dead body,' said Gordon glumly.

Fiona's hand went to her mouth, and she stared at him, aghast.

'Dead? Who's dead?'

'I don't know. A woman,' he replied.

'I told you a million times to lose the baby weight!'

'I didn't roll on top of her and crush her to death! She was just lying there, already dead.'

Penny's hand shot between them, waggling a bottle of water. Gordon gave her a grateful smile, unscrewed the top and poured water into his mouth, letting it overflow and stream down his beard. By the time he was done, he had mostly succeeded in dissipating the smell of sick; however, not quite enough for Fiona to risk a kiss.

Sergeant Wilson returned, looking grim.

She said, 'Poor soul. No obvious cause of death, so we'll have to see what the pathologist says. I've called for back-up. Ha! I always wanted to say that. You don't get much chance on an island with only Easy for company, and he's no back-up. He's just the stupid wee turdweasel who used all the crime scene tape to wrap his Christmas presents. Do you have any idea how difficult it is to order more crime scene tape? I had to swap three tasers with the Tayside cops for a box o' the stuff. I'm down to sixty-seven tasers now. Is it any wonder I'm in a bad mood?'

Jim and Gordon exchanged a complicit glance. They were both wondering whether Sergeant Wilson had ever been anything other than terrifyingly annoyed…slash deranged. In Jim's opinion, the woman probably came out of the womb wearing a stab vest and roaring at her mother,

'Stop giving me that tit milk shite, and take me to your nearest cow.'

'Right, listen up Losers.' the Sergeant continued, 'You may as well make yourselves useful and help me round up the crusties before the local cops get here.'

'Crusties?' asked Gordon.

'I was trying to be polite. But you're right, George. I should stick to *achievable* goals. Tree-huggers. Filthy hippies. Penny, help me out here. What's the phrase I'm looking for?'

'People who are camping on a hillside and exercising their democratic right to protest about a road being built in an area of outstanding natural beauty?' suggested Penny.

'Close but not quite.'

Sergeant Wilson thought for a moment, then her face lit up with a broad smile, and she declared, 'Foreskin-ninjas.'

She pointed up the hill to where the demonstrators stood, identical pink snoods covering their necks and mouths, and Penny couldn't help but agree that the Sergeant had a point, especially about the baldie one in the pink fleece.

Slapping her thigh with her riding crop, Sergeant Wilson barked, 'Off ye fuck, then. Round up the foreskin-ninjas and get them to stay in their camp. I'll guard the crime scene until my lot show up. Weasley, you can stay here with me if you're not up to it.'

Gordon eyed the crop uneasily and got to his feet.

'I'm fine,' he muttered, before making a beeline for the short, steep ascent.

The others watched as he leaned into the wind, trudging stoically uphill, the back of his dungarees flapping in the breeze.

'Is that a tattoo?' asked Penny, eventually.

'No, I think it's just a bit of heather,' said Fiona, picking up Gordon's anorak and hurrying after him.

By the time the group gathered at the top of the slope, Fiona had tied Gordon's anorak around his waist to preserve what little modesty he had left. They were talking to one of the people from the camp, who introduced himself to the others as Fergus. He was a huge, shaggy bear of a man; a solid six-footer, powerfully built with a long, matted thatch of auburn hair that spilled over the pink snood. Like most of the protestors, he was dressed in jeans and fleece which had seen better days.

'Welcome to the Colony,' he said, gesturing to a cluster of tents behind him. 'We all love a fresh face here. Especially yours, Fiona.'

He wrapped a thick arm around Fiona's shoulders and pulled her into a hug. Penny was shocked by the familiarity and hoped they weren't all going to be hugged like that. Poor Fiona looked like she was suffocating. Yet, Penny noted with some surprise, she wasn't struggling. Rather, she was hugging Fergus back.

'Do you two know each other?' she asked.

Abruptly pulling away from the hug, Fiona took a deep breath and regarded her companions uneasily.

'There's something you need to know, she said. 'Fergus is my brother. Well, half-brother, I suppose. Same mum, different dads.'

Picking up on Fiona's unease, the friends looked to each other for a cue until, smiling warmly, Mrs Hubbard stepped forward and shook Fergus' hand.

'It's lovely to meet you, dearie. Fiona, why didn't you tell us you have a brother?'

Fiona, visibly uncomfortable, was frantically trying to think of a suitable reply, when Fergus stepped in and saved her the trouble.

'Because I've been in prison for the past fifteen years. For murder.'

CHAPTER 4

A long silence followed Fergus' announcement, broken only by the awkward shuffling of feet.

Eventually, Mrs Hubbard cleared her throat and said, 'Murder, dearie? Was it maybe an accident? Or a mistake?'

'Nope. I was the enforcer for a gang, and I was involved in a shooting. I got a reduced sentence for helping the police get the main players but make no mistake, I'm not a good man. Which is probably why Fiona hasn't told you about me.'

'Cordon bleu,' said Eileen. 'I don't think I've ever met an actual murderer. Have you murdered anyone recently? Because there's a woman just down the hill, and she's dead as a doormat.'

'Eileen!' exclaimed Fiona, shocked.

'I was only asking because if Fergus murdered her, then we could all be back at the hotel by teatime.'

'Is that what the fuss was about?' asked Fergus, his voice hoarse.

He sat down heavily on a stone and rubbed his forehead in his hand. When he looked up again, there were tears in his eyes.

'Can you describe the woman?'

Everyone stared expectantly at Gordon, who was busy adjusting his dungarees and tightening his anorak around his waist. Sandra Next Door gave him a sharp poke in the ribs and nodded at Fergus, who was waiting anxiously for a reply.

'Eh? What?' asked Gordon.

'Stop fiddling with your bum. The dead woman, you idiot. What did she look like?'

'Erm...eh...she had on a green jumper. Long, dark brown hair, I think. Like, middle eastern maybe. Quite thin. Oh, and her nose was pierced.'

'Layla,' Fergus breathed. 'Oh God, Layla.'

Fiona laid a hand gently on her brother's shoulder, and he flinched. She persisted, rubbing his back as he took deep breaths, struggling to compose himself.

'Who was she to you, Fergus?' asked Fiona quietly.

'My girlfriend,' he said, his voice catching in his throat. 'Oh, this is well and truly fucked up. I knew something was wrong. She went into Inverurie to meet a friend yesterday and she should have been back by evening.'

'Did she have a phone with her?' Penny asked, reluctant to bluntly ask the obvious question.

'Aye, I called her. Dozens of times. But she's gone off before without telling me, and the reception around here is shite.'

'Sergeant Wilson is treating it as a crime scene. Do you think someone could have killed Layla? Do you know who she was meeting? Maybe they know something,' Penny suggested.

Fergus' cheeks reddened and he snapped, 'What is this? Twenty questions? I'll get enough of that from the police. Whether there's a crime or not, you know who'll end up in handcuffs, don't you? Me.'

'You'll have people to vouch for you, no doubt,' said Jim, stepping in to defuse the situation before it escalated. 'Penny's asking because we've done a lot of investigating before. She just wants to help.'

Fergus looked at Fiona. 'Is this true?'

'Yes,' she told him. 'We've solved a few murders and caught a few baddies. That's why we're here. Police Scotland are giving us a bravery award, believe it or not.'

'God, I really have been out of touch. When did we last speak? It must be five years ago. I thought you were moving to the back of beyond to be a farmer. Are you a private detective now?'

'No, I'm still a farmer and we're a weight-loss group.'

'A crime solving weight-loss group?'

'Aye.'

Despite his distress, Fergus managed a short bark of laughter.

'Do you have any idea how ridiculous that sounds? What do you call yourselves? Thinvestigators? Sugar-free gumshoes? Pie Spies? No, no, I have it. Weighty Watchers.'

'Losers Club,' said Penny flatly. 'Do you want our help or not?'

His amusement evaporating as quickly as it had appeared, Fergus sagged and said, 'Aye, go on then. As soon as they find out who I am, they'll have me away in cuffs. At least I'll know somebody's got my back.'

'Then let's start with why you're here,' said Penny.

Fergus explained that after his release from prison, he had initially drifted in and out of hostels; however, the temptations of the drugs world and easy money were always there. Realising that his old life might catch up with him, he'd decided to go off-grid.

'Aren't you supposed to be on parole, dearie? Don't you have to check in with your parole officer?' asked Mrs Hubbard.

Fergus smiled. 'You've been watching too many American cop shows, Mrs Hubbard. For my own reasons, I asked not to be considered for parole. I left the prison on licence for six months, then that was it. I was a free man.'

'And you ended up on Bennachie because...?' Penny prompted.

'I met Layla and she wanted to get away. Something to do with her family. We heard about this group of activists who were recreating the old Bennachie Colony - the twenty-first century version, anyway - while they tried to stop the new road being built.'

Fergus pointed to the groups of brightly coloured tents arranged around firepits behind him.

'Transport Scotland want to build a dual carriageway around the bottom of Bennachie to make a fast link between Aberdeen and Inverness. We've been protesting. Blocking the surveyors, demonstrating at local meetings, getting the press on side. And we live here, among the old Colony crofts. Their wells are still there from two hundred years ago, so we have water and we've been able to grow our own crops in the kailyard. The locals have mostly been fine about it, although a few are saying that we're a nuisance and destroying the hillside.'

'Yet it must have been incredibly hard, living here over the winter,' said Penny.

'It was, but we got by. We're funded by a charity based in Aberdeen. The Climate Change Collective - CCC. They're always up here, bringing us food and things.'

Fergus removed his snood and flattened it out to show them the logo, explaining, 'They give us clothing and enough money to provide the basics.'

'What about Layla? What's her story?' Penny asked.

Fergus looked uncomfortable and shifted his gaze towards the bank of Scots pines to his left.

'She had some trouble with her family. Her dad's Egyptian, and I think he disapproved of her lifestyle, so she left home. We met in Kemnay Library.'

'Oh, that's a good library. Number seven on Trip Adviser,' Eileen assured him.

Fergus smiled weakly and said, 'I'd been drifting around

the North East, doing odd jobs, and she was in Kemnay visiting a university friend. I came in to use the library printer a few months ago, and we got talking.'

'Is this the same friend she was meeting in Inverurie?'

'Aye. Anni-Frid Mackie. Her mother was a big ABBA fan, apparently. I remember Layla laughing about that.'

Tears pricked Fergus' eyes once more and he used the heels of his hands to roughly wipe them away.

'She was such a bright star. My bright star.'

This time, his efforts to compose himself failed, and he dissolved into heaving sobs. Fiona squatted down and wrapped her arms around him. He didn't resist, instead hunching forward into her embrace and allowing himself to be comforted. Fiona glanced over her shoulder to Penny and shook her head to signal that the time for questions was over. For now, at least.

Penny, Sandra Next Door, Eileen, Jim and Mrs Hubbard moved away, giving Fergus space to be with his family. The other protestors had gathered on logs around a large firepit in the centre of the clearing and, clearly realising that something was wrong, were casting curious glances at the group.

'Can we sit with you?' Jim asked, gesturing to one of the logs.

'Depends,' said a woman in a blue hoodie.

Whereas the others were in their twenties, this woman was older. It was difficult to say exactly how old because she had the haggard, prematurely lined face of a drug addict. Her missing front teeth rendered her speech slightly slurred.

'I'm not sure what a seat can depend on,' said Jim. 'If it depends on the tiredness of my feet, I can tell you that this morning I've been made to stand in a riding shop while a hellion with an inventive set of curse words tried on fifteen pairs of jodhpurs and pronounced them all as making her fanny look like a burst cushion on a cheese wire. Then I was dragged up a bloody big hill. My feet are telling my arse to glue itself to that log immediately. Now, if it depends on you wanting to know what's going on further down that very hill, then I'm the man with the story.'

The woman flashed him a toothless grin and said, 'I was only going to ask if you had a spare cigarette. But thanks for sharing. Sit yourselves down.'

Sheltered as it was by trees, the clearing felt like an oasis of calm away from the cold, stiff breeze that had accompanied the Losers Club friends on their walk so far. The firepit cast a welcome warmth and, Jim noted with some longing, was the source of the delicious smell of sausages. Some of the demonstrators were toasting them over the open fire, the drops of fat hissing and sending up small showers of sparks. Jim looked on with envy. Sausages are so versatile, he decided. Unlike any other food, you can cook them in a myriad of ways, *and* they're great for willy jokes. Bugger addressing haggises... haggi?...haggis, he thought, sausages should have their own PO Box! He'd have to tell Penny that one. He could, however, sense that now was not the time and gave himself a silent high five for emotional intelligence, before tuning Radio Jim back into the conversation.

Penny was explaining that Layla's body had been found and that Sergeant Wilson had requested the demonstrators stay together in the main camp until the police could speak with them. Their reactions to the news appeared to be genuine shock, and they spoke over one another in their haste to find out more.

'Are you sure it's Layla?'

'Dead? But she was fine yesterday.'

'How?'

'Scary lady with riding crop and strapping thighs is a police officer?' asked the older woman, seemingly as stunned by this as she had been by news of the murder. 'I thought she was raising money for charity, dressed like that.'

'She's an acquired taste,' Jim replied. 'Sorry, I don't know your name.'

'Claire. And this is Jake, Aaron, Phoebe and Dani. I see

you've met Fergus. Poor Fergus. He'll be heartbroken. Him and Layla were planning a trip to Orkney in the summer.'

'I thought you were here for the long haul to stop the road,' said Jim.

Dani shook her head sadly and said, 'We come and go. Claire and I have only been Colonists for a couple of months, but Aaron and Phoebe have been here since the beginning. People go off to support other causes or go back to their families. Usually there are about thirty of us, but the others are at a public meeting with the council today. Do you know what happened to Layla? How she died?'

'Sergeant Wilson doesn't know,' said Penny. 'Had Layla been in the camp long?'

Jake replied, 'She was one of the new ones as well. Maybe since December, just before Claire.'

He looked to the others for confirmation, and they nodded in agreement.

'She said she was having trouble with her dad,' he continued. 'Not sure what it was, exactly. I think he works for Aberdeen University. A scientist or something. I overheard her on the phone to him one day, and she was really angry. Said she was ashamed. Told him there was no way back for her.'

'No way back? What did she mean by that?' asked Jim, pre-empting Penny's next question.

Jake didn't know, and Jim looked around the group to check if the others had anything to add, but they merely shrugged.

'When did you last see Layla?' he asked.

Dani took up the reins, telling him, 'Yesterday morning. She said she was going to walk to Pitcaple and get the bus into Inverurie from there. Claire, you walked down the hill with her. Did she say anything to you?'

'Just that she was going to meet a woman friend for lunch and did I need anything from town. She didn't say who she was meeting, but I got the impression they weren't from

Inverurie because she asked me if I knew where it would be best to park. Anybody from the town knows that the back of the car park behind New Look is free.'

'Did Layla have any enemies?' asked Penny. 'Was she involved with anyone or anything she shouldn't have been? Did she take drugs?'

'Absolutely not,' Dani replied, her tone firm. 'She was very anti-drugs. She told me she'd had a problem with them but had been clean for years. She didn't even want anyone smoking weed around her. Everyone in the camp liked her, as far as I know, although she was one of the quieter ones. Didn't talk much about herself. Helped out a lot with getting the kailyard ready for planting and pitched in with the chores. She spent most of her time with Fergus, so he'd probably know more than us.'

Phoebe tucked her hands into the pockets of her fleece and muttered, 'It's weird to think that she went out yesterday with plans, and today she's never coming back.'

'We'll probably all be gone soon anyway,' said Claire glumly.

At Jim's questioning glance, she added, 'That's what the public meeting's about – the alternative road plans. There's a rumour they've decided not to build the road here after all, so I suppose that will be it for our Colony.'

'Not me,' said Aaron. 'I'm staying.'

'You might survive the summer, but there's no way you'll survive another winter up here without the money from CCC,' Claire told him.

'I bet the minute we're gone, they'll change their minds and build the road here,' said Phoebe. 'I'm with Aaron. I'm staying.'

They sat in comfortable silence for some time, the Colonists no doubt contemplating the demise of their small community, Penny and Jim mulling over everything they'd just heard and Sandra Next Door quietly fuming about the lack of hygiene in the camp.

It was clear that Mrs Hubbard had been thinking along the same lines because she suddenly burst out, 'How do you even wash your hair? Would you like me to bring you some shampoo? I have a few bottles going spare. I didn't like to say, given the circumstances, but some conditioner wouldn't do Fergus any harm. Oh! I'm so sorry. I'm not very good with long silences, dearies.'

Mrs Hubbard clapped a hand over her own mouth, her cheeks reddening as she realised that she may have offended the Colonists.

'Cordon bleu, Mrs H,' said Eileen.

'Maybe if you finish that story from earlier about squatting in nettles,' said Jim in a mock stage-whisper, 'nobody will notice that you just called them dirty.'

'Don't worry,' Claire reassured her. 'We've been called a lot worse.'

'Foreskin-ninjas at the ready!' bellowed a voice from below.

Sergeant Wilson appeared at the top of the steep path, panting slightly from the climb. One hand reached inside her stab vest to scratch at her right breast.

'That's the problem with all this running up and down hills,' she said as she reached the group. 'Stuff gets sweaty. Och, I can't reach inside this thing. It's too tight. I need a stick. Does anybody have a stick?'

While the Colonists stared dumbfounded at the Sergeant, Sandra Next Door gestured around her and said, 'You're in a wood. I think even you, with your questionable detective skills, might manage to find a stick.'

Ignoring her, Sergeant Wilson picked up a twig from the ground and thrust it inside the vest, working it vigorously back and forth.

'Ah!' she groaned in satisfaction. 'That's a relief. I decided I'd take a leaf out of Weasley's book and go commando today. I thought it might help with the yeast. Aye, top half only. If that goes well, I'll try the bottom half tomorrow, although I might need a longer stick.'

She extracted the twig, gave it an experimental sniff and handed it to one of the two policemen who had just staggered to a halt beside her.

'PCs Kirk and Chapel,' she announced. 'The holy pair. They're here to have a word. Losers, you come with me. We're going to go back to the hotel and leave this to the locals.'

Confused, Penny protested, 'But we were–'

'Sticking your noses in as usual. The scene's secure and there's a team on their way from Aberdeen to do the interesting bits. Our work here is done. Giddy up! There's a hotel jacuzzi nozzle with my name on it.'

Sergeant Wilson tapped the side of her nose and waggled an eyebrow at Penny.

'Yeast.'

CHAPTER 5

Disregarding everything she had ever said about healthy lifestyles, Penny ordered afternoon tea for herself and her companions. They now sat in the hotel lounge, in front of plates of tiny sandwiches, eyeing up cake stands heaving with miniature scones, small eclairs, tartlets and cakes.

Gordon, freshly showered and wearing an old Iron Maiden t-shirt over a pair of Sergeant Wilson's jodhpurs, was seated on a leather wingback chair, holding forth on the subject of vegetables.

'What exactly is cress, when it's at home? A decoration. No flavour. So why bother putting it in a sandwich? You may as well give me an egg sandwich, without the cress. I wouldn't even notice. Cress is the most pointless vegetable on the planet.'

'What are your thoughts on okra?' asked Jim, genuinely curious. This conversation was right up his alley.

'I think Ms Winfrey is a very fine interviewer and an inspirational lady,' Gordon declared.

'Almost as good as David Lettuceman,' said Jim, nodding gravely.

'Will you two shut up?' said Penny, exasperated. 'Have you heard anything more about Layla, Sergeant Wilson?'

'No. Acting Chief Inspector Dunderheid is coming to the hotel to take George's statement. He said he had to come anyway, to drop off some things for the awards ceremony, so he'd kill two birds with one stone. I told him to bring reinforcements. It would have to be a fucking boulder to kill Big Bird over here.'

She jerked a thumb in the direction of Gordon, who looked mildly hurt and self-consciously tugged his t-shirt over his belly.

'Dunderheid. Is that his real name?' asked Eileen.

'Aye. That's his name.'

'Really?' said Penny, highly sceptical.

'It seems a strange name,' mused Mrs Hubbard. 'Now, are you sure you haven't got it mixed up? I had a penpal at school called Fara Tucker and for a whole year, I addressed all my letters to Tara–'

'I am hurt and offended that you doubt me. If you don't believe me, you can ask him yourself. He's over there.'

A tall man in black uniform stood in the doorway. He was in his mid-forties, with neatly clipped brown hair and the lean, slightly craggy appearance that had first attracted Penny to Jim.

Not bad, she thought, watching him nod in recognition to Sergeant Wilson. She noted that a change seemed to come over the Sergeant. On spotting her boss, she had stood up and arranged her face into a rictus grin. This was interesting. Penny didn't think she'd seen Sergeant Wilson attempting respect before. It took all her self-control not to whip out her phone and take a photo so she could prove to everyone back home that this had really happened.

Slightly flustered by her attraction to the policeman and Sergeant Wilson's unusual behaviour, Penny approached him and held out her hand.

'Chief Inspector Dunderheid, pleased to meet you. Penny Moon.'

The Chief Inspector's face darkened, and he flicked a glance towards Sergeant Wilson, who quickly rearranged her features into an expression of innocent surprise.

'Acting Chief Inspector Hunter Deed,' he corrected, shaking Penny's hand.

He moved towards the group, and behind him, Penny shot the Sergeant a murderous glare.

The woman never moved. She had once more adopted the rictus grin and said, obsequiously, 'Good afternoon, sir. I apologise for Penny. Let me introduce you to everyone.'

Hunter Deed seemed relaxed and friendly, happy to share a pot of tea and help himself to a fondant fancy, yet his grey eyes were watchful. He chatted informally with the group at first, getting to know them a little before bringing them up to speed with the events that day.

'I can't say too much, obviously. We've notified the victim's family and a forensics team is still going over the scene as we speak. At the moment, it's being treated as an unexplained death, pending the outcome of the pathologist's examination.'

'When do you think that will be?' Fiona asked.

'We should know more tomorrow, but strictly between us, our initial thoughts are that it's probably drugs-related. An overdose.'

'But she didn't take drugs,' said Penny. 'According to her friends, she was very anti-drugs.'

'I can't share all the details with you. I'm sorry about that. I just want to reassure you that we're doing everything we can to find out what happened to the victim.'

'The victim,' snorted Fiona. 'We know that she's my brother's girlfriend, Layla.'

'As I said, we're doing everything we can.'

'What about Fergus?' Fiona asked.

'We haven't made any arrests in connection with this incident,' he assured her. 'Until we know more, we're treating it as an unexplained death.'

'I'd like to help with the investigation, boss,' said Sergeant Wilson.

'You're on rest days, Martisha. There's no need for you to help. We have plenty of boots on the ground already, but thank you for the offer.'

'I'd rather help than sit around here drinking tea,' the Sergeant insisted.

'I said no, Martisha. You're too close to one of the witnesses.'

'With all due respect, sir–'

Deed, aware that her next words were unlikely to contain any respect at all, cut in, firmly telling the Sergeant, 'I'm not going to change my mind, so please don't ask again.'

He turned to Gordon, who had managed to sneak a third fondant fancy when Fiona wasn't looking and was now wearing a suitably grave expression, oblivious to the pink icing and cream pasted to his beard.

'Erm, you might want to get that,' said Deed, gesturing with a finger to his own chin.

Gordon's tongue flicked out and captured a spot of cream, before just as quickly flicking back in again. He glanced sideways to check whether Fiona had noticed. She had, but her worries were much larger than Gordon's expanding belly, so she paid him no heed.

'I've asked the manager if we can use his office while I take your statement,' Deed continued. 'Are you ready to start? You can take your tea with you.'

The moment they'd gone, Fiona began to pace the room. The napkin she had been twisting in her fingers fell unnoticed to the floor, as she threw her hands up and said, 'We have to tell Fergus. With his history, if they think it's drugs-related, he'll be the first person they look at. They'll assume he got the drugs and made her take them, or even worse, *forced* her to take them.'

'And what do you think?' asked Sergeant Wilson. 'Would he have supplied her with drugs? Hurt her?'

'No! Look, I know it's a tired cliché, but he's no angel. He says himself that he's not a good man. Yet he's a different man from the one who went to prison. What you don't know about us is that we didn't have a good life. When I was five, our mum overdosed on heroin. I was taken into foster care and ended up with a family who adopted me and loved me. Fergus was ten and not so cute. My older brother stayed in a children's home until he was sixteen, so what sort of life do you think he had?

'By the time he was thirteen, he was running away from the home and dealing drugs. By the time he was twenty, he was an enforcer for the gang, and by the time he was twenty-five, he was doing fifteen years for being in the car during a drive-by shooting in Glasgow. He wasn't the one holding the gun, but it didn't matter.

'None of that excuses what he did. All of that made him realise that he could either spend his life going in and out of prison, looking over his shoulder, or he could take control and walk away. He chose to walk. He chose to stay under the radar and get on with his life, away from that world because the alternative was a premature death when the gang caught up with him. There were at least four attempts on his life while he was in prison. Eventually, someone would succeed.

'I am one hundred percent sure that if they test Fergus, the worst they'll find in his system is cannabis. He wouldn't have risked going back to prison by supplying hard drugs to Layla or anyone else. If she took drugs, she either got them herself or someone else was involved.'

Fiona looked around wildly, her eyes wide, begging the others to believe her.

'Sit down, Weasley,' said Sergeant Wilson. 'I'll be straight with you - it's not looking good for Fergus. I thought if I took part in the investigation, I could keep an ear to the ground, but Dunderheid knew exactly what I was up to. I can still do that through some well-placed colleagues, but if this turns out to be murder, it'll be handed over to the Major Investigation Team in Aberdeen and they're a closed shop, so that only gives you maybe a few days to convince Dunderheid that Fergus wasn't involved.'

'How do we do that?' Fiona asked.

'For a start, I can't be seen to be connected with anything you do. I can't use police resources to help you, and if you break the law, you're on your own. And we all know that you're a bunch of sneaky bastards, so you'll probably break the law at some point.

'Three possibilities that the police will be considering here - Layla willingly obtained and took the drugs on her own; Fergus or someone else supplied them and either coerced or encouraged her to take them without meaning to kill her; or someone deliberately injected her and made it look accidental. The first option is an unintentional overdose, the second is possibly culpable homicide and the third is murder. If they suspect Fergus was involved, he'll be arrested.'

Penny mulled this over for a few moments then said, 'We know that Layla was anti-drugs and had been clean for years, so the most likely scenarios are coercion or murder.'

'Dunderheid will be focussing on options one and two,' said Sergeant Wilson. 'He won't consider murder unless there's direct evidence. Fergus was the person closest to Layla and has a history of drug dealing and violence. He has the connections and the ability. Senior officers love a slam dunk. It's like police Viagra. Dunderheid is probably a human tripod right now, thinking of all the shiny things he'll get to wear when he's promoted.

'To convince him that Fergus isn't involved, you should concentrate on finding an alternative explanation for who could have either forced her to take drugs or got close enough to stick a needle in her, and why. If I were you, I'd start by having a full and frank discussion with your brother, Weasley. He'll tell you more than he'll tell my lot.'

Relieved to finally be feeling less helpless, Fiona said, 'Thank you. I know you tried to stick your neck out for me, and I won't forget it.'

'Aye, well, it's nae Make a Ginger Happy Day,' said the Sergeant gruffly. 'There's a complaint on Dunderheid's desk and I'm hoping for some reflected glory to take the sting oot of it. Ernie on the Other Side said I held his false teeth hostage for three days to make him confess to stealing a Mars Bar from Paula McAndrew's paper shop.'

'And did you?' asked Jim.

'Aye, but that's nae the point. Him and Mrs Hay went on a geriatric shoplifting spree because apparently life is boring when you're in your nineties. They had to be stopped. Anyway, he knew his teeth were fine. I sent him a photo with the ransom note every day.'

Jim shrugged.

'Fair enough. What was he complaining about, then?'

'Somebody allegedly rubbed chilli on them before I gave them back.'

'Somebody?'

'Aye, it's a complete mystery,' snapped Sergeant Wilson, standing up and glaring at the group. 'Stop asking stupid questions about Ernie's teeth and get on with whatever you need to do to save Fergus. Make calls, speak to folk, be sneaky bastards. Just don't fucking involve me.'

She stalked out of the lounge, leaving the others to stare after her in surprise.

'I suppose she's right,' said Penny.

'Yes, anyone could have put the chilli on Ernie's teeth,' said Eileen.

Sandra Next Door rolled her eyes heavenward and sighed, 'Lord, save me from these people.'

'They totally could have,' Eileen protested. 'I watch telly. Folk tamper with evidence all the time. Someone could have bribed Easy or picked the lock to wherever she kept the teeth.

Or, and I think you'll agree that this is the most likely explanation–'

Penny held up a hand to stop her friend right there.

'Pooh Bear, you're my best pal in the whole world, but if this is something to do with aliens or ghosts, I swear I'll make you lick Sergeant Wilson's itchy boob stick.'

'I was going to propose that someone could have hypnotised Sergeant Wilson to do it,' said Eileen haughtily. 'I will ignore your threatening behaviour, Rubber Duck, and I suggest we get on with proving Fergus had nothing to do with Layla's death.'

Penny conceded with a nod and explained, 'When I said Sergeant Wilson was right, I meant that if we're to exonerate Fergus, then we have to show that Layla was murdered. That she'd never have willingly taken the drugs and that someone other than Fergus had a reason to want to harm her. I don't know how we do that. Any ideas?'

'Maybe we could find out where the drugs came from,' Jim suggested.

With a small gasp, Mrs Hubbard put down the slice of lemon drizzle cake she'd been inspecting and said, 'Years ago, Mrs Brown on South Street had her hedge stolen by the very man who sold her the seedlings. It turned out she'd grown a lovely cannabis farm for him. She didn't know, of course, and the lad was just a petty criminal at the time. Yet that was only the start of his career. He lives in Aberdeen now, and I hear he is the main man for drugs in these parts.'

'What are you thinking, Mrs H?' asked Jim.

'That never in a month of Sundays did I think that I'd be asking Minky Wallace if she could arrange for us to talk to her dad.'

Impressed with her ingenuity, Jim offered Mrs Hubbard a high five and explained to Sandra Next Door and Fiona, 'Penny, Eileen and I were at school with Minky Wallace from Cuppachino. She's the only decent one in that family. The rest are a bunch of criminals. Her dad and sisters moved to

Aberdeen over twenty years ago. Although, I'm sure I heard that he was in prison for arson.'

'Not so, dearies,' said Mrs Hubbard, settling in for a good gossip. 'Mrs Hardman told Charlie from the butcher's who told Ivy at the hairdresser's who told me that Minky's Uncle Isaac was the big man in Aberdeen, but he got put away for setting fire to a rival's house, with the wife and kids in it. Isaac Wallace ran things around here, but while he's away in the Big Hoose, Donald Wallace is in charge.'

'I'm confused,' said Eileen.

'Why am I not surprised?' sneered Sandra Next Door.

Ignoring her, Eileen asked, 'He committed arson, and somebody gave him a big house?'

'The Big Hoose. Barlinnie jail,' Jim explained.

'The important thing is,' said Penny, 'Minky Wallace's dad is the top gangster in Aberdeen, so we need to ask Minky if she can persuade him to help us.'

'But we don't even know what drug it was,' Eileen pointed out.

A voice from outside the lounge door shouted, 'It was probably heroin.'

'I thought you'd gone,' Jim called back.

'Fuck off, turdnugget.'

'You fuck off. You were supposed to have done that already anyway.'

'As if I'd leave you lot completely unsupervised. It would be like you lending Easy your wank mag collection and expecting it to come back without the pages stuck together.'

'We do have the internet nowadays.'

'Do you have something you'd like to confess?'

'What? No! I'd never do that.'

'Aye, right. Do you hear that, Penny? Jim's got his onanism problem firmly in hand.'

This was followed by a delighted cackle, and despite Jim's outrage, Penny couldn't help but give a small snicker of her own.

'If Janey Godley out there's done, can we get on with agreeing a plan?' asked Sandra Next Door.

'Aye, I'm not here anymore. I've definitely gone away,' came the voice from beyond the door.

Penny took a moment to marshal her thoughts, then said, 'We need to split into groups. I suggest that Fiona and Gordon try to get more information from Fergus. Anything he can tell us about Layla's background, her friends, what she was doing the day she left. Does anyone know if she ever made it as far as Inverurie, or did she come to harm on the way back?

'Eileen and Sandra Next Door, would you mind going back to Bennachie tomorrow morning and talking to the Colonists? The ones who were away today should be back by then. One more thing - even though she's only been there a short time, that Claire seems to have taken charge. Find out what people have to say about Layla *and* Claire. Claire was the last one to see Layla alive. I don't know what it is, but something feels off about her.'

'She's certainly past her use-by date,' muttered Sandra Next Door sourly.

'Mrs Hubbard,' Penny continued, 'would you come with Jim and I to see Donald Wallace? I'll call Minky in a minute and ask her to arrange a meeting with him. In the meantime, if you can think of any skeletons in his closet that we can use to encourage his co-operation…'

'My superpower,' Mrs Hubbard agreed.

'The Avengers assemble,' shouted the voice from beyond the door. 'Iron Man, Hulk, Thor. Have I missed anyone out? Oh yes, Wank Boy and the fucking Curtain Twitcher. Hooray. We are all saved.'

'Finally,' said Penny, raising her voice to be heard above the stream of invective being hurled in the direction of Sergeant Wilson by Jim. 'Finally, we need some internet research into Layla and the rest of the Colonists. And before you say anything, no, not the kind of internet research Jim likes doing.

'Fiona, do you think you can get their personal details from Fergus today? Even just surnames and where they're originally from will do.

'Eileen and Sandra Next Door, could you ask our hacker friends to do a deep dive into them please? Are they who they say they are? Financials, criminal history, anything that could give someone a reason to kill Layla.

'We'll regroup to discuss results tomorrow lunchtime.'

Tasks agreed, everyone slowly drifted off to make their arrangements until only Penny and Jim were left in the lounge.

'I don't know about you,' she said, snuggling up to him on the leather sofa, 'but I could do with a lie down. It has been an exhausting day, and it's far from over.'

Jim slung an arm around her and kissed the top of her head.

'Aye, well, all that sexual tension must be tiring.'

'What do you mean?'

'I ken fine that you fancied Dunderheid.'

'Only because he looks a bit like you. With a few more muscles.'

'Oh aye? I bet he doesn't have a furry belly button, an extra-long armpit hair and a weird lump on the back of his knee. See? You've already got the superior model, so no need to settle for the likes of Dunderheid.'

Penny gave a short snort of laughter and leaned down to kiss said belly button through Jim's fleece. These moments where they relaxed into easy banter were the best. It had been a long road to get to the point where they had this confidence in each other. Somewhere along the way, they'd managed to ditch the doubts and the emotional baggage, and just be.

'I suppose I better call Minky,' she sighed, reluctant to move.

'You know she fancies you, don't you? I told her about the

cold feet in bed, the hairy toes and the incessant farting, but it didn't seem to put her off. Give her a call, then maybe we could have a lie down for an hour. Play your cards right and I'll even let you put your cold feet on my warm knee lump. Hopefully, Fiona's doing the same as we speak. Phoning Fergus, I mean. Not sleeping with me.'

'One thing about Fergus puzzled me,' said Penny.

'What's that?'

'When we told him about Layla's death, he seemed shocked and upset, but he never asked how she died. Wouldn't that be one of your first questions?'

Penny bit her lip and locked eyes with Jim, watching comprehension dawn.

Eventually, he nodded slowly and murmured, 'Unless you already know.'

CHAPTER 6

Gordon couldn't believe they were doing this to him; they were making him walk up Bennachie again. Worse, now that Mrs Hubbard was no longer with them, everyone was going at a much faster pace, especially Sandra Next Door who was using a sweeping brush as a walking stick.

To be fair, thought Gordon, Sergeant Wilson's jodhpurs were comfier to walk in than his dungarees, even though she'd made him wear underpants. He did an experimental lunge. There was something liberating about the stretchiness of jodhpurs. You just didn't get stretchy men's trousers. Fiona was making him go shopping for new trousers later, and Gordon wondered if perhaps a detour into the women's department might be in order.

Ahead of him, Sandra Next Door was discussing strategy with Eileen.

'I know we need to find out about Layla and Claire,' she said, 'but while we're there, we may as well see if any of them know about the murder. We'll prioritise the ones who were around in the days before Layla left.'

Eileen enthusiastically agreed to the plan, although she had no idea how they were going to put it into action.

Sandra Next Door assured her, 'It's about being organised, and I thrive on order. Watch and learn, my friend.'

As soon as they arrived in the Colony, Fiona and Gordon went off in search of Fergus, leaving Eileen and Sandra Next Door with the other Colonists. Their number was much larger this time, and Eileen wasn't sure how she was going to talk to almost forty people by lunchtime; however, she hadn't factored in Sandra Next Door, who stood on a large rock and shouted, 'Who hasn't been in camp for at least three days?'

Ten hands went up.

'Do you have someone who can verify that?'

Ten heads nodded.

'Did you give this information to the police?'

Ten heads nodded and a voice piped up from the back, 'Aren't you the police?'

'I'm your worst nightmare, son,' said Sandra Next Door. 'An angry woman with a broom.'

'Aye, a real live witch,' Eileen confirmed, earning herself a dirty look from her friend.

Not to be outdone, the wag shouted, 'Where's your pointy hat?'

In response, Sandra Next Door jumped down from her perch and handed the young man her sweeping brush, before instructing the ten people to "tidy up this muckhole" with such force that no one else dared challenge her further.

'Back to the rest of you,' she said. 'Who here first joined the Colony yesterday or today?'

A smattering of people raised their hands, and Sandra packed them off to help with the cleaning operation.

'Minus the six we spoke to yesterday, we're down to fourteen,' she told Eileen. 'Not an exact science, but these are the people most likely to have been around when Layla left and who need to account for their whereabouts in the twenty-four hours between her leaving and her being found.'

'God, you're good,' breathed Eileen.

They took seven people each and had soon whittled them

down to one person of interest, a young woman who introduced herself as Kendra Lawson. She was a little cleaner than her cohorts, her long blonde hair framing a pretty, heart-shaped face, and although she was dressed in the same combination of fleece, anorak and jeans, even Sandra Next Door could recognise the expensive brand names. Just another trust fund baby looking for a cause, she thought bitchily. Although she clearly hasn't cleaned her teeth this morning.

'So, Kendra,' said Sandra Next Door, offering the woman a breath mint, 'you were in camp the morning that Layla left. Did you talk to her?'

'Of course. I share…shared a tent with her. She said she was going into Inverurie to meet her friend for brunch. Anni-Frid Mackie. Look, Layla and I were friends, and I don't think I know anything that can help you figure out who killed her.'

'Killed her? Have the police told you that someone killed her?'

'No. I thought…maybe the others said…I don't know. I just assumed that she'd been killed.'

'Erm, okay. How did you two become friends?'

'Actually, we knew each other from school. We both went to St. Margaret's School for Girls in Aberdeen. She was in the year above me, so we didn't hang out so much at school. It was more before and after school. She lived near me, and we'd walk to school together, then sometimes do our homework at each other's houses. We were friends, but not best friends. She was always very reserved and didn't have a big group of friends. I think it's to do with her dad, Professor Hamdy. He did something at Aberdeen University, but I got the impression there was a lot of family money. He was really strict, and Layla wasn't allowed to do girl stuff, like going to the cinema at the weekends or hanging around with boys.'

'No boyfriends?'

'Not when we were at school. We lost touch after we went

to university. I went to Edinburgh, and she went to Aberdeen. I didn't see her again until we bumped into each other here.'

'You said her dad was strict. What about her mum?'

'Her mum died in a car accident in the Middle East when she was three. It was just her and her dad. She told me once that her dad's job brought them to Scotland. Oh, I remember now. He was a geologist. He worked for an oil company before he worked at the university. It's so sad that her whole family is gone.'

'What do you mean by gone?'

'Her dad took his own life in January.'

'Oh, that *is* sad. Layla must have been devastated.'

'She was. She told me they'd argued a lot because she didn't agree with his job.'

Kendra held up a hand in anticipation of Sandra Next Door's next question.

'Don't ask me what that was all about because I don't know. I can only guess it was something to do with oil. Layla was really passionate about the environment and belonged to a lot of climate change groups. She even took part in Just Stop Oil roadblocks last year. Her boyfriend, Fergus, might be able to tell you more about her arguments with her dad. All I know is that she was in bits when he died and blamed herself.'

'Why would she blame herself?'

'I don't know. Ask Fergus. He was the one that brought her into the Colony in the first place.'

'Did Layla have any enemies that you're aware of?'

'I don't think so. I can't see how anyone could dislike her. She was self-contained, but not unsociable.'

'Was Layla close to anyone else in the camp?'

'She got on well with Claire. They were both early risers, so they'd go for a morning walk together most days.'

'What's Claire like? How did she come to be in the Colony? She seems much older than the rest of you.'

Kendra shrugged and said, 'She's alright, I suppose. She

can be bossy and quite loud sometimes. Maybe argumentative. But who isn't? I think we've all become frayed at times, living here over the winter.'

'Did she have a lot of influence over Layla?'

'I'm not sure what you're trying to say. They went for morning walks together. I didn't notice anything unusual, if that's what you're asking. Layla didn't open up to many people, and you'd have to ask Claire if she opened up to her.'

Sandra Next Door wasn't sure what she was trying to say about influence either, so she let it slide and repeated, 'How did Claire come to be at the Colony?'

Kendra gave this some thought, before replying, 'I don't know. This is going to sound strange, but when I think about it, Claire talks a lot and says very little. What I mean is, she's loud and chatty, always happy to give an opinion, but she hasn't said much about herself. Not that I've heard, anyway. You could ask the others. They might know more than me.'

Sandra Next Door thanked Kendra and went to join Eileen, who was sitting by the firepit, cup of tea in hand, chatting with some of the group who were supposed to be tidying up. Sandra sent them scurrying off to finish their chores and brought Eileen up to speed with what Kendra had told her.

Her account complete, she asked, 'What about you? Found out anything useful?'

'Not really,' said Eileen. 'A lot of them are getting ready to move on. They've achieved what they came here for. The road's going to be built elsewhere. Some of the people who've been here for ages are making noises about staying in the Colony, at least until the end of summer. I suppose it must feel like home to them.'

Sandra Next Door gazed around the camp, her lip curling in disgust.

'If I had to live here, there would be a lot more than one murder. Have you seen Fiona and Gordon?'

'They headed back down a while ago. Fiona had a face like thunder, but I was speaking to someone at the time, so I didn't ask what was wrong. I hope Gordon hasn't burst another pair of trousers. Can you imagine explaining to Sergeant Wilson that you've wrecked her new jodhpurs?'

'We should get going as well,' said Sandra Next Door. 'Give me a minute first, though.'

It took more than a minute, perhaps ten, for Sandra to retrieve her broom and inspect the neat piles of firewood, tents swept of debris and stacks of clean plates. Eventually, she announced a generous seven out of ten for effort and left the Colonists with a sharp admonishment to "keep it like that, or I'll be back to skelp your backsides."

Fiona and Gordon were waiting in the car park. Fiona was in the midst of what everyone in Losers Club called "doing a Sergeant Wilson," namely screaming swear words and threatening the future fertility of Fergus' manly parts. Gordon appeared to be trying to calm her down but was in fact only risking his own manly parts.

'Fiona,' said Eileen sharply. 'This isn't like you. What's wrong?'

Fiona's cheeks were flushed, and tears welled in her eyes as she roared, 'It's bloody Fergus. He's gone. Left the Colony. Vanished. When I spoke to him yesterday, I told him to stay put. He knows that you're all helping me, and he decided to run off anyway. I'm so sorry. After everything you've done.'

Eileen put a comforting arm around her, and Fiona dissolved into heaving sobs.

'I feel so ashamed of him,' she squeaked. 'He's not even answering his phone.'

'It's okay,' Eileen reassured her. 'He's the idiot, not you.'

Her voice still constricted by emotion, Fiona whined, 'He's made himself look guilty. Maybe if I hadn't been here or got involved, he'd have stayed.'

Eileen hugged Fiona before peeling her away and gently passing her over to Gordon. He held his wife tightly and murmured into her hair, 'You're not responsible for anything Fergus does. Ellie-Minty, yes. A grown man who happens to be your big brother, no. Remember that time Ellie-Minty did a projectile poo down the front of my dungarees? That was your fault.'

Through her sniffles, Fiona managed a weak laugh.

'And remember when the wee minx was so sick, it got me heaving then you heaving too, and we all had to stand in the shower in our clothes to clean off? Your fault. And the time you played peek-a-boo, and she smiled her first smile? Again, your fault. What about when she had a fever and you had to stay up all night holding her? All your fault.

'You're a good person darlin'. Your brother was always going to make his own choices. Now, it's up to you whether you want to carry on trying to save him from himself or let him deal with it on his own. Either way, nobody will be judging. With the possible exception of Sergeant Wilson.'

'She'll say I should kick his arse into next week,' said Fiona, wiping her nose on Gordon's anorak which, despite his efforts with a bottle of hotel shampoo, still smelled faintly of sick.

Sandra Next Door gave her a wry smile and assured her, 'That's the censored version of what she'll say. Tell her that Gordon peed in her jodhpurs. That'll distract her.'

'Don't tell her that!' Gordon exclaimed, his voice a couple of octaves higher than usual. 'I'm staying here. I…I'll camp with the Colonists, I'll use Fergus' tent… or I'll move to America, no, no, I'll defect to North Korea.'

'And sell state secrets on composting toilets?' asked Sandra Next Door. 'We're only asking you to make a small sacrifice for your wife.'

'That's enough,' said Eileen. 'Sandra Next Door, you know fine that you're just trying to annoy Sergeant Wilson.'

'Granted, but the thought of Gordon selling composting toilet secrets to North Korea has cheered Fiona up. She's feeling sorrier for him than herself, eh? So, no more shilly-shallying. Let's get back to the hotel, see what the others have found out, then agree what we'll do next.'

CHAPTER 7

The call to Minky Wallace had gone rather well, Penny thought. The café owner had asked her if she was still with that lanky streak of piss, Jim Space. Penny had said that she was, then pointedly enquired as to whether Minky was still seeing Grant Hay.

'I will give you a call should that change,' said Minky.

'My answer won't change,' Penny assured her. 'How's the new carrot cake working out?'

'Och, now you're just flirting with me. It's selling like…I was going to say hot cakes, but you know what I mean. Your Hector's a baking genius. If he ever gets tired of working for Jimmy Gupta, he could set up on his own.'

'He needs to finish his baker's apprenticeship first. He does, however, have a brilliant chocolate cake recipe, if you're willing to make a trade.'

Penny had explained their predicament and, despite Minky being somewhat reluctant to get in touch with her father, she had eventually agreed to set up a meeting provided Penny gave her the secret to Hector's Victoria sponge. Penny wasn't sure how her son would feel about this, and she suspected that she might end up forking out for the fancy food mixer he had his eye on. This was turning out to be a very expensive favour.

Minky had called back that morning, which was why Penny, Jim and Mrs Hubbard now found themselves standing outside The Marine Arms in Seaton. The sign above the pub was peeling and one of the windows had been boarded up, seemingly for quite some time, Penny thought, judging by the black streaks staining the panel. All in all, the place had seen better days.

She could see that Jim was nervous. This area may only be a stone's throw from the quiet cobbles of Old Aberdeen, but poverty rendered them a million miles apart.

His eyes flickered warily to the surrounding houses; a uniform series of granite Victorian tenements playing sentinel to their modern cousins, the soulless communal boxes thrown up by an idealistic council in the heyday of social housing, before time and deprivation leached all hope from their poorly rendered walls. Behind the flats, high-rise blocks loomed like the grim spectre at the food bank. For there could be no feasting here. At least, not until you'd sent the bairn down to the shop to top up the meter card.

The teenage denizens, clad in fake Armani, hunted in loud packs, their lack of school attendance underscored by the graffiti on the corner store and the shouts and insults they hurled at the few older people foolish enough to pass by their hard-won territory of the wall outside the betting shop. Yet what these children lacked in education, they more than made up for in razor-sharp instincts. They spotted the easy prey hovering outside the pub and, moving as one, began to saunter over.

Jim's heart began to pound as adrenaline flooded his system. He didn't mind a fair fight, but these feral creatures probably emerged from the womb carrying knives, and he knew that he'd be no match for them. Aw buggeration, he thought, I've no choice. Penny might manage to take a couple out, but that still leaves…what?...seven? Shit, they're nearly here, and the leader in the middle looks much bigger close up.

Panic was just starting to set in, when he felt himself being nudged aside, and Mrs Hubbard stepped forward.

'Hello, dearie,' she said to the strapping lad with the big gold chain and the sneer. 'We're from the Macaroni Pie Foundation and we're looking for volunteers to test our pies. We provide an all-expenses trip to Edinburgh and pay £200 a day, just to get your opinion on our delicious pies. Is this something you'd be interested in?'

The teen looked baffled. He'd come for a fight, yet instead, here was this a weird old lady offering him macaroni pies.

'Eh, do ye have any samples, like?'

'Not today. We're only recruiting volunteers today. Trying to get in ahead of the Skirlie Society.' Mrs Hubbard shook her head sadly. 'They're a devious lot. They throw in free mince and tatties to get people to sign up, but you won't get a fancy trip to Edinburgh if you volunteer with them. The Macaroni Pie Foundation is the real shizzle, dearies. All I need are your names and contact numbers.'

She dug inside her second biggest handbag then handed a battered notepad and pen to the leader. The rest of the pack huddled round, making sure their details were recorded on the list.

A few minutes later, Mrs Hubbard collected the notepad, but not the pen, and stored it carefully inside her handbag.

'Thank you very much, dearies. I'll be in touch. Now, if you'll excuse us, we need to talk to a very nice man called Donald about a batch of heroin.'

With that, Mrs Hubbard opened the pub door and stepped smartly inside. Penny and Jim crowded in closely behind her, anxious to get away from the teenage gang.

'Bloody hell, Mrs H,' Penny hissed. 'What just happened?'

'Confuse the enemy, dearie. Reverse the narrative. Remember all those business courses I did last year? There was one on psychology, and it was full of useful tips. Plus, now I have all their details to pass on to the police. Fo' shizzle.'

'Will you stop saying shizzle. You're not Vanilla Ice. You're a seventy-something year old woman with a very large handbag and Marks and Spencer shoes, standing in a run-down pub in a ropey part of Aberdeen, where everyone is staring at us.' Penny gulped. 'Everyone is staring at us, Jim. Do something.'

The problem with being a six-footer, thought Jim, is that people expect you to be able to handle yourself. Jim did not want to handle anything in this place. For a start, the level of hygiene was Sandra Next Door's worst nightmare, and for a very decisive finish, the patrons were the lean, mean adult versions of the Lord of the Flies candidates outside. What was it Mrs Hubbard had said? Reverse the narrative? Jim wondered if running away would count. How far could he even get with Mrs H slung over his shoulder in a fireman's lift? And what about Penny?

He was saved from further internal debate by Mrs Hubbard, who once again confidently stepped forward and said, 'Hello, dearies. We're from the Stovies Protection League. Don't worry – we're not collecting money. We're here to raise awareness about the threat to the traditional Scottish meat and potato stew. Who likes stovies?'

Virtually every hand in the room went up and within ten minutes, Mrs Hubbard had the names and email addresses of fourteen new members of the Stovies Protection League. By the time Donald Wallace arrived, she, Penny and Jim were firmly ensconced at a table with Amsterdam Clark, Fingers Corrigan and Benzo McDougall, all of whom were surprisingly nice people if one ignored their alternative sources of income.

At Donald's arrival, a hush descended over the bar, and the patrons began to melt away. Amsterdam and Fingers, who until a moment ago had been arguing over which one of them would take the minutes at the next SPL meeting, suddenly remembered that they had urgent appointments elsewhere; however Benzo, slightly slower on the uptake, remained seated, until one of Donald's three goons tapped him on the shoulder and said, 'Get tae fuck, Benny.'

The tension was once more broken by Mrs Hubbard, who stood up, smiled broadly, and said, 'Oh, wee Donald Wallace. It's grand to see you after all these years. And look! You've had triplets.'

She eyed the goons, all of whom sported shaven heads and the acne scars of habitual steroid users. They were almost identically dressed in black jeans and sports jackets, their muscles straining at the seams. Donald himself oozed gangster chic; cutting a dash in the snappy grey suit, the Rolex, the slicked-back steel grey hair. He may have been short, but he carried himself with an air of authority that Mrs Hubbard didn't recall from his days of dragging up three wee girls on Vik; however, the viciousness was still there, in the beady eyes behind the designer glasses.

'Very funny, Mrs Hubbard,' he said, his tone making clear his low tolerance for jokes at his expense. 'Welcome to my office. Mindy said you need a favour.'

Who the heck is Mindy, Penny wondered. It took her a moment to make the connection. Of course, she thought. The man would hardly call his own daughter Minky, even though that's what the whole island, and even Minky herself, called her. Mindy. Must remember to say Mindy.

Jim was having his third panic attack of the morning. He just knew that Penny would fuck this up by calling the man's daughters Minky, Manky and Poopy. Every fibre of his being was now focused on silently transmitting a single thought to Penny's brain - Mindy, Mandy, Poppy, Mindy, Mandy, Poppy, Mindy, Mandy, Poppy.

'Thanks for seeing us,' said Penny. She eyed the peeling wallpaper and bare floorboards, every surface stained and sticky, the light from the windows diffuse through decades of cigarette tar and the wire mesh that held the glass in place. A faux-velvet bench, once a deep red but now faded to a sickly salmon pockmarked with cigarette burns, ran the length of the walls. The tables in front of it were nailed to the floor and the cheap plastic chairs were unlikely to be much use in a bar fight.

'Nice office,' she offered. 'I'm Ming…dy's friend, Penny. This is Jim. We need some help with finding out about someone who died from a drugs overdose.'

Penny explained that the police were fairly certain that Layla's death was caused by an accidental overdose but that she and her friends were trying to show that it was murder. Earlier, she had agreed with Mrs Hubbard and Jim that they wouldn't mention Fergus. If Donald Wallace had any links to the people who were looking for him, it might only add to his troubles. They had to tread very carefully here.

Wallace listened patiently to Penny's abridged tale of woe, then leaned back, letting his suit jacket fall open as he languidly stretched an arm over the backrest of the bench.

'What do you expect me to do about it?' he asked.

'We want to know if there were any unusual heroin purchases,' Penny told him.

'It's not like Tesco, dear. There's no receipts and a money back guarantee. It's cash only and it's done away from CCTV.'

'I just thought someone, a dealer perhaps, might have noticed if they weren't selling to their usual customers. They must get a lot of repeat customers and even new customers are likely to be of a type. We were wondering if maybe one of them has had a customer that didn't fit. Someone who stood out. They could tell us, and we'll tell the police.'

Wallace looked at her appraisingly for a few moments, then said, 'My problem is that if you find this person and it comes back to one of my dealers, all roads lead to me.'

'Your dealers must get caught all the time,' Jim pointed out. 'What happens then?'

'They keep their mouths shut, do their time and they're

looked after financially. Holiday pay, if you will,' Wallace countered. 'But you want someone who will agree to tell you, and by extension the police, that they sold heroin to a particular person. A dealer who will hand themselves in and give evidence. That's a very expensive proposition because not only do I have to give them holiday pay, but my bottom line is hit while they're off the street.'

'I don't know what to do about that,' said Jim. 'We could club together and give you some money. And I still have my Marks and Spencer vouchers from Christmas. You could have those.'

'Ten thousand pounds,' Wallace sneered. 'That's my price. I doubt your Auntie Mabel was quite that generous with the vouchers.'

He turned to Penny and gazed at her through narrowed eyes.

'You have a diet club, yes? It's quite big, I hear. Branches all over Scotland. I might consider waiving my finder's fee if you would consider taking me on as a partner. I can recoup the money through profits.'

Penny gazed steadily back at him, but her stomach was churning. She knew exactly why Wallace wanted a slice of her empire. It had nothing to do with profit and everything to do with laundering his dirty money. She was in way over her head with this man. Inwardly, she cursed herself for a fool. How could she have been so naïve as to think she could waltz in here and get this wicked arsehole to agree to help them out of a sense of altruism and some loyalty to his daughter? She was going to have to say no, and Donald Wallace did not look like a man to whom you said no. The awkward silence stretched as she faced Wallace across the pub table, their eyes locked.

'Och, it has been lovely catching up with you, Donald,' said Mrs Hubbard. 'It brings back so many wonderful memories. Do you remember that time the horse got loose in the town square and your Poppy jumped on its back and rode it away? And Mrs Taylors cat? The wee thing used to follow Mandy home from school every day and sit howling on your doorstep. It moved in with you in the end. Then there was Dazzle-gate. Do you remember? It's such a funny story. Maybe the triplets would like to hear it. Oh, listen to me going on about nonsense again. I was just telling everyone the other day that I'm no good with long silences. I get all anxious and start to babble. Would you like to hear about Dazzle-gate, boys?'

The pink spots on Wallace's cheeks were a few shades darker than the faux-velvet bench. His arm no longer rested casually along the backrest. As Mrs Hubbard spoke, he had hunched forward and was now glaring at her with murderous intent.

Through gritted teeth, he said, 'Fine. I'll waive the finder's fee on this occasion. Give me your number, and I'll get back to you.'

'I always said you were a good boy underneath, Donald,' said Mrs Hubbard, her tone of cheery kindness unaffected by the menace in his voice. 'Will I let Mindy know you send your love?'

It was only when they reached Jim's car that Penny realised how tense she had been in the oppressive atmosphere of the pub. They quickly got into the old Land Rover, slammed the doors then breathed a collective sigh of relief.

'Oh my God, Mrs H,' Penny exclaimed, throwing her head back and closing her eyes. 'If you hadn't been with us, I don't think we'd have made it out of there in one piece.'

Jim turned the key in the ignition with a shaking hand and said, 'If you hadn't pulled that macaroni pie stunt, I don't think we'd have even made it *in* there in one piece. I was all set to throw you over my shoulder and leg it.'

'What about me?' asked Penny. 'Were you going to leave me behind?'

'You did those self-defence classes last year,' Jim reminded her. 'I figured you could slow them down for us. Thanks, Mrs

Hubbard. Bugger me with an Arbroath kipper, you really saved the day.'

From her perch in the back seat, Mrs Hubbard leaned forward and gave them each a reassuring pat on the shoulder.

'Och, it was nothing, dearies, but I'd be very glad if you could put the foot down and get us out of here, Jim. Now, is anyone interested in the Campaign for the Preservation of Big Pandrops?'

CHAPTER 8

Relieved as he was to emerge from his experience in Seaton unscathed, Jim couldn't help but reflect on what would have happened if things had gone the other way. It wasn't enough to thank Mrs Hubbard and move on. They had a responsibility towards their families and businesses to stay safe. Yet over the past eighteen months, he had repeatedly found himself in dangerous situations, and it wasn't normal. This time in particular, things were far more serious. They lived on an island in the back of beyond, for God's sake, where the biggest drama of the day was Mary taking the batteries out of the smoke alarm so she could get on with burning the dinner in peace. What did they know about drugs and gangsters and fucking idiots who camped halfway up a hill to stop a road being built? Penny would go as far as it took to help Fiona, but it was all getting out of hand, and something must be done about this.

'You're very quiet,' said Penny, stretching out on their hotel room bed. 'Wotcha thinkin'?'

'I was thinking about your mother taking the batteries out of the smoke alarm. It's a bit like what's happening here.'

'What do you mean?'

'We're doing stuff without any thought for the consequences.'

Penny sat up and regarded him steadily, a flicker of concern in her eyes.

'I get the sense that you're trying to say something without saying it.'

'In that case, I'll say it. This morning, anything could have happened. How would the twins or your parents feel if something happened to you? What about me or Mrs H? Can you imagine explaining to Douglas Hubbard that we'd put his Minty at risk? He nearly lost the heid when she got shut in the freezer with a corpse. How do you think he's going to react to us taking her to a rough part of town and sitting her down with a gangster?'

'He's going to realise that none of us knew it was a rough part of town and that she's a grown woman who can make her own decisions. Anyway, just because we came across a few bad eggs, you can't say it's all like that. The place is probably full of good eggs too.'

'That's not the point, Penny. We have to stop taking stupid risks.'

'You mean stop helping Fiona prove her brother's innocence?'

'If that's what it takes.'

'I'm all for not taking risks, but I won't stop helping Fiona. Look, we couldn't have known what was going to happen today. Things sometimes just happen. You could have crashed the car on the way there, Mrs Hubbard could have tripped over a loose paving stone, whatever. Life doesn't come without risk, and if sometimes that means taking on some extra risk to help a friend, well…'

Penny shrugged.

Frustrated, Jim said, 'You don't take the batteries out of the smoke alarm so you can burn the dinner.'

'You're being ridiculous. There's a greater good here. For starters, we convince the police to catch Layla's killer and get Fergus off the hook. And for seconders, someone speaks for Layla. She's the real victim in all of this, not that you care.'

'I care, but I care about you, us, more. You need to stop this and let the police do their job.'

Penny stared at him in mute outrage. Jim could see the explosion about to happen but felt powerless to prevent it.

'Speak to Dunderheid,' he pleaded. 'Go to the newspapers and put it all over social media. There are ways to pile pressure on the police without getting directly involved. I mean, step back.'

It was almost a relief when the explosion came.

'You mean let Fiona down,' Penny roared. 'You mean let them put Fergus in prison for something he didn't do, while the real killer goes free.'

Jim felt his own temper rising and, despite digging his fingernails into his palms in an effort to remain calm, there was a definite increase in volume as he argued, 'It probably won't even come to that. They might say she took the drugs herself.'

'Except we know she didn't take drugs.'

'Do we? Do we? Pray tell how we know that.'

'You know perfectly well. Fergus and everyone we've talked to has said she didn't do drugs.'

'And we're supposed to take everyone's word for it? Whoopee doo. Saint Fergus said it, so it must be true. Saint Fergus was the only one who knew her well, and he hasn't turned out to be very reliable. Eileen says he's disappeared off the face of the earth!'

'Fiona believes he's innocent, and that's good enough for me,' shouted Penny.

Jim threw his hands in the air and walked to the door of their hotel room.

'Do what you like,' he snapped. 'I'm out.'
'Fine.'
'Fine'

He opened the door and glanced back, giving her a final, disappointed shake of his head.

'Great friend you turned out to be,' yelled Penny to his disappearing back.

Jim didn't respond. The door closed with a quiet click that somehow felt louder and more pronounced than a thundering slam.

Penny flopped back onto the bed and took a few deep breaths. In truth, Jim had a point, yet turning her back on Fiona and Layla was something she simply couldn't do. Neither could she think how she was going to explain Jim's withdrawal to the others when they met at lunchtime. Lordy, this was a full-on Michelin starred dog's dinner.

Acting Chief Inspector Hunter Deed laid the document on the table and rubbed his eyes. The pathologist's preliminary report supported a conclusion of death by overdose. They were still waiting for some of the blood results to come back, but the syringe they'd found next to the body contained traces of heroin.

'Give me your thoughts, Mac,' he said to the man in the chair opposite.

The predicted rain had held off long enough for them to take a chance on sitting at an outdoor table at the Inversnecky, Aberdeen's famous beachside café. Yesterday's breeze had died away, but the cool North East air tended to discourage the good burghers of the town from dining al fresco before June. Thus it was that their conversation was interrupted only by an inquisitive seagull and a resentful waitress with an infected nose piercing, who much preferred to serve people indoors where it was warm and where normal people sat on a grey, March day.

Detective Sergeant Callum MacCallum, Mac to his friends, cautiously leaned back in his chair, sensing the wooden slats strain beneath his weight. He was a stocky man, whose long working hours and sweet tooth were slowly nudging him towards heavyset. His thick, waterproof jacket, not so long ago a snug medium, now stayed permanently unzipped because he couldn't both fasten it and have adequate arm movement.

He regarded Deed's slim figure with some envy. In all the time he'd known the boss, Deed hadn't changed at all. Sure, there were a few extra lines. But the guy still had all his own hair, worked out three times a week and, when not in uniform, could make Primark pants look like Savile Row. Mac knew Deed was married to the job, but he reckoned that his mistress was a fancy steam iron. It would be great if for once, he didn't look like he slept in a trouser press; if for once, he could come into work in a shirt where only the bits you could see had been ironed. Then he'd forget, take off his jacket and everyone would know.

'Earth to Mac.'

Deed's voice penetrated Mac's idle daydream of his boss in ketchup-stained joggers.

The DS shook himself and said, 'Sorry, I was miles away. The case, yes. There is little doubt that it was a heroin overdose. The question is, did she jump or was she pushed? We know the head wound occurred not long before death, but we can't say exactly when. Same with the bruising on the arm and the grazed knees. The rock beneath her head was bloody, so she could have simply toppled backwards and hit her head. Someone could have grabbed her arm to help her up and she stumbled. That's why the pathologist can't rule out trips and falls at this stage. But the fact that her sleeve had been pulled over the tourniquet does suggest that someone else was there when she took the drugs. No fingerprints on the tourniquet or syringe.'

'Which is odd, wouldn't you agree?'

'Certainly would, boss.'

Hunter smiled at his friend and reminded him, 'I'm not

your boss anymore, Mac. We've known each other for twenty years, and we're not on duty.'

'Old habits, sir...Hunter...no, it doesn't feel right. You'll just have to put up with boss, boss. As I was saying, I'd expect to see the victim's prints. Yet all these things - the bruising, the prints, the sleeve – they're not proof that someone else was there. Then we come to the contents of her bag. Nothing in there to show habitual drug use. Show me the photos again. Something bothered me when I looked at them the first time.'

Deed reached into his pocket and withdrew a sheaf of images he'd printed earlier; the contents of Layla Hamdy's bag were preserved from every angle in a curious still-life. Mac laid them out in front of him and focused his mind. When he'd first seen the photos, everything had seemed very ordinary. The bag itself, some tampons, a keyring, phone, bank card, pen, a few pound coins – exactly what one would expect in a woman's bag. But there was something he'd unconsciously picked up on during that first pass. Something that itched his brain.

'The keyring,' he murmured.

Deed lifted the photograph and peered at it closely. The keyring was a plastic skull wearing headphones. There was nothing remarkable about it. It appeared to be the sort of cheap, novelty item that people would buy as a stocking filler.

'Hmmm, I don't see anything.'

'Exactly,' said Mac. 'It's what you don't see.'

He took his phone from his pocket and quickly typed. Deed watched him scroll down whatever he was looking at, then stop, back up, stop again.

With a satisfied grin, Mac turned the phone screen towards Deed and said, 'Look.'

An Amazon page was open and there, among a selection of plastic pineapples, penguins and bumble bees, was the skull. Only it wasn't simply a skull. The rest of the skeleton was attached, alongside a brief description – "32GB USB Flash Drive Memory Stick Skeleton Headphones Gift."

'The memory stick's missing,' said Deed. 'It's a good start, but the absence of things doesn't get us anywhere. We need to speak to Fergus. I sent someone up there to get him this morning, and he's gone.'

'I thought you said his sister would keep him there.'

'I was relying on her presence to prevent him from doing a runner. I couldn't arrest him, yet I know he knows something.'

'Are you going to hand the case off to MIT?'

'No. Until we know different, it looks like a straightforward drug overdose. No point in complicating things until they need to be complicated.'

'I'll have a word with intel. They might be able to help us track down the dealer,' said Mac. 'Everything is circumstantial, though. We need something solid if we're to complicate anything.'

'Thanks Mac. I better get going. I'm covering the late shift, for my sins.'

'The sooner things get back to normal the better.'

'I second that,' said Deed, tucking thirty pounds under a saltshaker. 'Order yourself another coffee and tell the waitress that if she manages to get all the way out here without tripping over her bottom lip, she'll find a decent tip. Thanks for your help with the case.'

Deed's car was parked a short distance away, on Beach Boulevard, and he used the walk to think through the next steps in the investigation. Unfortunately, everything was pointing to Fergus, and the man was a drifter, so pinning him down was proving to be a challenge. The Colonists were being uncooperative, and he was waiting to hear back from the woodentops he'd sent out to visit Fergus' old haunts. There was no social media trail to follow. In fact, outside of the newspaper reports covering his original trial, there was barely a trace of Fergus online.

Deed was just coming to the conclusion that he would have to talk to the sister, when his phone rang. At first, he didn't recognise the voice on the other end.

'Hiya. Is that Chief Inspector Dunderheid.'

'No, it's Acting Chief Inspector Hunter Deed.'

'Oh. Aye. Erm, sorry about that. It's Jim here. Jim Space. We spoke the other day when you took Gordon's statement. Remember? Ginger beardy bloke in women's horse-riding trousers?'

'I thought you were the untidy one in the fleece?'

'I meant Gordon. Aye, I'm the one in the fleece. More tidy underneath the fleece though. A bit like yourself. Not that I fancy you or anything. It's just that my girlfriend said you have nice muscles. I have an extra-long armpit hair, though.'

'Good to know. What can I do for you, Jim?'

'Sorry, I'm nervous and talking shite. Here's the deal. I need to talk to you, but I'd prefer to explain in person. Is there someplace we could meet?'

The hotel restaurant was almost deserted by the time Losers Club convened at the same large, circular table where they'd eaten all their meals so far. Except this time, only six of the eight chairs were taken.

'I take it Sergeant Wilson's still keeping her distance,' said Penny, as she took her place.

'I certainly am, turdnuggets,' said a voice from a nearby table.

'Where's Jim?' Fiona asked.

Thankful that she'd had some time to consider how she would massage the truth, Penny replied, 'I don't know. We had a huge fight and he walked off.'

'Is he coming back? Maybe if I talk to him?' Eileen offered.

'The answer to both questions is I don't know,' said Penny. 'He's not answering his phone, so I have to assume he's sulking somewhere in the hotel. No doubt he'll calm down and come back when he's ready. Would you mind if we get on with the updates, please? If nothing else, I need the distraction.'

Any further questions about Jim were forestalled by the arrival of the waitress, who gushed and chirruped her way through today's specials. Soon, there followed water, then bread, then fish knives, then drinks, then main courses, then ketchup for Gordon, then the waitress again.

'Is everything alright for you?' she gaily asked.

'No, everything is not alright,' said Sergeant Wilson from three tables away. 'I came here to discreetly spy on these people, and instead it's busier than a cheap cocktail bar on Black Eye Friday.'

'Everything's wonderful, dearie,' Mrs Hubbard assured the startled waitress.

When they were finally alone, Penny told the others of their encounter with Donald Wallace that morning, concluding, 'Now, it's a case of waiting for him to get back to us with a name, then we'll speak to the dealer.'

'I'm not going back to Seaton,' Mrs Hubbard declared.

'You're not going anywhere,' said Penny, mindful of her argument with Jim. 'If I have to meet with him, I'll do it somewhere safe. What about you, Fiona? Any word from Fergus?'

'Not a peep. He could be anywhere. I'll keep phoning him.'

'Sounds like Eileen and I are the only ones who didn't come away empty handed,' crowed Sandra Next Door. 'We spoke with Kendra Lawson, a school friend of Layla's. They lost touch when they went to university then reconnected at the Colony, purely by coincidence.'

'It's actually quite sad,' said Eileen. 'Layla's dad was a geologist working at Aberdeen uni, Professor Hamdy, and he took his own life in January. Her mum died years ago, and now with Layla gone, there's nobody left.'

Not to be outdone with interesting news, Sandra Next

Door said, 'On the upside, she and her dad had a falling out about his job.'

'That's an upside?' Penny asked.

Sandra Next Door gave a small snarl in Penny's direction, then continued, 'From what Kendra said, Layla's dad must have been doing private work for the oil industry. Layla was well-liked but kept herself to herself.'

'What did Layla study at university?' Fiona asked.

'Good question,' snapped Sandra Next Door.

'And the answer?'

'Obviously, if I knew the answer, I'd tell you.'

Eileen could see Fiona's colour rising, so rushed to intervene before all out war could be declared and Fiona found herself fielding daily visits from the Vik council complaints team about everything from the length of her grass to the improper use of outbuildings. Sandra could be both fiercely loyal and gloriously vindictive.

'Let's talk about Claire,' Eileen said. 'Sandra Next Door's results were similar to mine, in that people find Claire abrasive and loud, yet they like her well enough. She's taken over as their main go-between with the charity that's been supporting them. Although she seems chatty and open, nobody knows anything about her background. Claire and Layla would often go for walks together, so Claire probably knows far more about Layla than she's letting on. That's pretty much everything we found out.'

'Oh no, it isn't,' gloated Sandra Next Door, preparing to triumph in her one-sided game of one-upmanship, 'Firstly, for someone who was close to her and shared a tent with her, Kendra didn't know very much about present day Layla. She kept referring me to Fergus and the others. Secondly, at the beginning of the conversation, she said Layla had been killed. None of us have ever mentioned to the Colonists that Layla was killed. Just that she died.'

'The police won't have said anything either,' interjected Sergeant Wilson. 'Carry on. I'm not here.'

'There might be a reasonable explanation. Did you challenge her on it?' Penny asked.

'Is my name Sandra Next Door? Of course I did. She thought she'd heard it from someone else.'

'There you go, then,' said Penny. 'Sorry, that wasn't meant to sound dismissive. It's just that you've managed to gather a fair bit of information, but I'm not sure what we can do with it. Any ideas for next steps?'

Gordon, who had been quietly using a napkin to rub a ketchup stain off the crotch of his jodhpurs while he listened, tentatively raised a hand, as if requesting permission to talk.

'Seems to me that all the people who knew Layla well are being very sketchy about her. It's like people know something and aren't telling. But there's a friend we haven't spoken to yet. The one she was meeting that day?'

Five pairs of eyes were staring intently at him, and Gordon gulped. He was an under the radar sort of guy; the man behind the beard; the quiet, mysterious, sexy one. He relied on Fiona to do his talking, but he could see that she was too busy plotting the downfall of Sandra Next Door, so he'd spoken up. And now they were all looking at him. They were smiling at him. Gordon didn't think he'd ever made five women smile at the same time, and he was very suspicious of all this smiling business.

He slowly lowered his hand and mumbled, 'Just saying, like. Gordon out.'

'That's a good idea, dearie,' Mrs Hubbard told him. 'Does anyone remember her name?'

Fiona thought for a moment, then said, 'Anni-Frid Mackie. She's Layla's university friend and she lives in Kemnay.'

'Brilliant,' Penny smiled. 'We'll pay her a visit this afternoon. Kemnay's a fairly small place, so we should be able to find an address. On that subject – Eileen, could you add her and Professor Hamdy to the hackers' research list? Any word from them, by the way?'

Eileen said, 'Still waiting. Ivan and Ashov are on it. Fiona phoned Fergus yesterday afternoon and got details of a lot of the Colonists, but it would have taken ages to get round them all, so I told Ivan to look at Layla, Fergus and Claire first. I asked them to check the charity as well.'

'I hardly think the charity's a priority,' Sandra Next Door observed.

'Although it pains me to agree with Sandra Next Door,' said Penny, 'there's more than enough for Ivan and Ashov to do with five people to research.'

'Weed whackeur,' said Eileen, giving her friend a mock salute.

'Oui d'accord,' Penny automatically corrected, used by now to Eileen's enthusiastic but tenuous grip on the French language.

'That as well.'

'I think I'll have the chocolate cheesecake for pudding,' declared Sergeant Wilson, apropos of nothing. 'Where's that damn waitress? What did you say to her, Mrs Hubbard? It's almost like someone frightened her off.'

While Penny coaxed the waitress out of the kitchen, Eileen googled Anni-Frid Mackie, filtering the search results until, just as Gordon tucked away his last sweet morsel of apple crumble, she gave a short squeal of delight.

'I've got it! The Old Manse on Kirk Road.'

Sandra Next Door immediately stood up to leave, but was interrupted by Gordon, who said, 'Where are you going? It was my idea, so I should be the one to go.'

This was an unexpected turn of events, thought Penny. Having a single good idea had turned Gordon into a bit of a feisty one.'

'I'm the people person,' Mrs Hubbard reminded them. 'I deal with people all day, every day.'

The debate over which of them should visit Anni-Frid was finally settled by the person with the deciding vote.

Sergeant Wilson loudly decreed, 'Fuck's sake. If you lot

were paid in brain cells, Fred and Fanny Features would be the only ones coming close to minimum wage.'

Fiona and Penny tried very hard not to look smug in the face of Sandra Next Door's fury over the decision, but they knew they were fighting a losing battle so hurried out to the hotel car park before their expressions could slip.

'I have Jim's spare keys somewhere,' said Penny, rummaging through her handbag. 'I'm sure he won't mind if we take his car. It's roomier than your van.'

In front of her, Fiona drew to a halt and said, 'Erm, not sure that's going to be possible.'

'Why not?'

'Look.'

Penny looked up, then looked around, then looked at Fiona.

'His car's gone,' she said, baffled. 'Where could he be?'

CHAPTER 9

Fiona's fruit and veg van stood out like a turd on a rosebush in front of the Old Manse. The house was a beautiful slab of Victoriana, with deep bay windows, decorative curlicues, and a wide, gravel drive which swept to a perfect semicircle in front of smooth, granite steps. Neat lawns either side were shaded by ancient oaks and impeccably trimmed hawthorns, to create a picture-perfect rural idyll. Oh, to live here. Penny felt an immediate stab of envy for Anni-Frid, followed by a spiteful slither of satisfaction when she noticed that there, tucked away in the background like the seedy relative who stares just that little too long at the children during family parties, was a very ugly 1970s garage. For goodness' sake Penny, she rebuked herself, you've been spending far too much time with Sandra Next Door. You need to apply an Eileen antidote as soon as you get back to the hotel.

It was little wonder that her thoughts had strayed towards the negative. She had spent the short drive to Kemnay in a state of anxiety, frantically phoning Jim. The calls went to voicemail, so she'd sent a series of texts, each more worried than the last, until he eventually replied with "I'm fine. Busy."

He was, at least, alive, but his sharpness left her with the gnawing sensation that something was very wrong.

She carried the internal boulder of doom into Anni-Frid's kitchen, responding on autopilot to the woman's welcoming smile and offer of coffee, while her mind turned over all the things that could be keeping Jim busy at half two on a Wednesday afternoon.

As Anni-Frid bustled between kettle and cups, Fiona gave Penny a gentle nudge with her elbow and whispered, 'Stop worrying about Jim.'

'It's not so much Jim. It's whatever he's up to. He may not have agreed with me, but he's never been disloyal before.'

'What do you mean by disloyal?'

Realising she was straying dangerously close to telling Fiona that Jim had opted out of helping her, Penny hissed, 'Shh. I'll tell you later.'

Anni-Frid set three mugs on the breakfast bar and effortlessly glided onto a high stool. She was a tiny creature with short, blonde hair and elfin features. It was like watching a fairy alight upon a blade of grass, Penny thought. As opposed to her own clumsy scramble, which was more akin to showjumping in a forklift truck. It didn't help that the seats seemed to be made of ice rink, moulded to fit pixie bums. Penny's bottom lacked any of the qualities associated with pixies. Rather, if one were pushed to compare it to a mythological creature, it veered towards the gnome. Not the earth spirits guarding underground treasures; more the chunky porcelain chappies with the fishing rods. Which was why Penny had wedged herself against the breakfast bar and was ignoring her burning thighs and stomach muscles as she pushed her heels into the footrest to support her weight - because there was no way she was sliding off in front of this elfin-featured, pixie-arsed baggage with the perfect house.

'Are you alright?' asked Anni-Frid.

'I'm fine,' said Penny, her voice a strangled croak.

'It's just that you look like you need the loo. The downstairs one's broken, but there's one upstairs.'

Penny attempted to arrange her features into something approaching nonchalant and relax her vocal chords.

'I'm fine,' she assured the woman.

'Thank God for that,' said Fiona, who had taken one look at the stools and made the wise decision to stay standing. 'I thought it was the brussels sprouts from lunch. I was worried I was going to have to drive all the way back to Inverurie with you beside me, farting for Scotland.'

It was no use. Penny gave in to the inevitable, relaxed her legs and let herself slide off the stool.

'Sorry, I'm not built for these plastic barstools,' she said.

'They're awful, aren't they,' Anni-Frid agreed. 'I insisted on getting them, despite the horrific price, because they'd go with the new kitchen. Then they arrived and they were dreadful. So uncomfortable, but I made such a fuss about getting them, that I can't tell my wife. Why don't we take our coffees through to the living room?'

Whereas the kitchen had been all sleek counters and glossy modern chic, the living room was country comfort, with layered fabrics and deep sofas. Penny found herself anxious about spilling her coffee on a sofa cushion that probably cost more than she earned in a month.

She really had to get over her current harumph. Her agitation over Jim was making her quite sneery, and it wasn't fair on others. Anni-Frid had lost her friend, for goodness' sake, and poor old Fiona certainly didn't deserve to be on the sharp end of Penny's mood. Other people had far bigger worries than an irritating git of a partner who'd gone off on one. She resolved to file Jim in the pending tray and stop being a snipey twat.

'Your home is beautiful, Anna-Frid,' she said. 'It's good of you to make the time to see us, and we're so sorry about Layla.'

'Thank you. Call me Annie. All my friends call me Annie

and…and I can't quite believe that I'm never going to see one of my best friends again.'

Penny instinctively wanted to reach out to the woman, put an arm around her and tell her it would be okay. Except it would never be okay, so she once again muttered a platitude about being sorry and asked, 'How did you find out about Layla?'

Annie's eyes were glistening with unshed tears as she explained, 'The police rang this morning. They were going through the contacts in her phone looking for a relative to notify, not that there are any since her dad…passed away. Some cousins in Egypt, I think. I told the policeman if he couldn't track down a relative, let me know and I'll take care of things. Although I've no idea if there's even a will.'

Fiona smiled warmly at the woman and said, 'You're a good friend, Annie. Maybe Fergus knows about a will.'

Annie glanced up sharply at the mention of Fergus. Her mouth tightened, and she regarded Fiona with suspicion.

'How do you know Fergus?'

'I'm his sister. He told us Layla met you for lunch on the day she died, which is why we thought you might be able to help us.'

'I don't understand. Help you with what?'

'It's complicated,' said Fiona. 'We suspect that Fergus knows something he hasn't told us about Layla's death. I don't know if you're aware of his history, but sufficient to say that he used to be involved with drug dealers. I assume the police told you that Layla died of a drug overdose?'

'Yes, and that's ridiculous. She didn't do drugs. She had a spell at uni where she was partying hard and taking a lot of cocaine, but that was mainly a rebellion against her dad. She hasn't touched booze or drugs in years.'

'We agree. We don't think she would have taken drugs willingly.'

'So, are you saying someone…?'

'Killed her. Yes, perhaps. Probably. Whatever the case, due

to his past, Fergus is likely to be the main suspect. We're worried that the police will be looking for an easy closure, so we decided to help him by investigating alternative explanations. The problem is that Fergus did a runner sometime last night and we don't know where he is.'

Annie looked away, staring into the empty fireplace as if mesmerised by imaginary flames. The silence lingered so long that Penny couldn't resist the urge to fill it.

She explained, 'We think that a couple of her friends at the Colony also know something and are holding back. We have some feelers out to find a dealer who sold heroin to someone who wasn't their normal type of customer. Can you think of anything about Layla that might help us?'

'It doesn't surprise me that Fergus has done a bunk,' said Annie bitterly. 'He's not the reliable sort. I don't know what Layla saw in him. I told her so, too, but she wouldn't listen.'

Fiona stiffened at this, and Penny could tell that she was struggling to maintain her composure.

Her voice was tight and formal when she said, 'Whatever you think of Fergus, I have no doubt that he loved Layla and that her death was as much of a blow to him as it was to you.'

Penny lightly touched Fiona's arm in a gesture of solidarity and repeated, 'Can you think of anything about Layla that might help us? Was she in any trouble? Did she seem as if something was bothering her when you met for lunch?'

'Look, I know you both want to get Fergus off the hook,' said Annie, 'but I don't think there's anything I can tell you. It might be best if you go.'

'Maybe she confided something in you?' Penny pressed.

Annie's cheeks were flushed, and she once more directed her gaze towards the fireplace.

'No. I don't have whatever answers you're looking for. It's time for you to go.'

Penny held up a hand to placate the woman, which she belatedly realised was a futile gesture, as Annie was now determinedly staring anywhere but at her guests.

Her tone gentle, Penny said, 'I'm sorry. Layla's death must have been a terrible shock. We didn't mean to upset you. Would you mind if I use the loo before we go? I think those brussels sprouts are taking hold after all.'

Following Annie's directions, Penny left Fiona sitting in awkward silence and climbed the thickly carpeted stairs. She hoped that the rooms above were equally carpeted because she had absolutely no intention of using the bathroom. Penny wondered how long a bad bout of the sprouts would buy her. Ten minutes? If her previous housebreaking adventures were anything to go by, she could get a lot done in ten minutes. Conversely, she had also been caught, beaten up, kidnapped, coerced into supplying treats to a recalcitrant cat and hidden in a wardrobe from a murdering psychopath. So, there was that.

Recalling Jim's angry words, Penny did a quick risk assessment. Pixie-arse was much smaller than her, plus Fiona would be on Penny's side if it came to a fight. Then there were the self-defence classes and…*and* the fact that they'd been invited in, so technically she wasn't burglarising anything this time. Plus, she didn't intend to steal anything; it was just a poke around. Annie wasn't talking, so there must be evidence of nefarious things somewhere. It stood to reason!

The first room she came to was the bathroom. Unless Annie kept mysterious things in waterproof bags inside her cistern like in the movies, Penny didn't think she'd find anything there. She shut the door heavily, making enough noise to reassure any doubters that she really was using the bathroom, then she crept across the hall to the next door, which turned out to be a guest bedroom. A quick look inside wardrobe and drawers revealed only an old copy of Frock In Hell by Yvonne Vincent, which was an excellent read but not what Penny was looking for.

Two more spare rooms followed, one of them filled with junk and an abandoned exercise bike, which Penny was tempted to smuggle back to the hotel for Gordon. She felt sorry for him because she knew he was desperate to lose the pounds he had piled on since Ellie-Minty had turned his nights into a gruelling, baby-placating snackfest. Most of the time, he and Fiona were too exhausted to care what they looked like, and he'd even turned up at Mrs Hubbard's shop in his nightwear a few weeks ago. Which wouldn't have been too bad, had his nightwear not consisted of a jumper three sizes too small, Fiona's pink slippersocks and a pair of Spiderman boxers. Mrs Hubbard counted herself blessed that he hadn't been going through his commando phase at the time.

To Penny's relief, the second last door revealed Annie's bedroom. The woman was clearly an advocate of the "out of sight, out of mind" school of thought because the room was the complete antithesis of downstairs' neatly choreographed homeliness. The bed was unmade, dirty clothes lay piled on top of a small chest, and a pair of knickers looked like it had become permanently welded to a sheepskin rug. The open drawers speeded Penny's search, and she took little care to disguise her rummaging on the basis that everything was so haphazard that no one would notice that she'd replaced a t-shirt in the sock drawer. It didn't take her long to conclude that there was nothing to find beyond an extensive supply of indigestion tablets and a shockingly large dildo. Annie really should see a doctor about that, Penny thought, although she wasn't sure if she meant the top end or the bottom. Perhaps, she mused, the shenanigans at the bottom end sort of pushed everything up and caused the reflux at the top. She'd share this theory with Jim later and get his thoughts on the matter. Or perhaps she wouldn't.

Penny sighed and placed Jim back in the pending tray, before quietly closing the bedroom door and trying the next room. Bingo. She had hit the motherlode. This room was no less chaotic than the last; however, the mess consisted of documents and a computer. The advent of the post-lockdown home office was a boon for any would-be burglar or nosey parker. If Annie's life had anything to reveal about Layla, it would be here.

Penny rifled through the paperwork on the desk, searching for anything that mentioned Layla. She wished she had learned to speed-read. There were dozens of documents, some potentially relevant but many of them personal bank statements and records relating to what appeared to be an investment company called Juniper.

Uninterested in Annie and her wife's financial affairs, Penny moved on to examine the contents of the filing cabinet.

The top drawer contained a plethora of folders marked in a bold hand as containing what she considered life debris - electricity bills, birth certificates, insurance documents and so on. The bottom drawer, however, yielded a collection of newspaper clippings and printouts, all of which seemed to be about energy companies.

'She and Layla must have had a shared interest in environmental causes,' Penny whispered to herself.

She pulled out one report, which contained a transcript of a Scottish Parliament debate on renewable energy. It concluded that the inevitable decline of the oil industry meant that the focus had shifted towards new sources of energy, and declared that Scotland, with its sparsely populated wilderness and boundless supply of water, must position itself to fuel the nation.

The next document made Penny pause. It was a printout of an email from Elaine Bear. The signature gave her title as Cabinet Secretary for Net Zero, Energy and Transport. Why would Annie have this? There didn't appear to be anything contentious in the message. The author was merely agreeing to a meeting with someone called Johnny and suggesting that he come to party conference so that she could introduce him to some like-minded individuals.

Realising that she didn't have time to become sidetracked, Penny replaced the documents in the drawer and stood up. She looked around the room, wondering where else Annie might have stored evidence. She had already given the computer mouse an experimental click, but the screen had requested a password and she didn't have enough information to make an educated guess.

She was just about to leave, when a photograph on the desk caught her eye. It was lying on top of an iPad, partially covered by a mortgage statement. Annie must have been looking at it recently, Penny reckoned, very recently. The picture was of two young women in cap and gown, proudly holding a certificate. Her eyesight wasn't up to the task of reading the certificate, but she recognised the two women; it was Annie and Layla. Without thinking, Penny slipped the photograph into her pocket and left the room, closing the door quietly behind her.

She tiptoed to the bathroom and flushed the toilet, washing her hands so that they would be plausibly damp in the unlikely event of any farewell handshakes; then she made her way downstairs.

The only sound in the living room was the loud ticking of the mantel clock, an ornate monstrosity presumably chosen by whichever designer was responsible for the rustic styling. As soon as Penny entered, Fiona shot to her feet and made all the polite leaving noises, despite the fact that they were practically being thrown out. Wordlessly, Annie escorted them to the front door, then shut it firmly behind them. Penny couldn't be sure, but she thought she heard the sound of a lock clicking home.

'That was interesting,' she breathed, glad to be away from the atmosphere of unspoken wrath.

'It sure was,' said Fiona. 'Listen, about the sprouts. You're not going to fart all the way home, are you? Because we can call you a taxi. We're not far from Aberdeen, so there might even be an Uber. You'd like that, wouldn't you? You've never been in an Uber before. It's much better than a Vikster, which is really just Brian Miller driving around the island in the hope that somebody will flag him down or give him a hand job in the back seat.'

Penny snickered at this and said, 'He once offered me a free ride home if I bought him a fish supper. Margaret from the chip shop had banned him for stealing a pickled onion from the big jar on the counter. He gave me a tenner and told me I could throw in a battered sausage for myself. You don't get that with an Uber. And no, I won't be farting all the way home. The brussels sprouts thing was just a ruse.'

'A ruse for what?'

'Get in the van and I'll show you; also, you wouldn't believe what I found down the side of her bed.'

The drive back seemed to quicker than the drive there. Penny reviewed in her mind what they had discovered so far. Precious little, she concluded, other than that everyone is hiding something. She couldn't wait to take a closer look at the photograph. Fiona had promised to lend her the magnifying glass Gordon had brought to keep an eye on an ingrown hair on his toe. His belly had come between him and his ability to reach his feet, so he was often to be found standing with one leg on the dressing table by the window, magnifier in hand, attempting to pick the bugger out with Fiona's tweezers. Which, in Fiona's opinion and presumably that of hotel guests walking in the garden, wouldn't be so bad if he wasn't going through his commando phase.

As they pulled into the hotel car park, Penny reflected that there was no need for her to envy Annie's perfect life. She wouldn't exchange her own life with these wonderfully deranged people for all the money and designer houses in the world. Why, she might even keep Jim.

CHAPTER 10

Fingers Corrigan and Amsterdam Clark looked up from their game of cards as the pub door opened. Fingers' first reaction had been a tense wariness. Strangers were not welcome here, yet despite the marauding gangs of teenagers outside and the simmering undercurrent of violence within, the odd oblivious newcomer still occasionally made it as far as the bar. Fingers stood, intent on telling the stranger to leave before Benzo got back from the toilets and decided to use his face as a beermat. However, as soon as the man moved away from the door, her face broke into a smile.

'It's okay,' she said, anticipating a show of aggression from Amsterdam. 'It's Donald's pal, the stovies guy. Fit like, Jim? I thought the first meeting wasn't til next week.'

'I'm not here for the meeting. I was hoping to see Donald. He said he'd be in this afternoon.'

'He'll be here shortly. Sit yourself down while you wait. Do you want a drink?'

Without waiting for a reply, Fingers called on the barman to pour a pint of the good stuff, then tapped the pack of cards and asked, 'Will I deal you in?'

'Aye, go on. What are we playing?'

'Snap.'

'Snap?'

'Winner takes all. So far, Amsterdam has fleeced me of the proceeds of last night's Craigiebuckler job. I'll warn you, he takes no prisoners. I'm down a laptop, two Rolexes and a bonnie china dog.'

'You're one to talk,' Amsterdam protested. 'You got me for a grand from the travel expenses kitty. Donald's going to kill me if he has to get the bus again.'

'I don't have anything to bet,' said Jim. 'I haven't…erm… pulled any jobs recently. Too busy with the Stovies Protection League.'

'Perfectly understandable,' said Amsterdam, nodding sagely. 'Tell you what, we'll play the next game for fun. Loser gets a round in.'

Jim, who was fairly sure his current pint would put him over the drink drive limit, resolved to lose and order himself a coke. Or an orange juice. It probably wasn't wise to ask for coke in this place, lest you found yourself the unwilling recipient of a wrap of Charlie, and that would definitely be worse than drink driving.

'Right. Fun,' said Fingers, as if unfamiliar with the concept of having a good time for no reason. 'I'm dealing. Aye, the cards, not the shite people around here shove up their noses for…what do you call it again?...fun.'

'Och, haud yer wheesht and deal the cards,' said Amsterdam, giving Jim a surreptitious wink.

Three orange juices and a dislocated finger later, Jim was just snatching his hand away from Amsterdam's overenthusiastic snap, when Donald Wallace arrived with his trio of minders. As before, the pub went silent, and people began to shuffle towards the door; however, at a slight nod of the head from the gang boss, they shuffled back again, and normal pub business resumed.

Donald took his seat at the same table, ousting a courting couple who had been so busy swallowing each other's tongues that it had taken them a full minute to notice the three goons hovering expectantly nearby. Eventually, the largest of the goons had planted a meaty hand on the lad's shoulder and roughly extracted him from the girl's face. Jim half expected to see their tongues, still locked together, stretch out then spring apart. He gave himself a slight shake, realising he'd been spending way too much time watching the Disney channel with Ellie-Minty.

'I have what you were asking for,' said Donald, as Jim sat down opposite him. 'The dealer's name is Ryan Richardson. He'll meet you outside the Old Torry Community Centre in an hour. If you're going to hand him over to the police, you'll need this.'

Donald handed Jim an envelope with a name and a mobile telephone number scribbled across the top.

'Auld Jock will make sure Ryan's looked after. Text this number once you're done. And tell Mindy to stop giving *my* number out to every Tom, Dick and whatever your name is.'

Donald leaned back on the bench and took his phone from his suit pocket, indicating that the audience was over, but Jim wasn't finished yet. He didn't have the information he came for.

'One more thing,' he said, causing Donald to frown and pointedly set his phone on the table. 'It's why I wanted to meet rather than do this over the phone. Do you know someone called Fergus...?'

Jim hesitated, realising that he'd never been told Fiona's brother's surname.

'Fergus, big guy, brownish red hair,' he finished lamely.

'Would that be Fergus who works in the amusement arcade down at the beach or Fergus the hairdresser in Kintore?' sneered Donald. 'Fuck's sake, go home and stop trying to play with the big boys.'

'Fergus the enforcer,' Jim persisted. 'Mrs Hubbard says that the more your memory improves, the less she remembers Dazzle-gate.'

This wasn't true, of course. Mrs Hubbard had no idea that Jim was here, and he felt a small twinge of guilt for bringing her name into it.

Donald heaved an exaggerated sigh and said, 'Fine. I know who Fergus is. What about him?'

'Is he working for you?'

'You're straying into dangerous territory, pal. Fergus worked for Chancer Neish in Glasgow, until he was put away. A jailing that coincided with the arrests of some of Chancer's top men and the seizure of several kilos of product from his home. Lucky for him, most of his product hadn't made its way south yet and was safe in my warehouse in Inverallochy, but Chancer isn't very pleased with Fergus, so if you know where he is, I will be happy to pass the message on.'

'I was going to ask you the same thing. If you know where Fergus is,' said Jim, trying to mask his unease at the viciousness in Donald's tone.

'Do I look like I run a missing person's service? If Fergus knows what's good for him, he'll be keeping his head down. Now, if you don't mind, we're done here.'

Donald picked up his phone and began to scroll through his messages, signalling that the meeting was well and truly finished. With a muttered thanks and a wary glance at the goons, Jim pushed back his chair and staggered clumsily to his feet, knocking the table.

'Watch it,' the largest goon warned.

'Sorry,' Jim mumbled, putting a hand on the edge of the table to steady it. 'Sorry. I'll just get out of your hair.'

'You taking the piss?' the goon asked, pointing at his shaven head.

'No!' squeaked Jim, quickly backing away.

He was halfway to the door when a voice called out, 'Is that you going? Will you not stay for another game?'

Fingers was waving the pack of cards at him, so Jim had no choice but to make a detour.

'Sorry, I have to meet somebody, but here,' he tossed a ten-pound note onto the table, 'have a drink on me.'

'Very kind of you my good man,' said Amsterdam, signalling to the barman to pour another. 'We'll see you at stovies club next week, eh?'

Jim almost felt sorry for Fingers and Amsterdam. They may not have been the most upstanding members of society, but there was a decent streak in there.

'Aye, stovies club, next week,' he said and, conscious of every eye in the place on him, strolled casually towards the exit.

The tremors began as soon as the fresh air hit. If asked, he could not have explained how he made it to the car and how he was able to drive the short distance to the loading bay behind an industrial launderette, where two men waited in an old van.

On legs like jelly, Jim stumbled to the van, threw open its rear door and scrambled in. The men inside stayed seated, watching as he lay panting on the floor.

'You did great,' Deed assured him, leaning forward to close the door. 'Far better than we expected.'

'Thanks for the vote of confidence,' Jim puffed.

'You did a grand job,' said Mac. 'We're no nearer finding Fergus, but you've managed to clear up a burglary, and now we know where Donald keeps his shipments.'

'I got this as well,' said Jim, sitting up and handing Deed the envelope Donald had given him. 'I'm supposed to text someone when I've finished with the dealer. I think it might be the phone number for a dodgy police officer.'

A frown creased Deed's forehead as he read the details on the envelope.

'We'll hang onto this, if you don't mind,' he said tersely.

He passed the envelope to Mac then bent to help Jim remove his coat. Deftly, he detached the top button and slid it into a hard, plastic case, before tucking the coat into the compartment beneath a console, on which stood the monitor that he and Mac had been watching while Jim was in the pub.

'Donald Wallace in full HD,' he chuckled, tapping the display. 'Better than anything on the BBC. Thanks, mate. It's been impossible to get our own people inside that pub, never mind anywhere near the man himself.'

Jim slowly breathed out and said, 'God, I can't believe I did that. After everything I said to Penny about not taking risks.'

'It was a controlled risk,' Deed assured him. 'We had a whole team on standby in case anything went wrong. When you told us what you and your friends had been up to, it was too good an opportunity to pass up.'

'Aye, well, I won't be doing that again.'

'Did you plant the bug?' Mac asked.

'Just at the end there, when I was standing up. I knocked the table and stuck it on the underside while the bodyguard was giving me a telling off. What if they find it when they're cleaning?'

'Cleaning? In there?' Mac laughed.

'Point taken,' said Jim. 'I won't need to go to court about any of this, will I?'

'No. You're a CHIS,' said Deed.

Seeing Jim's baffled expression, he clarified, 'Covert Human Intelligence Source. Anything you give us is sanitised before it's passed on. That means we record it in such a way that nobody can tell where it came from. Then we develop the intel into things which we *can* tell people about.

'Take the warehouse, for example. Now we know roughly where it is, we can use aerial photos to identify likely premises, check the land register and even take the drugs dog for a walk around the village. We also have the bug, and we have Donald Wallace's phone number – rich sources of intelligence on their own. There are plenty of ways to take this forward that don't involve you. Most importantly, as promised, your details are kept strictly confidential.'

'But Donald Wallace might guess,' said Jim. 'Who else knows that the warehouse is in Inverallochy?'

Deed replied, 'Probably a lot more people than you realise. We'll be building the case against Donald for months, and by the time we take him down, you'll be a distant memory. Whatever you do, don't go back to him asking questions, and don't let any of your friends contact him either. To be on the safe side, it might be best not to tell anyone what you did today.'

'I wasn't intending to,' said Jim, shrugging on his fleece. 'Although that was mainly because Penny will be fuming if she finds out that I gave her a lecture on not putting people at risk, then willingly threw myself into a nest of vipers. Do you need anything else from me? Do you want to meet the dealer?'

Deed glanced at Mac then shook his head.

'No, just report back on anything the dealer tells you. We can pick him up later, if we need to. I'll have a quiet word with Sergeant Wilson and make sure she reports everything to me as well. She won't like it, but she'll understand, once we get the swearing out of the way.'

Jim gave him a sympathetic smile and said, 'In that case, I suppose I better get myself off to Torry, then go back to the hotel. It'll be dark soon, and everybody will be wondering where I am. God, now that it's over, I'm bloody hungry. And I need a pee. All that fucking orange juice.'

A few minutes later, clutching Mac's scribbled directions to the Old Torry Community Centre, Jim got into his car and reversed out of the launderette loading bay. Behind him, Mac closed the van door, turned to Deed and proffered a handshake. Deep in thought, the boss ignored the gesture and signalled to his colleague to take a seat.

'We're no closer to finding Fergus or the missing memory stick,' he said, 'but we'll get some nice results from today. I'll keep up the official hunt for Fergus. You carry on digging in the background.'

'Or you could just close it as an accidental overdose,' Mac suggested.

'Indulge my curiosity. Even though we don't have much to go on, my gut's telling me that there's more to this than meets the eye. According to Gordon's statement, Fergus never asked how Layla was killed, which begs the question, was he already aware of her death? That might point towards him having given her the drugs and, by extension, killing her. Or he may have found her body and deliberately left it there for someone else to stumble across. Either way, it's likely that he took the memory stick.'

'That's cold, boss. How could you do that to someone you supposedly love?'

'Yes, it's cold,' Deed agreed, 'but he's a hard man who has had to make a lot of difficult choices in life. There's something on that memory stick that he doesn't want anyone to see. Something worth killing for. Find Fergus, and I'm almost sure you'll find the memory stick.'

'I'm on it. I'd offer to do more, but I have a pretty full workload as it is.'

'I appreciate the unofficial help. One more small favour, though. Can you get the intel on the burglary to CID in Ellon, and MIT will want the drugs intel.'

'No problem. And Auld Jock?' asked Mac.

'You know what to do. Nobody else needs to know about him for now,' said Deed, with an air of finality. 'Can we stop off at your place on the way back to Inverurie Police Office? I need to change back into uniform so I can carry on pretending to give a shit about how many traffic stops we've done this month.'

CHAPTER 11

The sun was making a last-ditch attempt to show its face before night came to claim the city. The granite buildings on one side of the street cast deep, cold shadows, and on the other, sparkled into sharp focus, casting off the afternoon drizzle like a bawdy showgirl.

At the end of Abbey Place, the Old Torry Community Centre was dressed in its Sunday best, neatly painted and perfectly adorned with hanging baskets, its noticeboards proclaiming a wealth of wholesome activities that belied the poor reputation of the area.

Jim wasn't quite sure what he'd expected, but it certainly hadn't been a pair of cheerful red doors, enticing him into late afternoon T'ai Chi with Tom. He sensed that there was a lot more to Torry than the junkies and jailbirds that Mac and Deed had warned him about.

His second surprise of the hour was Ryan Richardson. Jim's entire knowledge of the drugs world was informed by Trainspotting, and he'd been anticipating a wired Rent Boy type with pupils the size of dinner plates, yet the man who stood on the Community Centre doorstep was a freshly ironed version of Matt Damon in the Bourne Identity, all fit and lean and impossibly cool in a black coat and sunglasses.

Jim pulled over beside him and lowered the passenger-side window.

'Are you Ryan?' he asked hesitantly.

'The very man,' replied Ryan, removing his glasses. 'Donald Wallace said you need to talk to me. I hope you don't mind meeting here. It's Zumba at six, and I don't want to be late.'

Jim gestured to Ryan to get into the car and wound the window back up.

'My mum told me never to get into cars with strange men,' Ryan joked, as he settled into the passenger seat. 'If you drive round the corner, we'll be able to talk without some twat chapping on the window and asking for a fix.'

Jim did as he was asked, manoeuvring the Land Rover to a quiet spot on an adjacent street. He tried to think of some light conversation, some chit chat to gloss over the awkwardness of having this man in his car, but his hail fellow well met failed him, and all he was left with was the faint hope that this spot wasn't too quiet.

Picking up on Jim's unease, Ryan said, 'Calm down. Nobody will touch you when you're with me, and I'm a businessman, not a robber.'

'You're not what I thought you'd be like,' Jim commented.

'You were expecting some skanky lowlife, off their tits on their own product? Nah, if you want to survive, it's brains not veins. I'm working my way up, just like I would in any other organisation. Hard graft, earn the trust of the boss, dress like you mean to be taken seriously, etcetera.'

'How old are you?' Jim asked.

'Twenty-three.'

Just a boy, then. A daft laddie who thought he was immortal.

'Did Donald tell you that whatever you say here will be passed on to the police?' asked Jim.

'I know they'll be knocking at my door, but taking the fall is a good career move.' Ryan tugged a mock forelock. 'I plead guilty, your honour. I have no previous convictions, and a big sob story. Please don't send me for an all-inclusive stay at the Grampian Hotel.'

Seeing Jim's utter bafflement, he clarified, 'The jail in Peterhead. I'm not worried and it probably won't come to that anyway.'

'Ah, right, aye,' said Jim, unsure how to respond. It wasn't like he could empathise with the guy or trade war stories. Ryan had this cocky, Jack-the-lad thing going on that made Jim feel like a country bumpkin let loose in the big city.

'I once injected myself with horse tranquiliser,' he offered.

Ryan nodded knowingly and said 'Ket. One of my top sellers. Did you have a good trip?'

'I've no idea. The horse kicked, the needle slipped and I was unconscious for the whole thing.'

'You were actually injecting a horse?'

'Aye, it's what I do. I go to farms and see to the animals. I'm up Randy Mair's all the time.'

Ryan did a slight double-take at this, but Jim didn't notice. He was on a roll. He was going to convince this big city lad that things in the countryside were cool.

'Sometimes I'm there for hours, but I get a lot of satisfaction from it. Then, when the wee foals or whatever appear, I say to myself, "You did that, Jim." That's the thing about living in the country. It may not be high-powered or sexy, but you can still get pleasure from your work.'

Ryan was regarding Jim with horrified fascination.

'What about sheep?' he asked. 'Do you do sheep?'

'Aye, sheep, dogs, cows, anything that moves. I've had a fair few goldfish in my time, but they're tricky little buggers.'

'How does that even work? Do you just dangle your willy in the bowl or something?'

Jim shot Ryan a look that said he thought the lad was a puppy short of a full litter. He clearly didn't appreciate the nuances of being a country vet, Jim decided, his self-confidence reasserting itself.

He said, 'You have to be very gentle with them. Anyway, I'm not here to tell you about how I treat animals. Donald told me you have some information about one of your customers.'

'That's right,' said Ryan, visibly relieved at the change of subject. 'Two of my customers, I suppose. You asked about any unusual buyers; someone who stood out from the crowd. I think these two fit the bill.'

He took his phone from his pocket and scrolled through his photographs, muttering, 'Hang on. I do a lot of business on Snapchat and Insta, so I always have to go through a hundred photos to find what I want. Ah! Here, take a look. This pair came to my door last weekend.'

On the screen were a man and a woman. They appeared to be around forty years old and were smartly dressed. If Jim had seen them in the street, he wouldn't have looked twice. They were so very ordinary. Her dark brown hair was scraped back into a ponytail, and she wore a floral-patterned blouse. He wore a casual shirt and blazer.

'At first, I thought they were a couple of social workers who'd got lost,' Ryan explained. 'Or someone's parents come round to complain that I'd ruined their wee darling's life. Hazards of the trade, you know – angry people.'

Jim took the phone and splayed his fingers to zoom in on the faces, saying, 'Older and smartly dressed. I see why they're not your average customer, but surely you must get sales among the middle classes. I read that a lot of professional people take recreational drugs these days. What made this pair stand out?'

'They came in person. I do a delivery service, like Drugaroo, and I don't get many people coming to my door these days, so that was weird for a start. I thought maybe they just liked doing it nineties style. Old folk like yourself are into that personal service thing instead of technology.'

'And, so?' Jim prompted.

'So, they look like professional people, but the woman asked for heroin, and you don't get the professionals using heroin. It's all coke with them. Your modern heroin user is eighteen to twenty-four or some old junkie who managed to get through the past few decades without getting HIV off a needle-share in some shithole squat. Or they're from Dundee.

'I told her she'd be better off ordering online. There's a loyalty card on the app – you get ten percent off your fifth delivery – but she said she didn't want to leave a digital trail. They were both really confident, like they'd done this before, so I didn't think much of it at the time.'

'You sold them the heroin, then?'

'Aye, not there on the doorstep, mind you. I'm not daft enough to keep the stuff in my flat. I invited them in for a chai latte and phoned one of the lads on bikes to swing past on his way to his next delivery.'

'Weren't you worried they might be undercover police?'

Ryan grinned and said, 'Naw, there was no smell of bacon. Anyway, the polis use the young ones straight out of recruitment.'

'Did you get their names? Did they say anything that might give us an idea of who they are?'

'She called him Derek and he called her Lucy. I don't think that's their real names because she slipped up once and called him Dave. Tried to cover it up by laughing and saying that was her brother's name, but you could tell, you know? His accent was from Edinburgh way.'

'They didn't talk about anything personal?'

'My dog was straight on his lap, and when I told her to get off, he said it was okay because he had a dog as well. He went on and on about this Jack Russell winning prizes at shows. Its name was something daft like Curious Bob Ramsay. Maybe that was the guy's surname? Ramsay? Dave Ramsay?'

'Maybe,' said Jim. 'It's something to go on, though. Is there anything else you can think of?'

'No. The gear arrived and I saw them off. That was it.'

'How did you get their photo?'

'My doorbell. In my business, you can't be too careful, so I have one of them video doorbell jobbies rigged up. This is just a screenshot. I can give you the video if you want. There's sound and everything.'

Jim did want. He wanted very much indeed. He gave Ryan his phone number and watched, impressed, as the younger man quickly clicked through a series of screens. Within a few seconds, Jim's phone pinged to let him know that a message had arrived.

'What are you going to tell the police?' Ryan asked.

'Only that these strangers pitched up at your door to buy heroin and whatever you found out about them. I'll share the video as well.'

'Nothing about my business model, though. That's classified information.'

'If they ask me, I'd have to tell them. But if they don't ask, I'll say nothing. Or you could go to them yourself and give them the information direct,' Jim suggested. 'That way you control the narrative.'

'Clipe on myself!' exclaimed Ryan in disbelief. 'Aye, like I'd do that. It's bad enough that my mum makes me go to the over 50's Zumba with her. Handing myself into the police would destroy my reputation.'

'Aye, well, Donald gave me a number to text once we're done here. I expect the man on the other end will make sure you're brought in and treated with kid gloves.'

Ryan took a deep breath, as if bracing himself, and said, 'No guarantees with the polis, though. If we're done here, I'll get back to the Community Centre. Then it's off home to put my affairs in order.'

As soon as Ryan had gone, Jim checked the piece of paper bearing the directions Mac had given him. At the bottom, Mac had copied the phone number for Auld Jock.

'Carry through Donald Wallace's instructions,' he'd advised. 'Don't deviate from the plan.'

Jim opened up a new text and entered the number, then typed, "Spoke to Richardson. Will tell police what he told me tonight. A mutual friend said to let you know."

He hoped that would be enough. He assumed that it would be unwise to mention full names yet couldn't think how else to phrase things. Hopefully Donald had given the man a heads up on the situation.

Jim took a moment to collect himself. It had been a long day, and he still had to somehow tell Penny and the others what he'd been up to, without telling them what he'd really been up to. He should probably call Penny. The sun had gone down and she'd be wondering where he was. He hadn't wanted to talk to her earlier because that might have meant confessing that he'd gone to Deed about their investigation.

He'd done it with the best of intentions, but he doubted Penny would see it that way. Despite his desire to do things in a way that would see them all safely back to Vik at the end of the week, Deed had talked him into meeting with Donald, wearing a wire and planting a bug. Which in turn meant he had to meet the dealer and text a corrupt policeman. Only, he couldn't tell her that. She'd get the abridged version, which would still earn him an earful, but it put Donald Wallace firmly in everyone's rear view mirror and, as per Deed's instructions, they wouldn't need to have anything more to do with him.

Feeling like a condemned man, Jim dialled Penny's number.

She picked up on the first ring, loudly berating him with an exasperated, 'Where have you been? You can't take off in a huff and ignore all my texts and calls. I've been really worried. We've all been really worried. Except Sandra Next Door. She said it was very peaceful and long may you bugger off. But the rest of us were worried. Eileen's on the point of holding a séance for you!'

'I've only been gone for an afternoon,' Jim pointed out.

This was the wrong thing to say.

'Hours!' Penny screeched. 'You've been gone for hours.

Fiona has enough on her plate with Fergus, and then there's Gordon's trouser situation. She doesn't need to be fretting about you as well.'

There was a pause, and Jim was about to say something in his own defence when he realised that Penny had only stopped to draw breath.

'You were the one who went on about not taking risks. I had to do all the burglarising on my own. That's hardly safe, is it? Is it? You've let Fiona down, you've let me down, you've let us all down.'

She seemed to have run out of steam, and Jim thought it might be his turn to speak. He wasn't sure what to say. A wee joke might calm things down. Yes, that was it, the power of laughter.

'Ooh, you're sexy when you're angry.'

He pulled the phone away from his ear and waited for the tirade to end.

When it did, he adopted his most contrite tone, the one reserved for particularly heinous crimes such as forgetting to put the bins out, and said, 'I'm sorry. If you'll let me explain…'

Eventually, Penny relented, and Jim gave her a heavily edited version of his day.

'I didn't want you or anyone else taking risks, so I got Donald's number off Minky and contacted him myself. I had to go back to that damn pub, but it was better the second time around. I played Snap with Amsterdam and Fingers, then Donald told me the name of a dealer and where to meet him.

'I've just finished meeting with him. He seemed a nice lad. He was off to Zumba with his mum. I'll tell you everything he told me when I get back.'

She appeared to be feeling a little more rational, although not entirely mollified.

The remainder of the conversation at Jim's end consisted of, 'Aye. Aye. I'll be there within the hour. Aye, okay. Could you order me a steak so it's ready when I get there? Aye, I know I'm capable of ordering my own tea but...aye, okay. I'll do it myself.'

Jim clicked the red button and put the phone on the passenger seat. All in all, that had gone better than expected. She hadn't booked him a separate room, although there was a good chance that this was because the magicians' convention had taken up every room in the place. He'd seen them arrive before he left. It had been very weird. One minute they were all in the foyer, being noisy and checking in, then the next they'd vanished.

Penny had told him to hurry back to the hotel because Eileen and Sandra had heard from the hackers. Jim looked at his watch. He had said he'd be an hour, but there was one last urgent thing left to do. Well, two. Send Deed the video and find a bloody toilet. Three orange juices, for fuck's sake. Three!

CHAPTER 12

Woman: With the racket that dog's making, you'd think if anyone was in, they'd have answered the door by now.

Man: We can try the other guy, but Chauncey said this one's more reliable. And he's clean.

Woman: We're not getting paid enough for this type of grunt work.

Man: Yes, we are. The client is paying for no link back to them, so we have to do this face to face.

Woman: Knock again. No, don't touch the doorbell. It's one of those video things, and the last thing we need is to be caught on camera.

[Sound of heavy knocking, followed by more frantic barking, then the door opening]

Woman: We're looking for smack?

Ryan: I think you've got the wrong flat.

Man: Chauncey Greig recommended you.

Ryan: Chauncey? Erm…aye. Right you are, come on in.

'What sort of fucking name is Chauncey?' asked Sergeant Wilson. She adopted a posh, English accent. 'Ooh, I'm

Chauncey Greig of the Chipping Norton Greigs, and my specialist subjects are silver spoons and being bummed to death at Eton.'

Sandra Next door gave her a thin smile and scoffed, 'The BAFTAs called. They said don't bother turning up.'

'It's the parents' fault. The poor soul can't help his name,' Mrs Hubbard pointed out. 'There's a lot worse than Chauncey.'

'According to Trip Advisor, there isn't a Greggs in Chipping Norton,' said Eileen, flicking through screens on her phone. She held up Google maps for them all to see. 'You'd have to travel to Moreton-in-Marsh for a steak bake and a yum-yum.'

'I really fancy a steak bake,' Gordon sighed.

Fiona poked his belly and exclaimed, 'You've just eaten a twelve-ounce sirloin and an apple crumble!'

'We didn't have starters,' said Jim, coming to Gordon's defence. 'I wouldn't say no to a steak bake. And chips.'

Giving Gordon a gentle nudge, he murmured, 'Aye, eh?'

Gordon looked hopeful. 'Aye?'

'Aye.'

'How?'

'Ye ken.'

'But?'

'No'

'No, aye?'

'Aye,no.'

'Mate'

'Pal.'

There followed a spontaneous manly hug, lasting no longer than the regulation three seconds, lest anyone think they were turning into women, then they broke apart to find Fiona eyeing them suspiciously.

'What are you two up to?'

'Nothing,' said Gordon.

'Aye, no, no, aye?'

Donning his best shocked expression, Gordon remonstrated, 'Jim was just being sympathetic to my plight, that's all.'

Fiona turned to Penny, who shrugged and said, 'They couldn't have been planning to sneak out for a chip supper later because I know for a fact that the chip shop shuts at seven on a Wednesday. It's ten to seven now.'

Both men looked more crestfallen than any crest had the right to fall, and Penny couldn't resist a cheeky wink and a tip of the glass towards them.

Raising her own glass, Mrs Hubbard asked, 'What time does happy hour finish? Would someone mind going to the bar for me? I'm feeling quite bloated.'

She settled back onto the sofa and rested her legs on a small footstool, then let out a long, low burp, before saying, 'Oh, goodness me. Like my Douglas always says, better in than out. Or is it better out than in? Which one's for the wind and which one's for the bedroom? Ooh, thank you, dearie. I'll have two sexes on the beach. It only counts as one when it's happy hour.'

She handed her glass to Fiona, who was taking full advantage of a few days away from breast feeding by making up for lost time with the vodka bottle.

They were in the hotel bar and, until a moment ago, had been huddled around Jim's phone, watching the video given to him by Ryan Richardson. Penny was letting Jim have his moment of triumph, biding her time until she breathlessly announced what she and Fiona had discovered in the photograph she'd borrowed/purloined from Anni-Frid's desk. Now, with everyone returned to their respective sofas and armchairs…well, not exactly armchairs, more those semi-armchair things that pretended to be armchairs by dint of having a low back that circled round barely far enough to allow one to rest an elbow…now that everyone was ensconced in their sofas and elbowchairs, it was time to start sharing.

'I know we all have big news today,' she began.

'I don't have any big news,' said Mrs Hubbard, with a small belch. 'Although I did have a lovely FaceTime with the Hollywood Knitting Club. There's a new member. Nice lassie. Och, what's her name? Likes a bowl of Cullen Skink. Something Weaver. Definitely Weaver because I remember thinking it was a really good surname for somebody in a knitting club. Much better than that Huge Ackman. For shizzle, the man does a grand Fair Isle, but I ask you, what sort of a name is Ackman?'

She regarded her companions expectantly, clearly anticipating general agreement that Huge Ackman was a ridiculous name. In the ensuing silence, the turning of brain cogs was almost audible, as everyone tried to think of something sensible to say.

'Is anyone else hearing this?' asked Sergeant Wilson. 'Sometimes I think your arseholes have closed up and the shit's had to find another way out. A minute ago she was saying that Chauncey was fine. Now she's worried about Ackman!'

'For someone who's not here, your own mouth seems to be contributing its fair share of shit,' said Sandra Next Door, with a scornful toss of her head.

'Do you have shares in Silvikrin?' the Sergeant sniped back. 'Or is it like an Exorcist thing? When you turn your head, your hair stays in the same place. I think it's the Exorcist thing. What does everyone else think?'

This caused more consternation than Mrs Hubbard's question. Fortunately, they were saved by Fiona, who returned from the bar with a tray laden with beers, vodka, wine and two sexes on the beach. Fully distracted by beer, Sergeant Wilson scowled at her friends and bade them carry on.

'As I was saying,' said Penny, 'We all have news. Anni-Frid Mackie wasn't very forthcoming today, but she did *lend* Fiona and I a photograph.'

Fiona produced the photograph and passed it around the

group. Reading glasses were produced as everyone tried to make out the wording on the certificate.

'Don't bother,' Penny told them. 'We borrowed Gordon's ingrown hair magnifier, and it says, "Strathbogie Prize for Excellence in Journalism – Anni-Frid Day and Layla Hamdy for an article on The Cost of Renewables." I looked it up, and it seems they both studied journalism at Aberdeen Uni.'

'Which chimes with what the hackers found,' said Eileen.

She pulled a tablet from her handbag, opened her notes and began to read.

'Anni-Frid Mackie née Day. Freelance journalist. Lives with her wife Cheryl, who's a painter. Didn't you say they had a nice house, Penny? I think Cheryl must be handy with a tin of Dulux. Anyway, yada, yada, yada. Specialises in reporting on climate change. Three arrests for breaches of the peace during demonstrations in Manchester and London. Social media loads of stuff. They've given a list of what she's posted in the past month. Lots of pictures of a dog and a few photos of her and Cheryl at various art galleries in Glasgow. One of them has a poster advertising the Cheryl Mackie Exhibition opening 6th of March. Maybe she was decorating the art gallery. I suppose it's handy to show folk you can diversify before you start throwing wallpaper up and giving them feature walls. Right, let's talk about Fergus.'

Eileen scrolled back a few pages.

'Fergus MacQuoid…is that how you say it? Mac Woyd?'

'Macoyd,' said Fiona, fiddling nervously with the strap on her dungarees.

'Fergus Macoyd. No social media. Rap sheet like the FBI's most wanted. Contract out for him on the dark web, but it's only for a thousand pounds, so no takers. Oh, he has a licence to drive a bus. Good for him. He could take Cheryl to her decorating jobs. Start a whole service for people who live in the countryside and need a bus to take them to work.'

'You mean a bus service?' asked Jim. 'Like the number 20 that runs between Aberdeen and Alford via Kemnay?'

'Exactly like that,' said Eileen.

'Maybe he could get a train driving licence too,' Gordon suggested with a sly wink at Jim, 'so he could run a train service. And he could build a railway and a station in Kemnay.'

'Now you're just being ridiculous, Gordon,' Eileen chided him. 'It takes years to become a train driver. There isn't much more on Fergus and they couldn't find anything on Claire, which is a story in itself.

'Moving on. Layla Hamdy, daughter of Ahmed Hamdy, Professor of Geology at the University of Aberdeen. Attended posh school for girls, studied journalism, dropped out in her final year for health reasons. Repeated the year and graduated with a First. Stint at posh hospital in England, presumably rehab.

'Worked for the Aberdeen Press and Journal for a year before disappearing off the face of the earth. Social media deleted, the works. Popped up a while later getting arrested alongside Anni-Frid. Inherited a lot of money and property from her father after his death a couple of months ago.

'Her father did a lot of work for oil and gas firms. Most recently, he was paid a substantial amount of money via a shell company. The hackers have offered to trace the money, but it'll take a while.'

'I don't think we have a while,' said Penny. 'Is there anything in what the hackers have found so far that gets us one step closer to convincing Dunderheid that there's more to this than Fergus being a twat?'

'Yes, there is. Here's where it gets weird. Someone else has been poking into Layla. The hackers found applications for a copy of Ahmed's will and land deeds. The application was submitted by a firm of solicitors, Cowrie Robert. They didn't look into Cowrie Robert, but they did check for other applications by the same firm and found deed transfers for fifteen farms along what was the proposed route of the new road, all around Bennachie.'

Eileen paused to let that sink in.

Jim sat frozen, his pint halfway to his lips, and Penny was leaning forward expectedly, watching while the others joined the dots. Of course, she'd got there immediately, yet it was Sergeant Wilson, sitting a few chairs away and still feigning official ignorance, who not only joined the dots, but added some new ones to improve the picture immeasurably.

'Close your mouth, Wank Boy. All this means is that somebody has been buying up the land. It's probably someone who was betting on selling it for a profit under compulsory purchase when the road was built. You'd make a tidy sum. My bet would be a dodgy politician. Who were the deeds transferred to? Did Layla or her dad own any property along the route?'

'I don't know,' Eileen admitted. 'I'll check. The hackers sent so much stuff, and it's taken me and Sandra Next Door all afternoon to organise it. We could easily have missed something.'

She looked to Sandra Next Door for confirmation. Sandra merely gave a sharp nod, reluctant to expose her weak underbelly to Sergeant Wilson's claws.

'Mistakes happen,' the Sergeant said, waving a hand breezily. 'We seized a bag of herbal cannabis off Stevie Mains just before Christmas. Turns out Easy shops in Scoops, you know, the loose foods place on North Street. Anyway, the lab got a hundred grammes of Italian seasoning, and his mother remembers nothing between getting her Christmas hamper and New Year's Day. But that's nae the point. The point is, what did you say the name of the dog was?'

Sergeant Wilson addressed this to Jim, who had laid his pint down and was imagining how horror-struck poor Easy must have felt, facing Sergeant Wilson when the lab report came in.

Determined not to fall victim to the same fate, he racked his brains to recall what Ryan Richardson had told him.

'Uh, Ryan said it was something like Curious Bob Ramsay.'

The Sergeant bared her teeth at him in a facsimile of a smile, and Jim swallowed nervously. Beside him, he felt Gordon shudder. A happy Sergeant Wilson was possibly more unsettling than an angry one.

'Time to rub together the two brain cells God gave you and hope for a spark,' she said. 'Say Cowrie the Scottish way.'

Dutifully, Jim said, 'Coorie.'

'If Coorie had a dog, what would you call it.'

'Coorie's dog.'

'And if the dog was called Robert?'

'Coorie's Bob,' said Jim automatically.

A second later, he jolted upright, his mouth once more hanging open.

'Something like Curious Bob. Coorie's Bob. You think the man who bought the heroin is connected to Cowrie Robert. That's genius.'

'It has been known,' said Sergeant Wilson, baring her teeth a little more widely.

Beside Jim, Gordon gave a quiet squeak.

'Hang on, what about the Ramsay bit?' Jim asked.

'I may be a genius, but I'm not omnipotent, mostly,' said the Sergeant. 'They give these pedigrees daft names. I would bet on Easy's life that the firm of solicitors is known locally as Coorie Bob, and either Ryan misheard, or the dog's owner works for the firm, and it was a play on words.'

Penny, who had been furiously turning everything over in her mind, said, 'We've got solicitors looking into Layla, acting for dodgy land purchases and buying heroin. How does all this connect with Layla's death? Why would these people kill her?

'Eileen, I think whatever you can find out about the land deals and whether Layla owned any property is going to be important. Also, could you ask the hackers to find out who Chauncey Greig is? If we can find him, it might help us identify the pair in the video. We can hardly wander into the solicitors' office and say, "Excuse me, can you tell us which two of your employees killed Layla Hamdy?"

'Oh, yes, and one more thing. What about looking through dog shows or Kennel Club records for Curious or Coorie Bob Ramsay? There might be something about his owner. Lordy, there's so much going on here, my brain hurts. Does anyone have any other thoughts?'

Fiona laid her empty glass on the tray, surprised that the vodka had disappeared so quickly. Beside it sat two empty cocktail glasses. She glanced across at Mrs Hubbard and noted that the woman appeared to be asleep. There would be no useful contributions from that direction, she thought wryly; however, she herself did have an idea. She had been quietly taking in everything that had been discussed, trying to sift through the information bomb that Eileen had dumped, and in all the talk of dogs and solicitors, something had been missed.

'Rewinding back a bit,' she said. 'Two things. Firstly, Claire. If she doesn't exist, who is she? Is she even linked to this at all? Secondly, Layla and Anni-Frid being journalists. Could that have any bearing on things? What if Layla was investigating the solicitors, found out something important and met Anni-Frid that day to pass the information on?'

Penny nodded. 'That makes sense. It could be something to do with the road building. Maybe she found out about the land deals. Sergeant Wilson, was there a computer or a notebook in her bag?'

'No, just the usual handbag stuff. Nothing on her phone either.'

'In which case,' said Fiona, 'She must have handed whatever it was over to Anni-Frid. We need to get back into that house and search it properly.'

'La la la, not listening,' said Sergeant Wilson, putting her hands over her ears.

A small belch and a hiccup alerted them to an impending

pearl of wisdom from the lips of Mrs Hubbard. The older woman was leaning back on the sofa, her eyes still closed. On the stool in front of her, however, her right leg gave a small twitch to signify that its owner was awake. When it came, her voice was one of a woman who had had far too much sweetie juice.

'No, you don't need to shearch, deariesh. Like Fiona shaysh, rewind. You've mished one vital clue.'

Mrs Hubbard paused for effect. Everyone knew that she liked a dramatic pause. They leaned forward, waiting for the big reveal. And waiting. Everyone knew that she liked to spin out her dramatic pauses just that little bit too long, so they waited some more. And waited. Mrs Hubbard gave a gentle snore.

'Oh, for God's sake,' snapped Sandra Next Door, poking her with a bony elbow.

Mrs Hubbard started awake and beamed at them.

'Ash I wash shaying, you've mished one vital clue.'

'If you do another dramatic pause,' Sandra Next Door told her, 'I'll lock you in your room for the rest of the trip.'

That woke Mrs Hubbard up. Her beatific smile faltered, and her speech sharpened.

'Anni-Frid didn't have lunch with Layla. She was at her wife's exhibition opening in Glashgow.'

Fiona and Penny locked eyes, each running through in her mind their visit to Anni-Frid.

'She's right,' Penny gasped. 'Anni-Frid never confirmed to us that they met up hat day. We based that on what Layla told other people. So, if she wasn't with Anni-Frid and passing her some information, who was Layla meeting?'

CHAPTER 13

It was late by the time Deed finally managed to close his office door, shutting himself off from the hubbub of the station.

A nasty pile-up on the Inverness road outside Huntly had diverted most of the shift away from Inverurie. His Sergeant had gone home early with suspected Covid, and the Inspector had been in court giving evidence all day, so Deed had accompanied his team to coordinate the various emergency services and ensure that procedures were followed so that the road could be opened quickly without compromising any evidence as to the cause of the crash. Although the smell of alcohol on the driver and the dead sheep on the road were something for the investigators to bear in mind.

Now, despite it being almost midnight, the building was awash with people chattering and winding down from what had been a traumatic scene.

Deed was lost in thought, contemplating an email marked urgent, so was unaware of the gentle tap at the door until it opened and Shotgun Shuggie's lanky frame appeared in the gap.

'I brought us a cup of tea, boss. I hear it was a bad one.'

Deed smiled gratefully at the man and waved him into the

only other chair in the small room. The office was bland and utilitarian, one of three shared by whichever senior officers happened to be on duty. With the North East division covering thousands of square miles across Aberdeenshire and Moray, being a cuckoo in someone else's nest came with the territory. However, as Inverurie was home to the traffic cops, and Deed was currently, in Mac's words, High Heidyin of the Broken Taillight, he could more often than not be found here, in his cubbyhole of choice. Which was, unbelievably, the Ritz compared to the broom cupboard that was Shotgun Shuggie's domain downstairs.

The Sergeant had been Deed's training officer when he joined the force, those many moons ago. Now close to retirement, he was, as he never stopped reminding Deed, a very important cog in the firearms licensing team. It was easy to dismiss firearms licensing as a bunch of old-timers talking to farmers, but this quiet, unassuming man had saved many lives through confiscating weapons and working with mental health services to keep his customers on the top side of the graveyard.

It was with this in mind that Deed made the decision to confide in the man.

'Here, look at this. It's about the overdose on Bennachie the other day.'

He swivelled his monitor around so that the Sergeant could see the email on the screen:

From: martisha.wilson63@scotland.pnn.police.uk

To: hunter.deed47@scotland.pnn.police.uk

Subject: Unpaid work

· · ·

Boss,

You ~~forced~~ told me to give you an update even though I'm on holiday. The turdnuggets have discovered that a firm of solicitors Cowrie Robert have been looking into Layla Hamdy. They think two people from the firm bought heroin a few days before she was killed. Wank Boy says he sent you video of them doing it. Aye – buying the heroin – nae doing it doing it. It's nae that kind of video. Although I'm very suspicious about Wank Boy's browser history. Cowrie Robert has also been buying up farmland around Bennachie. No details as yet. Layla is a journalist and possible motive for death is that she found out about the land deals. If so information is missing. She didn't meet Anni-Frid Mackie. They do know each other but Anni-Frid was in Glasgow. Turdnuggets want to know who she was meeting. Claire Barrow is an alias. Nobody knows who she is but she spent time with Layla. Clear links between Cowrie Robert and Layla's death. Nothing showing Fergus was involved. Weasley didn't make me say that. Also Fergus has a bus drivers licence. Clearly a big bus ~~weirdo~~ fan. Suggest you check bus station CCTV.

Respectfully yours,

Sergeant Martisha Wilson KBO, OMG, WTF

PS I have no idea how they found out this stuff because I was in the jacuzzi self-administering a colonic.

'What do you think?' asked Deed.

Shuggie tutted and shook his head, like a used car

salesman about to offer Deed an exceedingly low trade-in price for his old banger.

'Other than a complete disregard for paragraphs and commas? Looks like they have some suspects for you, but I don't know much about it. What do you have so far, apart from this?'

Deed needed a sounding board, yet despite Shuggie having his full trust, he had to be cautious about what he told him. It wasn't Shuggie, per se; more other people asking questions and Shuggie being forced to answer. It was no secret that they were friends. Deed had already strayed off-piste by setting Jim up as an informant. Then there was the memory stick. His gut was telling him to keep quiet about that. Finally, there was the fact that this was looking more and more like a murder, and he was treading on thin ice by not handing it over to MIT. If the ice broke, he didn't want to take Shuggie down with him.

He mentally sifted his findings so far and ordered them into a sanitised version of the truth.

'On Tuesday, Layla Hamdy was found dead from a drugs overdose on Bennachie. She was one of the Colonists, and according to them, she'd gone into Inverurie the day before to meet a friend for lunch. That's Anni-Frid Mackie in the email. The pathologist found some bruising. That, taken with the lack of fingerprints on the syringe and the state of her clothing suggest she wasn't alone when the heroin was taken. Nothing conclusive, mind you. Her boyfriend, Fergus MacQuoid, used to run with Chancer Neish's crew and is not long out of prison after a fifteen-year stint for murder.

'Those are the basic facts. It's also worth mentioning that Layla's dad took his own life a couple of months ago. I've looked into it and there was no suicide note, which is a bit strange. She and him didn't get on, by all accounts, but she was his only close family member, and they were regularly in touch. She was the sole beneficiary to his estate.

'Fergus was nearby when Layla's body was found.

Witnesses say he seemed distraught but never asked how she was killed, which raised a few eyebrows. This, his history and the fact that he's done a runner put him in the frame for supplying the heroin to his girlfriend.

'It looked like a fairly open and shut accidental overdose, except that everyone who knew Layla insisted she wouldn't have taken drugs. The pathologist confirmed that there was no evidence of prior drug use, but her medical records show a history of poor mental health and drug use when she was at university.

'Assuming all of this is correct, and she hadn't taken drugs in years, it would seem odd to start now on a hill in the middle of nowhere, on her way back from lunch with a friend. I began to wonder if Fergus had somehow forced her to take the heroin. Perhaps talked her into it or threatened her, and the dose was too strong for someone who's not an addict. That's pretty much where I've got to.'

Shuggie had patiently listened without interrupting, but now raised his hand to ask a question.

'Who are the turdnuggets?'

Deed smiled. 'Ah, Martisha does have a way with words. They're her weight-loss group. They've come over from Vik to get a bravery award on Friday. Quite a resourceful lot, and going by this email, they've somehow got much further on in their investigation than I have in mine. One of them, Fiona, is Fergus' sister. Another, Jim, broke ranks and told me that Fiona's convinced her brother had nothing to do with Layla's death. Apparently, they've been investigating to come up with an alternative explanation.'

'Which they have,' Shuggie pointed out. 'For a bunch of amateurs, they've come up with some solid stuff. How did they get a video of somebody buying heroin?'

They were into choppy waters here, so Deed chose his words carefully.

'You know Donald Wallace, yes? They're friendly with his daughter. I'm told she persuaded her dad to help them track down the dealer. I don't know how, but Jim got the guy to give him his doorbell camera footage. We'll pick up the dealer tomorrow, but he's small fry and will probably get a slap on the wrist provided he's willing to corroborate the video.'

'From what you've got here,' said Shuggie, 'this has moved on to possible murder. Personally, I think you're wasting your time looking for Fergus. If there's a clear link between Coorie Bob, the heroin and the victim, you need to hand this one over to MIT.'

'Coorie Bob?'

'Aye, it's what the locals call them. They're an Edinburgh firm, but tread lightly there, Hunter. Coorie Bob's the go-to solicitors for people with money, and they're not too fussy where the money comes from either. They represent anyone from celebrities to your gangsters like Donald Wallace and Chancer Neish. And they fight dirty.'

'Thanks for the heads up, Shug. Well, you've told me what I should do…'

'And I don't need to know whether you actually do it,' Shuggie grinned. He'd been around long enough to know what was at play here. First thing he used to tell the new recruits – CYOB – cover your own back.

They sipped their tea and reminisced awhile about old times and mutual acquaintances, until Shuggie announced he was going home to bed.

'What were you doing in work at this time anyway?' asked Deed.

'I often come in when it's quiet, to catch up on paperwork.' Shuggie waggled a warning finger at Deed. 'There's a lot more to firearms licensing than ticking boxes.'

Once he'd gone, Deed attempted to read a quarterly report on community engagement, but soon gave it up as a bad job. He wished he had half the dedication of Shotgun Shuggie, but there was no getting over the fact that he hated this job. The sooner he was out of here the better.

He had just closed his laptop and was about to head

home, when a sudden thought struck him. Something that Sergeant Wilson had said about buses and Layla not meeting her friend. Something that he and Mac hadn't picked up on, and he didn't think that Losers Club could have either. Everyone assumed that Layla had gone to Inverurie, but if she did, how did she get back? There was no bus ticket in her bag.

With a sigh, Deed sat down at his desk and opened the lid of his laptop. He wondered if Mac was still up. It was going to be a long night.

CHAPTER 14

'Day three thousand four hundred and ninety-six in the Big Brother House,' said Sergeant Wilson, scratching her armpit with a fork. 'All the housemates are getting to do the exciting bits and Sergeant Wilson is bored. Take me out. Do something with me.'

The Losers were rather subdued this morning. The scent of sausages and bacon which had so delighted them on Tuesday, now mixed with the smell of stale alcohol to induce a cold, queasy sweat.

Penny had taken up temporary residence by the orange juice dispenser and, having already refilled her glass three times, was now wondering whether it would be bad manners to ask for a chair.

Mrs Hubbard had declined to turn up at all. When Sandra Next Door and Eileen went to check on her, she had refused to answer the door, simply telling them to come back next week, dearies. Penny fervently hoped that her parents didn't FaceTime Fiona with daft baby questions today because if Douglas Hubbard heard that his Minty had overdone it on the sweetie juice, there would be hell to pay. They'd be loudly blamed for leading her astray, and whenever any of the Losers went to his shop for ice cream in future, they would find that the freezer had developed a mysterious fault which meant that ice cream was unavailable.

The thought of ice cream wasn't helping with the queasiness, Penny decided. Toast. That was the answer. Toast to settle the stomach, and a smear of jam to raise the blood sugar. Who was she kidding? A smear of jam because toast was boring. It was the distant cousin of crispbreads and rice cakes, both of which, in Penny's humble opinion, should be served exclusively in prisons. Surely the recidivism rates would go down if people knew they were going to do cardboard instead of porridge. Ha! She gave herself a notional pat on the back for the play on words and decided that she might be ready to join her companions now.

Toast featured heavily in the breakfast orders. The only person to brave a fry-up was Sergeant Wilson, who was surprisingly chipper and seemingly immune to the common hangover.

More for the sake of everyone's stomach contents than a desire to think about complicated murder things, Penny suggested the Sergeant sit at another table because they were going to discuss the case. Unfortunately, having argued with the woman and become the target of an expletive laden diatribe on the subject of fanny-faced bacon dodgers who make perfectly nice Sergeants move, Penny had unwittingly ensured that everyone was obliged to discuss the case. Nobody wanted to discuss the case. In fact, she was fairly certain that Sandra Next Door had hissed at her.

'We're all a touch delicate this morning,' she began.

'Speak for yourself, bogey-breath,' came the voice of Satan's stepchild from three tables away.

'We're all a touch delicate,' Penny repeated, 'but we need to make some decisions. Jim sent Dunderheid the video and Sergeant Wilson has given him a run-down of what we've found out. We couldn't sit on the Coorie Bob thing. The question is, do we think we've done enough, or do we carry on investigating?'

Fiona was unconsciously tapping her teaspoon against the table and gave a start when Gordon tugged it from her fingers.

He muttered, 'Sorry darlin', I know you're worried, but could you fiddle with something a bit quieter?'

Fiona snatched the teaspoon back and placed it on her saucer, before taking a deep breath in through the nose, and out through the mouth.

Trying to keep the note of accusation from her voice, she said, 'I understand why we need to inform Dunderheid, but if he agrees that this is murder, then he'll pass it on to another team and we won't know what they're going to do about Fergus. My vote is that we keep on keeping on.'

A quick show of hands settled the matter. Sergeant Wilson and Jim were for leaving things to the police. Gordon, Eileen and Sandra Next Door were with Fiona. Eileen then raised an extra hand for the absent Mrs Hubbard, giving Team Fiona a clear majority. Penny didn't think anyone noticed that she hadn't voted. Truthfully, her rational brain was with Jim, yet her irrational heart was with Fiona.

'Now we have to decide what to do next,' she said. 'I remember saying last night that we need to find out who bought the farms.'

'I did a quick Google,' said Eileen. 'We can get the information online from the Land Register. Cordon bleu, I wouldn't have known that a year ago. I think the hackers must be rubbing off on me.'

'What about the other things?' asked Fiona. 'Finding out who Claire is and who Layla met before she died?'

Penny had given this some thought the previous night, before the wine replaced her brain cells with laughing gas and the world began to whirl. Before Jim had carried her upstairs and gently put her to bed. Before the spins became too much, and she'd stumbled into their bathroom to purge herself of excess wine. Before she'd collided with him, the big weirdo, sitting on the loo in the dark. Before she'd been sick in his underpants. She shuddered at the memory and brought her mind back to the task at hand.

'I don't know how to find out who Layla met. The only person I can think of who might know something about Claire is Anni-Frid. Layla must have told her about the people she was living alongside. Although I don't think Fiona and I will be welcome if we pitch up asking more questions. Is anyone else up for another go at Anni-Frid?'

'We shouldn't be driving anywhere this morning,' said Jim. 'How about we start phoning round some of these farms that Eileen's looking into? Maybe the people who live there will talk to us.'

'You're taking the "safety first" approach, aren't you?' asked Penny, giving him a wry smile.

'Aye, plus you're still half-blootered from last night, and going by the faces around this table, you're not alone.'

'And I've got everyone's car keys,' said Sergeant Wilson.

Gordon looked shocked.

'You've got my keys? How did you get my keys?'

'Stole the maid's pass. Gets you into all the rooms. Sometimes, Weasley, I like to watch you when you're sleeping.'

Gordon looked like he might faint, and Fiona was about to assure him that she had their van keys, when a sharp voice stabbed the very centre of their hungover brains.

'Martisha Wilson! You leave Gordon alone!'

Sergeant Wilson started at the rebuke and turned to see Mrs Hubbard bearing down on her. The older woman was still in nightgown and slippers, her white housecoat billowing behind her in the draft from the door and giving her the appearance of an avenging angel in curlers.

'I was just having a wee bit of fun,' mumbled the Sergeant, crossing her arms defiantly.

Mrs Hubbard's jaw tensed, and for a moment, it looked like the hotel dining room was about to be the scene of a very rare event; an exploding Minty. Then her stance relaxed, and she slumped into the chair opposite the policewoman.

'You're bored, dearie' she said, her tone softening, 'and I am too. I couldn't get back to sleep, so I thought about the case, and I've decided that you and I are going up that darn hill again to speak to that darn Claire. We'll squeeze the darn truth out of her.'

Sergeant Wilson bared her teeth and forced her lips to curl.

'Oh, Mrs H, you are spoiling us. Anyone who says you're a filthy old muckraker will have me to deal with.'

'You're the only one who ever calls me that,' noted Mrs Hubbard.

'And I shall deal with myself later,' said Sergeant Wilson. 'Off you fuck, then. Curlers oot. Panty girdle on. Chop, chop.'

'I'm coming too,' said Sandra Next Door. 'Not that I want to spend time with *her*, but I'd enjoy squeezing the truth out of folk.'

'Bring a spade,' retorted the Sergeant. 'Because I'm nae stupid enough to leave your body lying around for daft, beardy gingers to find.'

'You shouldn't be driving,' Jim cautioned.

Sergeant Wilson gave him a withering look.

'They have these things…what are they called? Ta…ta…ta something.' She snapped her fingers. 'Cars driven by tax-dodging, nosey bastards. Talking of which, how's the husband, Sandra Next Door?'

Still bickering, the two women made their way to the hotel lift, closely trailed by Mrs Hubbard, whose housecoat once more billowed in the draft, affording those behind her the rather memorable view of the hem of her nightdress tucked into the back of a lacy thong.

'Ooh, Mrs H,' Penny whispered.

Jim grinned. 'I always said she was a saucy minx.'

'If you had to choose a bum,' mused Eileen, 'which would you go for? Hers or Gordon's?'

'Why would we be choosing a bum?' asked Fiona.

'Like if somebody puts a gun to your head and says, "Go on. Pick a bum." Or they kidnap Gordon and tell you that if you don't pick a bum, they'll send *his* bum back to you in pieces.'

'I can see where you're going with this, Eileen,' nodded Jim. 'You wouldn't want bits of Gordon's bum in the post. Imagine you were on holiday and came back to two weeks' worth of bum.'

'I am here. I can hear you, you know,' said Gordon. 'If you've nothing sensible to say, I'm going for a swim then a walk round the gardens to clear my head.'

'Oh, but I do have something sensible to say,' said Eileen, much to the surprise of her companions. 'While you've all been chatting, I got on with those searches. I've only done a couple, but the results are very interesting.'

She slid her tablet across the table, and the others leaned in to read the document on the screen.

'I don't understand,' said Penny. 'What are we looking at here?'

'The new owner of the farms is the same in both cases.'

'And?'

'Thermacorp. The company that bought the farms is the same as the shell company that paid money to Layla's dad.'

CHAPTER 15

Superintendent Nadia Gilani was perhaps one of the best bosses that Deed had ever worked for. A straight-shooter who, with her long, dark hair pulled into a tight bun and her gold-rimmed spectacles, gave off a no-nonsense vibe that kept her more senior officers firmly in check. Yet when it came to the junior staff, she was a down-to-earth, trusted ally.

Her office, Deed noted, was larger than his and south facing, the desk positioned so that, while he narrowed his eyes against the glare of the late morning sun, she was cast into silhouette - a shadowy interlocutor who wanted to know exactly why she should release him from duty for the day and pay for a trip to Edinburgh, when it was the Major Investigations Team's job to solve murders.

'What can I say?' said Deed. 'I sent them the report last night and they came back to me this morning saying it's all very thin, they have a lot on, and I have enough to close it as a bog-standard overdose.'

'Can CID take it?'

'No. I spoke to DI Patterson before I came to you. They've had some intel on a spate of burglaries in the West End and they're about to make a big arrest.'

'I really don't understand why MIT won't take the case. From what you've told me, there's a lot more to this than an overdose. Well, we're stuck with it, I suppose. Okay, go to Edinburgh, but take someone with you and put everything in writing. If this all goes tits up, I don't want us looking like we were trying to cut corners or circumvent the process. And keep me posted.'

Deed rose stiffly to his feet, trying not to let his relief show.

'Thank you, boss. If it's okay with you, I'll take Mac MacCallum from Bucksburn. That way we're not down a body in Inverurie.'

Gilani had already moved on to the next urgent matter in her inbox, so merely waved a hand to indicate both assent and that this meeting was over.

Mac, however, was less sanguine. When Deed popped into the Bucksburn office to deliver the good news, his erstwhile colleague was in a Teams meeting with a visibly irate Procurator Fiscal and a handwriting analyst from Gartcosh. Mac was perspiring beneath a large pair of headphones, so Deed could only hear his end of the conversation, but he wondered if the Procurator Fiscal or his friend's collar, tight enough to cause a neck muffin, were responsible for the blood pressure tablets on the desk.

Eventually, Mac removed the headphones and closed his laptop.

Vigorously rubbing his ears, he said, 'Idiot sent the wrong report, and now we're all getting it in the neck from the PF. What can I do you for?'

'Do you fancy a trip to Edinburgh?'

'What? Now?'

'Yes, now. A visit to Cowrie Robert Solicitors.'

'I thought you were handing that over to MIT this morning.'

'I tried, but they won't take it.'

'Why not? There's some strong evidence in there that Coorie Bob are up to their necks in the lassie's death.'

'I don't know. I got the impression they'd rather it went away. Let's just say there was some encouragement to close it as an overdose and move on.'

'You're sticking your neck out, doing the investigation yourself,' Mac warned.

Deed wondered if it was just him, or was the subject of necks coming up a little too often for one conversation? He gave Mac a quizzical look, but the man gazed back, his face a picture of blank innocence.

'I ran it past Gilani,' he said. 'She's fine with it.'

'Did you tell her everything? The last thing you need is her breathing down your neck because you didn't mention the memory stick.'

'Yes, she knows everything. She was the one that signed off on putting Jim Space into the pub. I had to tell MIT about the memory stick as well. I didn't want to, but it was a last-ditch attempt to get them interested. Their DCI pointed out that the thing could have been lost anywhere, anytime, if it ever existed. So, are you coming to Edinburgh or not?'

'Aye, of course,' said Mac. 'I'll save your neck yet again.'

'Okay, what's with the neck–' Deed began, then he saw his friend's face break into a wide smile.

Mac couldn't hold back the laughter that swept through him, making his man boobs dance to the tune of his shoulders.

'Oh, you should have seen your face,' he wheezed. 'You spent the last ten minutes of that Teams call staring at my neck. No, don't deny it. I saw you. If you must know, I put on an old shirt by accident today and didn't notice until I went to put on my tie before the meeting. Here, help me get the top button open before I stop breathing altogether.'

Deed obliged, grinning wickedly and saying, 'As Acting Chief Inspector, I can arrange for a move, you know. I think you'd make a great Community Liaison Officer.'

'What even is a Community Liaison Officer?'

'No idea, but I imagine it involves checking people's window locks and visiting primary schools. You'd look grand on one of them wee primary school chairs, with a head like a blueberry muffin.'

The good-natured banter continued all the way to the car, all the way down the A90 and all the way to George Street where, behind the smart façade of a nineteenth century townhouse, Coorie Bob Solicitors plied their trade. That was when things things got serious.

The discreet brass plaque to the right of the freshly painted, black door was the only indication that this was the premises of Cowrie Robert Limited. There was no sign or window sticker to announce the firm's presence. You were either in the know, or you weren't. Deed exchanged glances with his partner, then turned the handle.

'Good afternoon. Welcome to Cowrie Robert. Do you have an appointment?'

The young receptionist was straight out of the Insta influencer playbook, in a shirt carefully chosen to provide a hint of pectoral beneath an out of season tan. The sleeve was tucked behind a Hublot watch, which was either stolen, a fake or a gift because no matter how he dressed it up, this guy was minimum wage.

Within seconds, Deed had the receptionist sussed as someone who would initially resist any attempts to see his boss. He would be superior and dismissive. Deed would probe for any weakness in his defences, threatening to arrest him if necessary. Then there would be some flouncing on the young man's part, as he strutted to the boss' office, followed by humble pie and a garbled justification of his behaviour after his boss chewed him out for messing with the police. By the end, there would be meekness. Which meant there would be vulnerability, and Deed was not above exploiting a vulnerability when necessary.

Deed opened his wallet and held up his warrant card.

'We don't have an appointment. Chief Inspector Deed and Detective Sergeant MacCallum to see either Mr Cowrie or Ms Robert.'

'I'm sorry, they don't see anyone without an appointment. I could book you in for, hmm, next Thursday.'

'And *I'm* sorry, but crime doesn't run to a schedule. Could you let them know we're here please?'

'As I said, you would need an appointment. They're very busy people. Now, if you'll excuse me, officer, I have important clients to attend to.'

So far, so predictable, thought Deed, gazing round the unexpectedly modern interior. Clusters of empty cubicles, separated by frosted glass panels, took up the centre of the floor space. Around the edges were doors to what he presumed were offices and meeting rooms. Through the floor to ceiling glass panel at the back was a large conference room, beyond which, more glass led to an outdoor terrace.

Deed had done his research the night before. Cowrie Robert had certainly come up in the world since its days of representing minor drug dealers and petty thieves. Given a small tweak in life circumstances, the wee nyaff in front of him could have been one of the firm's old clients.

He sniffed the air and turned to Mac, saying, 'I don't see any clients waiting, but there's a strange smell. Mac, can you smell it?'

'Sure can, boss. Smells to me like something illegal. Maybe when you arrest him for obstruction, you should search his bag.'

Deed turned back to the receptionist and fixed him with a steely glare.

'If I searched your bag, would I find something illegal?'

The young man glared back.

'Fine. Wait there.'

So let the flouncing begin, thought Deed, giving Mac a wink.

Mac, who had played this game before, gave it thirty

seconds then whispered, 'I'm so sorry. Mr Cowrie will see you now. It's just that I'm not supposed to bla, bla, bla.'

An office door opened, and the lad made his way back to the reception desk, looking a little cowed.

'I'm so sorry. Mr Cowrie will see you now. It's just that I'm not supposed to–'

Deed held up a hand to stop him.

'No need to explain, son. You were only doing your job. I hope he didn't give you a hard time.'

Then finally, they were past the sentry, through the hallowed door of Kenneth Cowrie's office and being offered coffee by the man himself.

Not even the Chief Constable had an office like this, Deed thought. It was…shiny…just shiny. Yet Cowrie was quite the opposite. Everything about him, from his suit to his hair, was a drab grey. Had he not seen it for himself, Deed would never have imagined this dull, little solicitor surrounded by such glamour. The man clearly never came to work with a hangover because the sheer amount of glossy white and chrome would hospitalise your average functioning alcoholic.

'How can I help you, officers?' asked Cowrie.

His accent was the sort of posh Edinburgh that made its owner sound like they'd simultaneously swallowed a snooker ball and sat on the cue. Chalk end up. Deed and Mac knew full well that the man was dragged up in Leith in the years before the middle classes stole it and replaced all the prostitutes with dining experiences, but they were going to let the accent slide, for now. Get the measure of the man first.

'Thank you for seeing us at such short notice, Mr Cowrie. We're investigating a murder in Aberdeenshire, and two people have come to our attention whom we believe may work for you. We'd be grateful if you could take a look at this photograph and identify the subjects.'

Deed passed over his phone so that the solicitor could examine a still taken from Ryan Richardson's video. Cowrie glanced at it, then slid the phone towards Deed, shaking his head as he did so.

Mac leaned over and pushed the phone back across the desk, saying, 'If you wouldn't mind taking another look, Mr Cowrie, just to be sure.'

'I *am* sure,' the solicitor said. 'I don't recall meeting them, and I'm certain they're not clients.'

'Could they be subcontractors perhaps?' asked Deed, aware that a large firm like this could possibly subcontract out the scut work.

'We do take on independent contractors from time to time, but I'm afraid I wouldn't be familiar with their staff.'

'Would your HR manager be able to help?'

'Unfortunately, Sheila went home early today. Ladies' problems, I believe.'

'Does she have assistants? Maybe they know something?'

Cowrie's smile did not reach his eyes.

'Sadly, the entire staff is on a team-building event this afternoon. We'll be closing in ten minutes, so they won't be back in the office today. You appear to have had a wasted trip, gentlemen.'

'Just one more question. Do you know the name Layla Hamdy? Or Professor Ahmed Hamdy?'

'Not that I recall. Now, if there's nothing more I can do for you...'

Deed could see that Mac was about to protest so put a discreet hand on his arm to forestall him.

He said, 'Thank you again for meeting with us at short notice. We'll see ourselves out. Here's my card, just in case you think of anything more.'

The moment they hit the street, Mac rounded on Deed.

'You gave in far too easily, boss. That man's a snake. All his "I don't recall." He's hiding something!'

'There's more than one way to skin a snake,' said Deed. 'We weren't going to get anything out of him anyway. He's more slippery than an oil spill on an ice rink. Come on, there's a café across the road. I'll buy you a coffee.'

One coffee became two, as they sat at a table by the café window, watching the freshly painted black door opposite.

'Closing in ten minutes, my arse,' grumbled Mac.

Deed simply smiled and bade him be patient. Their quarry would soon emerge, and at least the coffee was good. To pass the time, they wrote their notes and scrolled through the news of the day, taking turns to make up the story behind the headline.

'Prince Edward shares why he doesn't shake hands with crowds,' said Deed.

'Because they wore out his last set of hands and his dad says if he breaks this pair then he's not getting any more,' said Mac. 'Streakers treated same as men who masturbate in a dark alley by law.'

'Seriously? That's a headline?' chuckled Deed.

'The Daily Telegraph, I shit you not.'

'Alright. I can't believe you're making me say this. An ancient law states that the men of Banff must meet in the passage by the bakery every Tuesday night, where they will… erm…share a giant biscuit. The streakers of Macduff are now obliged to join them.'

Mac's amused chortle came to an abrupt end when he spotted movement across the street. Cowrie was leaving his office. Without a backward glance, the man strode confidently along the pavement towards a taxi rank. Mac made to stand, almost knocking over his coffee in his haste, but Deed put out a warning hand, telling him to sit down and keep watching.

'I thought we were going to follow him, boss,' said Mac.

'That won't get us the information we're after. Give it a minute. Ah, here we are.'

As if on cue, the receptionist appeared on the front step. He turned to lock the door behind him, giving Deed and Mac time to run across the road and loiter casually by the building next door.

Deed considered that there was an art to "accidentally" bumping into someone. You had to have some forward momentum, but not too much; otherwise, you might injure the other party or, worse, yourself. You had to be careful to put on your surprised face after the bump and, most importantly, you had to pretend not to recognise the other person at first.

None of this was required. The receptionist turned in the opposite direction and headed briskly off down the street. Wrong-footed, Mac and Deed hurried after him, both regretting that Mac wasn't ten years younger and five stone lighter. It also occurred to them that they didn't know the young man's name, so couldn't even call for him to slow down.

Deed caught up to him first, with Mac not far behind, panting a little. His loud "excuse me" caught the attention of the receptionist, who immediately slowed and turned.

'Sorry, I didn't see you. Is everything okay? Mr Cowrie's gone home for the day.'

'We were hoping to have a quick chat with you, if that's alright,' said Deed. 'Can I buy you a drink?'

The receptionist eyed the wheezing Mac doubtfully.

'There's a decent pub round the corner, if you think he can make it that far.'

'You cheeky young pup,' said Mac. 'Mine's a pint, boss, since you're buying.'

The pub was small and, being slightly off the beaten track, its prices were quite reasonable for a central Edinburgh hostelry. The interior had been painted in trendy, modern shades of cream and grey, but the old wooden bar stood untouched, its deep, warm patina given central stage, as if to declare that nothing else mattered - drinking had happened here for hundreds of years and would continue for hundreds more.

They took their drinks to a table by the window, where the weak afternoon light barely penetrated the filthy panes.

'Thanks for speaking with us,' said Mac. 'Sorry, I don't know your name.'

'Liam. Liam Hardy, and I never turn down a free drink,' said the lad. 'I'm sorry about earlier. No excuse. I'm a right twat sometimes.'

'Us too,' said Mac, pointing at himself and Deed. 'Especially him, and he's the boss, so you'd think he'd know better.'

'Thanks Mac,' said Deed wryly. 'I'll be straight with you, Liam. Your boss wasn't overly helpful. We're looking for the murderer of a young woman about the same age as yourself. We have a photograph of a couple that might be connected and that we want to trace.'

He unlocked his phone and showed Liam the same video still that he'd shown Cowrie earlier. The young man took his time, eventually handing the phone back to Deed with a curt nod.

'I've seen the man,' he said. 'He's been in the office a few times, mostly to see Mr Cowrie. They're probably private investigators. Sometimes the firm needs extra information when cases are going to court or they need to persuade a client's husband to be more generous with the divorce settlement, so they use private investigators. Well, I say private investigators, but they're fixers too.'

'Fixers?' asked Mac.

'If you have a problem, they make it go away. I don't mean that I know they go around bumping people off.' Liam took a sip of his drink, then continued, 'For example, if you were bidding for a large building contract and you thought your competitor was going to win, these guys would start planting stories in the press or pay people to make complaints about a recent building project so that your competitor looks unreliable.'

'Do you know their names or the name of the firm they work for?' asked Deed.

'No. I'll check Mr Cowrie's calendar tomorrow and see if

there are any names in there. I don't know if they work for a separate firm. They have passes, so they might work directly for us.'

Liam pulled a plastic card and lanyard from his pocket and showed the officers his pass.

'It doesn't actually do anything. It's only an ID badge that HR give out. It's a pity you couldn't speak to HR today. They could probably have told you who those people are and who they work for.'

'Aye, it's a pity Sheila went home sick.'

'Who's Sheila?' asked Liam.

'The HR woman,' said Deed.

'We don't have a Sheila in HR.'

'I must have misheard,' said Deed, knowing that he hadn't. 'What about the rest of the staff? Do you think anyone else would know anything helpful? We didn't get to speak to them, what with them being on a team building event.'

Liam hesitated and seemed to struggle with his conscience for a moment, before saying, 'They weren't on a team building event. God, I hope I'm not going to get into trouble for telling you this. Mr Cowrie sent everyone home at lunchtime. He only kept me there because he needed somebody to answer the phones.'

Deed turned to Mac and their eyes met.

'Interesting,' he said. 'It's almost as if Cowrie was expecting us.'

CHAPTER 16

The magicians' convention was in full swing. A noticeboard by the hotel reception desk read:

Day 2 – The Modern Magician

The hat is no place for a rabbit

Sawing women, men and other gender identities in half

Lunch

Assistants – other body shapes can be glamorous too

Improve your hex life - using your wand responsibly

Jim was supposed to be meeting Penny for a swim but was instead poking about backstage, doing some excellent multi-tasking. He was successfully combining his curiosity as to how the magic tricks worked with his desire to avoid his girlfriend.

He wished he could magic up some answers about Thermacorp. He'd called a few of the farms owned by the company and discovered that they were still operational. "Business as usual," the farmers had assured him, yet they were strangely unwilling to answer any further questions. So far, he had resisted Penny's attempts to get in the car and go visit the farms in person, but he was starting to think that she was right. Not that he'd tell her, of course. He'd rather be locked in one of them there fancy boxes and run through with a sword.

Snooping through magic tricks was even better than getting a bravery award, he decided, if a little freaky. All these mysterious gadgets and piles of silk handkerchiefs and sharp objects and…ooh, what do we have here? He opened the door of a tall cabinet and immediately felt his sphincter give an involuntary spasm.

'Fuck! Oh, fuck.'

Gordon sat on the floor of the cabinet, his knees drawn up as far as his belly allowed. Jim gave him an experimental poke, just to check he wasn't an illusion, then jumped back and shut the door.

He gave his heart a moment to sink back down from his throat to his chest, before opening the door again.

There was nobody there.

'Bugger me with a Three-card Monte! I think I'm hallucinating Gordons. This must be what happens when you have toast for breakfast instead of sausages.'

He opened the door again, and Gordon was back.

'Fuck!' Jim exclaimed. 'How did you do that?'

Gordon looked up at him, misery etched across his face.

'Do what?'

'Never mind. Why are you in here?'

'There's been a wee snafu with Sergeant Wilson's jodhpurs, and I'm facing certain death, so I thought the best thing to do was hide. What are you doing here?'

'I was trying to think of ways to say that Penny was right without actually saying she was right.'

'Is there any chance you could sneak me into Inverurie to get new trousers? I was supposed to go shopping with Fiona, but she's all upset about Fergus, so I didn't like to remind her. And I can't tell her I've burst another pair.'

'That's not a bad idea,' said Jim. 'We can get trousers, *and* we can visit the farms.'

He checked his watch and gave Gordon a thumbs up.

'When we get back, I'll tell Penny that we went shopping and thought we may as well visit the farms while we were out anyway.'

'Why are we visiting farms?' Gordon asked.

'Because I phoned a few of the farms belonging to Thermacorp and the farmers aren't talking, so Penny says we need to visit them in person. Only she knows I don't want her gadding about doing risky things. But she's right. Only, I can't tell her that because it'll be like I'm going back on what I said about doing risky things. And, worse, if I admit she's right, she'll never shut up about it.'

'Have you two ever considered just having a good talk about stuff?'

'Says the man hiding in a vanishing cabinet to avoid his wife and Sergeant Wilson.'

'Fair point.'

Jim held out a hand and helped Gordon to his feet, pausing for a moment to inspect the damage.

'Ach, a safety pin should hold them together long enough for us to make it to the shops. Do they have dungaree shops in Inverurie?'

'I was thinking of something more stretchy,' said Gordon.

'You're on a slippery slope there, pal. We need to steer you back to non-elasticated waists. And I notice you've gone commando again. Come on, I'll lend...*give* you a pair of boxers so you don't get done for flashing in the changing rooms.'

The short drive from the hotel to the Country Clothing Emporium, the sartorial destination for the well-dressed farmer, took them past three chip shops. Both men agreed that if nothing else came from this trip, they had at least gained highly valuable local knowledge.

They parked in the Square, the hub of the town which, despite decades of oil boom and bust, had remained almost entirely unchanged. Jim recalled a school camping trip more than thirty years ago, where the only relief from endless hikes in the rain was being let loose in Inverurie town centre. He and his friends had marauded through the Square, setting the wreath on the war memorial tumbling and shocking the locals by smoking cigarettes on the town hall steps.

He remembered the ironmongers, a mercantile labyrinth which sold everything from paint to gardening tools to china souvenirs. He'd spent nearly an hour in there, desperate to buy his mum a dog or a ballerina, yet terrified by the handwritten notices on every shelf - Lovely to look at, delightful to hold, but if you break me, consider me sold. Wee Jimmy Space had been a skinny arrangement of arms and legs that had a tendency to grow an inch overnight and knock him off kilter. He could do untold damage in this shop, and he only had his five pounds holiday money.

Like a few of the small independents, the ironmongers was gone now, replaced by a chain selling premium brands, yet it made little difference. If wee Jimmy Space had been transported through time, he would barely have noticed.

The Country Clothing Emporium was a short walk from the Square, nestled among the boutiques and bridal stores that were scattered the length of the High Street. A little bell above the door tinkled its warning as Jim and Gordon entered in search of the elusive dungaree, and a very serious man in very serious hiking gear came out to check that he wasn't being robbed.

'I'm looking for some trousers, preferably dungarees,' Gordon told him.

'We do a good range,' said the man, settling himself onto a chair behind the counter. 'We're one of the few places in the area that supplies work clothes to the farmers. We also have strong boots, fleeces and mountain gear. You won't find your big-name brands, but we can't be beat on quality.'

Gordon and Jim exchanged excited glances. This was it – the ultimate man goal. They had achieved in half an hour what took many men a lifetime. They had found the only shop they would ever need. They had found their tribe. Jim felt strongly that there should be rousing music to mark this moment; it needed bagpipes and maybe a drum and snare. Och, dammit, a full pipe band belting out Scotland the Brave.

'Do you take orders online?' Jim asked, thinking ahead to their triumphant return to Vik, where he and Gordon would spread the word and be hailed as conquering heroes down the pub.

'Aye,' the shopkeeper nodded. 'Got to keep up with the times.'

'I think I might actually love you,' Gordon whispered.

'Well, I am very attractive,' said the man, his countenance deadpan, although Jim thought he detected a twinkle of amusement behind the eyes.

'This is the best shop I've ever been in,' said Gordon. 'It's a shame we're just passing through. I could spend the whole day here.'

'Thanks very much. Are you on holiday? We don't get many tourists in March, what with the weather. You can still get up Bennachie, though. There's a good, sturdy pair of walking boots on the bottom shelf, next to the steel toe-capped wellies.'

The man eyed Gordon's lower half with some distaste and added, 'If you're after a new pair of ladies' jodhpurs, they're on the top shelf on the left.'

'Thanks,' said Gordon. 'It's mainly the dungers I'm

looking for. And no, we're not tourists. We're on our way out to speak to some of the farmers around Bennachie. Has there been any local gossip about folk buying up the farms out there?'

'How many pairs of dungarees did you say you wanted?' the man asked.

'I'd say at least three,' said Gordon.

The man was silent.

'Okay, make it four.'

The man remained silent.

'And I'll take two pairs of the ladies' jodhpurs.'

'In which case,' said the man, 'you'll want to talk to Frankie Mitchell out at Glenmachie. The other farmers won't speak to you, but Frankie will if you tell him I sent you. Paul Jamieson. I've been supplying his checked shirts for twenty years.'

Gordon was rather pleased with himself. So far on this holiday, he'd had one good idea, located the chip shops and now he'd found out some very important information. A single question remained.

'Where will we find Glenmachie farm?'

Jamieson was silent.

'Do you have these fleeces in green?' Jim asked.

'Certainly do. Third shelf up on your right.'

'I'll take two.'

'In which case, I'll draw you a map,' said Jamieson, before turning back to Gordon. 'Now, about these dungarees. What size do you require?'

Gordon glanced uncertainly at Jim, then shuffled closer to the till. He helped himself to a sticky note from a plastic tub full of odds and ends, wrote a number on it, folded it and slid it across the counter to Jamieson.

'Your discretion is appreciated.'

Jim rolled his eyes and was about to pass comment when he felt a vibration in his pocket. He left his friend trying on dungarees and strolled outside to answer his phone, cursing under his breath when he saw the caller ID. So desperate had Gordon been to avoid Fiona, that they'd slunk out of the hotel without telling anyone, and now it would seem that Penny had discovered they were gone.

'Hello. You're through to Jim Space, sexy vet and all-round nice guy. I can't come to the phone right now because I'm too busy being downright charming. Please leave a message at the tone. Beep.'

'Jim. I know you're there. Your voicemail message is just you saying "Aye" then a beep. Where are you?'

'Shopping,' said Jim meekly.

'That's a load of old rubbish. You hate shopping.'

'I so am shopping! Look!'

Jim switched on the camera and turned his phone to face the shop. Through the window, Gordon could be seen wandering out of the changing rooms to ask Jamieson if he had any dungarees in the next size up.

'It's the best shop in the world,' Jim declared. 'Turns out I do like shopping. I just never found the right shop before.'

There was a lengthy pause while Penny absorbed this news, then…

'Is Gordon wearing your boxers?'

'Aye, well, you could hardly expect him to be rubbing his gentleman's area over things then putting them back on the shelf.'

'Erm, does that mean you're not wearing any?'

'No! They're a clean pair. Do you think I slipped my boxers off in the shop and lent them to him? We're good pals, but we're not *that* close.'

'The whole thing's a bit weird,' said Penny. 'You and Gordon going on a shopping trip.'

'If I tell you, will you promise not to tell Fiona or Sergeant Wilson?'

'What? That he's burst the jodhpurs?'

'God, Sherlock, how did you know?'

'Logic, dear Watson, and Fiona's not daft either. She'll

figure it out as soon as she sees that he's bought new dungarees. Just make sure you come back with some identical jodhpurs so that Sergeant Wilson doesn't do a Sergeant Wilson.'

'Alright,' said Jim. 'I'll see you in a wee while.'

'Define a wee while.'

'There's a chip shop here with an actual restaurant.'

'I'll see you in a couple of hours.'

Gordon wisely opted to wear the dungarees and had happily handed over his entire year's clothing budget to Jamieson by the time Jim re-entered the shop. Jim bought two fleeces as promised, and they left clutching four carrier bags and the directions to Glenmachie farm.

Despite the lure of the chip shop, neither man had any intention of making a delicious haddocky, potatoey, salty and vinegary detour. Although it pained them, they were on a mission impossible. Trousers then farmers. They were hardened investigators, seasoned wheedlers of information, international mannies of mystery. And they agreed that not even Tom Cruise could have tracked down the only dungaree seller in Inverurie who just happened to know a loose-lipped agriculturalist.

Later, locals would claim that they heard two strange men careening down the Bennachie road in a battered Land Rover, singing, 'Doot, doot, do-do. Doot, doot, do-do. Doot, doot, do-do. Doot, doot, do-do. Diddly-doo. Diddly-doo. Da-dum.'

By the time they reached Glenmachie, Jim and Gordon had notionally saved the whole of Scotland from dungaree disaster and were ready to apply the thumbscrews to any dissembling farmers in their path. They would swing through cattle barns on ropes and jump electric fences to get to the truth.

The reality, of course, was entirely different. They pulled up in a muddy yard and tiptoed across the concrete, trying not to get chicken poop on their trainers. Outside the farmhouse, a short, bearded man in orange overalls was tinkering with a tractor engine. He must have been around seventy years old, Jim reckoned, but the deftness with which he was wielding the spanner and the head of thick, brown hair gave the impression of a much younger man.

'Aye, aye, fit like?' said Jim, subconsciously dialling up the local dialect in an effort to fit in.

'Bonjour and foo is your doos,' said the man in a thick French accent.

Slightly taken aback, Jim's own accent now morphed into formal English.

'Aye, eh, hello. I am looking for Frankie Mitchell.'

'I am François Michelle,' said the man, wiping his hands on a rag.

'Nice to meet you,' said Gordon, 'but we're looking for Frankie Mitchell. Do you know where we might find him?'

The man sighed and gave Gordon a look that managed to combine both pity and resignation in equal measure.

'I believe you are confused, non? François Michelle. Around here, they call me Frankie Mitchell. They think it is a good joke. Ha, ha, very funny. But after thirty years…' The man gave a Gallic shrug.

'Sorry about that,' said Gordon. 'François, Frrrrançois. Haw hee haw hee haw, Ferrrrrançois.'

He rolled the name on his tongue as if testing it for compatibility with the rest of his mouth.

'Please, it is torture to my ears. Frankie is fine.'

'Thanks,' said Jim, flashing Gordon an exasperated look. 'We've been looking into sales of farms in the area and Paul Jamieson suggested that we talk to you.'

Frankie dipped his head and regarded the men suspiciously from beneath a pair of dark, bristly eyebrows.

'Are you police?'

'No, we're dieters,' said Jim. 'Look, it's a long story. Is there somewhere we could sit down?'

Frankie led them into the farmhouse; a two-storey stone cottage which had been extended to include an incongruously modern wooden box, complete with bi-fold doors and a glass balcony.

'It is the wife,' Frankie explained as they entered a glossy kitchen that would have graced any magazine. 'She is always watching the shows like Grand Designs. Malheureusement, we cannot have guests in the extension. I am a farmer, so she waits until after lambing for the underfloor heating.'

Over large mugs of tea, Jim explained how they were helping a friend look into Thermacorp, and along the way, had stumbled across the purchase by the company of several farms in the Bennachie area. Had Frankie been approached by Thermacorp?

'Not Thermacorp,' said Frankie. 'Shortly after they announced the road plans, me and many other farmers were contacted by some solicitors, I think, Cowrie Robert.

'What did they say?' Jim asked.

'They told us that their client was making steps to save Bennachie from the new road. How do you say it? A protected area for the natural beauty.'

'Area of outstanding natural beauty,' said Gordon.

Frankie raised his mug in acknowledgement and continued, 'They said if you sell us your farm we will make sure there is no compulsory purchase from the government. We have all the money and important friends to fight this. Do you have the money and important friends? Non, you do not. Sell us your land and we will lease it back to you. The road is stopped, you still have a farm, we can protect the beauty, and everybody wins.'

'Sounds reasonable,' said Jim. 'Did you sell?'

'Non, I did not. And I will tell you for why. It is all too good to be true. I asked about the client and Monsieur Cowrie said they were an investment company called Juniper.'

'An investment company?' asked Gordon. 'That's a bit weird.

'I think the same. "Why is an investment company saving the land?" I asked. "What is in it for them?" He says, "Fair dos and hunky-dory, Frankie. Maybe they will keep some of the land for a hotel and a golf course." I said no because I do not trust this deal, but he keeps coming back and coming back, more and more pressure to sell. Now, my fences are being broken, and my sheep are getting out. Or my machinery is broken, and it is expensive to fix. My workers don't come to work. No explanation. But Monsieur Cowrie has forgotten that I am a French farmer. I am born to fight. My son is born to fight. His son is born to fight. Three generations of Michelles will stand and fight the oppresseur.'

Frankie's voice had risen as he'd detailed the harassment and his fists were now pumping the air. Roused, Gordon stood up with a cry of 'Vive la revolution!'

Jim pulled Gordon back into his chair and asked, 'Have the other farmers had similar problems?'

'Pardon,' said Frankie, his eyes still blazing. 'I am very angry about this. None of the farmers held out for very long. The offer was raised, most took it, then the rest caved in to the pressure. They won't talk to you because they all signed a non-disclosure agreement. Which is also very strange, I think, non?'

Jim agreed that this was unusual, adding, 'But you must have done something about it. I mean, told people.'

'I tried to go to the newspapers and the police about this, but nobody is listening. A girl came to see me. She was going to write my story for a big newspaper, but she didn't call back, and I have heard nothing more.'

Jim leaned forward, very aware of his own heartbeat as he asked his next question.

'This journalist, did you get her name?'

'I have her card here somewhere. The first time she came, she recorded my interview. The second time, she had her little computer and typed tippy tappy everything. She showed me the article and I thought it was magnifique. Parfait. Restez là, I will look for the card.'

Frankie went off to another room, and they could hear

him muttering to himself as he opened drawers and cupboards. Eventually, he returned with a small, white slip of card and handed it to Jim, who quickly read it and passed it to Gordon.

Layla Hamdy
Freelance Journalist
layla.hamdy@gravynet.com

CHAPTER 17

On the lower slopes of Bennachie, Vik's version of Charlie's Angels was making its way up the steep bit.

'The dancing keeps you fit,' said Mrs Hubbard.

'The housework keeps you limber,' said Sandra Next Door.

'Dressing up in a giant bunny outfit when your suspect needs a bit of physical encouragement keeps you anonymous,' said Sergeant Wilson.

The others looked at her aghast.

She shrugged and said, 'Easy was going to do the Easter Policester talk at the school, so I borrowed his bunny costume and paid a wee visit to the interview room. Nobody's going to put in a complaint to Dunderheid that the Easter Bunny sat on them, are they?'

'Who did you sit on?' asked Sandra Next Door.

'Mr Long, coincidentally the deputy head at Port Vik Primary. He accidentally on purpose sent a picture of a dead rat to the PE teacher, who happens to be sleeping with Long's missus on the side. Anyway, Easy turned up at the school the next day for Easter Policester, the guy took one look and he's been off sick with trauma ever since. Problem sorted.'

Mrs Hubbard filed this nugget away for safekeeping. She was fairly sure that she wasn't supposed to tell anyone, but you never knew when a piece of information might come in handy.

They were nearing the top of the bank now and they could see some of the Colonists milling around. When they crested the hill, it became clear that something was wrong.

Upon spotting them, Claire rushed over. She was pale and jittery, and Sergeant Wilson's first thought was oh aye, she's coming down from something that I'm not supposed to know about. Yet the woman seemed inordinately relieved to see them.

'Can you help us? We're all ill. I don't know what it is, but I'm so worried about Dani. She can't even keep water down. It's been like this since last night and everyone's just getting worse.'

'Have you called an ambulance?' asked Sergeant Wilson.

'Our phones aren't working. They were supplied by the charity, but they withdrew their funding yesterday, and I think they must have somehow cancelled the phones. Phoebe, Kendra and Jake weren't too sick, so they went down to the village to get help. That was hours ago, and they haven't come back.'

An immediate change came over Sergeant Wilson. The rude, mischief-making devil was gone, and in its place was the police officer trained to deal with a crisis. It wasn't simply that she exuded authority. The change was physical too. She seemed to grow in stature and her voice became lower.

'Mrs Hubbard, call an ambulance. Tell them that...how many of you are sick?'

'Thirty,' said Claire. 'A few have left, but most of us voted to stay on the Colony for the summer. I don't know why I'm telling you that. Oh, God, I'm going to be–'

Claire rushed off towards the bushes and Sergeant Wilson turned back to Mrs Hubbard.

'Tell them that there are thirty people here who need treatment, with at least one urgent. Vomiting, the squirts, dehydration. Sandra, you're with me. We're going to check on everyone and triage them as best we can, then we'll give Mrs Hubbard an update to relay to the paramedics. Don't touch anyone or rub your face. I don't want us catching it as well. I am not spending my last hours shitting in a bush next to you, Sandra Next Door.'

Ignoring the jibe, Sandra rummaged through the contents of her handbag and extracted three face masks and three pairs of thin, blue plastic gloves.

'Are you shagging somebody in the forensics lab?' asked Sergeant Wilson, donning the mask.

Sandra Next Door sighed the deep sigh of someone who has a heavy cross to bear.

'They're for emergencies in case housekeeping don't clean my room properly. There's a bottle of bleach in here too, if you're thirsty.'

'Mind, I like my bleach with ice,' retorted the Sergeant. 'If you don't have any in that bag of yours, you'll find some down your knickers.'

Without waiting for a response, she strode off, yelling, 'Foreskin-ninjas, would the walking dead please come to the firepit in the middle?'

Between them, Sandra Next Door and Sergeant Wilson checked tents, the latrines, the kailyard and anywhere else they thought they might find a Colonist. They took notes of names and Sergeant Wilson returned to the walking dead at the firepit to check if they'd missed anyone.

A bedraggled soul dully lifted his head and mumbled, 'The only problem is, nobody's sure who left and who stayed. Somebody could have wandered off in a bad way, and none of us would know.'

Sandra Next Door found Dani lying on a thin mattress in one of the tents. The young woman's face was covered in a sheen of sweat and she was shivering violently. She didn't have the energy to talk, simply giving Sandra a pleading look before her eyelids fluttered closed. The ground beside her was awash with vomit, and the smell of faeces had hit Sandra the moment she lifted the tent flap. Someone had clearly been trying to take care of the lass judging by the bowl of water and the cloth which lay near her head.

'You poor thing,' said Sandra Next Door. 'Help is on its way. Let's get you cleaned up.'

She lifted the edge of the sleeping bag and immediately dropped it. Normally, she thought, the advantage of being a cleaning hobbyist is that you've seen so much filth nothing fazes you. But this is a whole other level of gruesome. It's like a swimming pool down there.

'Whoof. Have you been at the fermented herring again? You know it doesn't agree with you,' said a voice behind her.

'Not now, Martisha. Come here and help.'

It was difficult to manoeuvre in such a small space, but between them they lifted Dani onto a blanket so that Sandra Next Door could mop up the mess with a towel. Sergeant Wilson stripped Dani's clothes, using the water from the bowl to clean her before wrapping another thick towel around her lower half. Both women retched their way through the exercise, but by the time they were done, Dani was more comfortable.

'We need to make her drink,' said Sandra Next Door, pulling a bottle of water from her bag. 'God, she's just a kid. She was fine yesterday. They were all fine yesterday. Is it a virus? Bacterial? What could spread this quickly?'

'I don't know. It could be something they ate or drank,' said Sergeant Wilson.

She shuffled to the tent opening on her knees, preparing to leave, then paused and turned to look at her fellow Loser.

'Just a thought,' she said. 'Don't let anyone drink the water from the well.'

When Sergeant Wilson returned to the centre of the camp, Mrs Hubbard was still on the phone, updating the paramedics and guiding them to their location. She paused briefly to let the crowd know that an air ambulance was on its way, then went back to her call.

'Foreskin-ninjas,' shouted Sergeant Wilson. 'Stop puking and listen. I want you to go back to your tents and gather all the bottled water. Take it here and share it out. Do not drink the water from the well. I repeat, don't be arseholes and do as you're told.'

Holding the phone to her chest, Mrs Hubbard sidled over to the Sergeant and said, 'The air ambulance will be here within half an hour for the urgent casualties. Normal ambulances should arrive soon. It'll take the paramedics hours to get up here and see to everyone, so I've said we'll get as many as we can down the hill to the Visitor Centre.'

'You're not such a useless old baggage after all, Mrs H. Any who aren't taken to hospital won't be going back up the hill tonight. I'll ring the local bobbies and ask if someone can arrange a place for them to stay.'

'Do you really think it's the water, dearie?'

'I've done farts that have spread slower than whatever's ailing this lot. They're using the water for cooking, bathing and drinking, so the water's the most likely culprit.'

Mrs Hubbard's lips folded into a determined line, and she gave a curt nod.

'When they come back with their bottled water, I'll get as many as possible down the hill. If you and Sandra Next Door stay here, I'll give the emergency services your numbers so you can coordinate with them. Goodness, I never expected this. I thought we'd have a nice wee wander, you'd shout at Claire, then we'd go into Inverurie for a cup of tea. Where is Claire? I haven't seen her since we arrived.'

Sergeant Wilson looked alarmed. Claire was in no fit state to be wandering. The lassie had looked on the point of collapse. Without another word, the Sergeant strode off at speed, back towards where Claire had met them on the brow of the hill.

She stared at the patch of bushes into which the woman

had disappeared earlier and roared, 'Are you in there, Claire? If you're shitting in there, I hope your arse is aimed downhill.'

There was no response, so she tried again.

'If I have to come in there and get you, I better not slip on something nasty. I've lent my other pair of jodhpurs to Gordon, and he's spilled so much ketchup on them it looks like he's on his man period.'

Still no response. With a savage "Fuck!" Sergeant Wilson picked up a big stick and prodded the bushes, peering between the branches. Beyond the initial tangle, there was a path which led downhill into the trees. Mining the depths of her swear word collection, the Sergeant pushed through and began to scout around for her quarry.

The light was dim here, filtered as it was through the towering Scots Pine. Underfoot, the ground was spongy and slippery with needles, making the terrain hard going, and more than once Sergeant Wilson struggled to maintain her balance in stiff riding boots. It wasn't long, however, before she spotted a patch of red, bright against the unrelenting browns of the forest. Claire's coat.

Claire was slumped against a tree, her legs splayed in front of her, her head resting against the rough bark. Even from a distance, the Sergeant could see that her eyes were closed and that she was unnaturally still.

'Fuck, fuck, fuckity, fuck. You better not be dead. I'm not coming all the way down this bastarding hill just to find out you're dead. If you're dead, I'm leaving you here.'

The moment she reached Claire, Sergeant Wilson fell to her knees and pressed two fingers to the woman's neck. There was a pulse, but it was faint. Breath steady but shallow.

Shit, bollocks, bums.

Sergeant Wilson wasn't sure what to do. She couldn't carry Claire back up the hill to the Colony on her own. She'd have to call Sandra Next Door and tell her to come down and help. Buggeration. She didn't have Sandra's number. She'd deleted it from her phone because she got indigestion every time she scrolled past it.

She stood up and dialled Mrs Hubbard.

'Minty. I've found Claire. She's in the woods and I can't get her back up on my own. Can you text me Sandra Next Door's number? No. If I had it, I wouldn't be asking you for it. Aye, I did have it. What? Because every time I see her name it makes me think of lemons. Eh? No, not the sweetie kind. Sour lemons. I don't like lemons. They give me indigestion. Fuck's sake, just text me the number.'

Sergeant Wilson's phone beeped, and she screwed up her face when she saw Sandra's number. With a sigh, she dialled.

'I've got Claire. I need a hand to get her back up to the camp. Push through the bushes where we last saw her. There's a path through the trees. And bring some indigestion tablets.'

She squatted down next to Claire and pulled the ends of the woman's anorak together, trying to fasten the zip to keep the cold out.

'I'm quite good in an emergency,' she said. 'Calm and very diplomatic. I think I might be a fucking people person. I'll make sure that Dunderheid puts it in my next appraisal.'

Claire's eyelids fluttered, and her breathing became ragged.

The Sergeant tapped her face, saying, 'Claire, can you hear me? Claire?'

The woman's mouth opened, and her breath hissed between dry lips.

'Don't try to talk,' said Sergeant Wilson. 'Help is on its way.'

Claire's whisper was barely audible.

'Frankie.'

'Save your energy. Don't worry about this Frankie gadgie.'

Claire's whisper became stronger, and she tried to move her arms.

'Frankie says…'

'Relax'

'Frankie says…'

'Relax.'

'Frankie.'

'Look, if you're trying to get me to say don't do it, I'm not going to. It's nae a fucking nineteen eighties disco.'

Claire lapsed back into unconsciousness, leaving the Sergeant to her one-sided conversation on the musical merits of Karma Chameleon and who was the best looking one in Duran Duran. By the time Sandra Next Door arrived, she'd moved onto her theory that Bob Geldof survived on a diet of his own bogies.

'There's definitely a vitamin deficiency there,' she concluded. 'Although he seems like a very nice man and I'm sorry for all his troubles. Ah, Sandra Next Door, good of you to join us.'

Together, she and Sandra managed to carry Claire up the path. They found an alternative route which didn't involve pushing through bushes and eventually deposited Claire gently by the fire pit.

There were only half a dozen Colonists left, the others having staggered down to the Visitor Centre like sick little ducks behind old mother duck Hubbard. Those that remained were too weak to make the two-and-a-half-mile trip, so sat quietly on the ground, sagging against the log benches and listening for the sound of helicopter blades in the distance. There was little more that Sandra Next Door and Sergeant Wilson could do. Once they had hauled mattresses and sleeping bags from tents to keep their patients warm and comfortable, they built a fire in the firepit and settled down to wait.

The quiet in the clearing was almost eerie. Even the birds seemed to have sensed that something was wrong, their presence marked only by a faint rustle in the trees. The whump of rotors when it came seemed unnaturally loud.

They watched as the helicopter, its yellow livery bright

against the grey sky, landed on the area of heather where Gordon had found Layla two days ago. Only two days, thought Sandra Next Door. It felt like a lifetime.

The medics took Claire first, assuring them that another helicopter was on its way for Dani. One by one, the helicopters circled back to collect another Colonist so that, by mid-afternoon, the Colony was an empty, desolate place full of discarded sleeping bags and empty tents.

Exhausted, Sergeant Wilson and Sandra Next Door made their way down the rocky path towards the Visitor Centre.

'I wonder what happened to Jake, Phoebe and Kendra,' said Sandra Next Door.

'Mysteries are like Chinese takeaways,' mused Sergeant Wilson. 'You think you've had your fill, then five minutes later you're hankering for more. I told the local cops and they've sent out a search party from Pitcaple. No doubt we'll hear they've been found spewing their guts up in a layby at Chapel of Garioch. I asked my colleagues to send a team up to the Colony to test the water too.'

They walked on in companionable silence, thinking their own thoughts and trying not to trip over any rocks.

After a while, Sandra Next Door cleared her throat and said stiffly, 'You did a good job back there, for someone with the people skills of an angry wasp.'

Her voice gruff, Sergeant Wilson replied, 'You didn't do so badly yourself, for the love child of Ted Bundy and Rose West. Anyway, I do so have people skills. I did lots of people skilling today.'

The walk continued with no further exchanges until they finally joined Mrs Hubbard at the Visitor Centre. Over Sergeant Wilson's objections, she enveloped them both in a warm hug.

'Thank goodness you're here, dearies. I called us a taxi when you said you were on your way down and it should be with us any minute. I was starting to worry it might get here before you.'

Even Sandra Next Door cracked a smile at the thought of going back to the hotel.

She said, 'If I never go up Bennachie again, it will be too soon.'

'You've gone and jinxed it now,' Sergeant Wilson complained, gearing up for an argument.

To Mrs Hubbard's relief, her outrage was cut short by the arrival of the taxi. Bowing to the Sergeant's refusal to sit next to her nemesis, Mrs Hubbard got in the back with Sandra Next Door, leaving the police officer to irritate the driver from the front seat.

The driver was a chatty sort, happy to share "worst ever passenger" stories with Mrs Hubbard, talk about the best handheld vacuum cleaners with Sandra Next Door and tell Sergeant Wilson to bugger off when she tried to help herself to one of his mints, but like many of his ilk, he liked a good chinwag about politics.

'What about this leadership election eh?' he said. 'The news is saying that Elaine Bear is set to win. I wouldn't mind that. She's done well with all the subsidies for offshore windfarms and not spoiling Scotland. People like me need the tourists to keep coming and that's not going to happen if you fill the bonnie bits with great, muckle windmills. Fuelling the nation, that's what she calls it.'

The women, mindful that their beautiful island was under threat from one of these offshore scourges, professed little interest in politics, so he tried again.

'I hear there was some excitement up Bennachie today. 'Did you catch any of it?'

'No,' snapped Sergeant Wilson, before Mrs Hubbard could open her mouth and spend the next ten minutes giving him a blow-by-blow account of every vomit on the way back down the hill.

'Somebody said it was the Colonists taken ill. It's a shame. They're not a bad lot. I often pick them up from the Visitor Centre when it's too wet for them to walk to Pitcaple for the bus. I picked up that lassie on the day she was murdered. I canna tell you how sad I was to hear of it. She was one of my regulars.'

Sergeant Wilson's ears pricked up at this and she began to regret having been so cantankerous. She bared her teeth at the driver, forcing the corners of her mouth to turn upwards.

'She was a friend of a friend,' said the Sergeant, stretching the truth almost to breaking point. 'We're all devastated. What sort of places did she like going?'

'Mostly Inverurie. I think she'd meet friends there. Then she was up at a farm. What's it called? Let me think. Glenmachie, the Frenchie's place. It's not too far from Bennachie, but quite a long walk when you're a couple of women on your own. Nowhere's safe these days. You see the news and it's terrible. Women being attacked, and then there's what goes on behind closed doors. We didn't used to have all these rapists and paedophiles when I was young. I'm telling you, I wouldn't want my daughter to be–'

'On behalf of all women, thank you for being an ally, but can we stick to the fucking point? Please,' said Sergeant Wilson, still trying to be pleasant but suspecting that there might be a slight undertone of impatience bleeding through.

'Martisha Wilson.'

Mrs Hubbard's voice sounded a warning note from the back.

'What? I said fucking please.'

'We're sorry about her,' said Mrs Hubbard, leaning forward to speak to the driver. 'She's…different. You were saying our friend was with someone when she went to the farm. You'll appreciate that we didn't see much of Layla when she was up there on Bennachie. We'd like to know more about her last days. Do you know who she was with when she went to the farm?'

The taxi driver stared ahead at the road for a few moments, deciding how helpful he wanted to be given the attitude of the heathen beside him, then his good nature won out. He glanced in the rear-view mirror and his eyes met Mrs Hubbard's.

'Fair enough. But if she fucking swears at me again, I'm chucking her out.'

Sergeant Wilson looked like she had something to say on the matter, but Mrs Hubbard laid a hand on her arm and said, 'Quit while you're ahead, dearie.'

'Your friend went to the farm twice,' said the taxi driver. 'The first time was a couple of months ago, near the beginning of January. The second time was Monday, and that's when she had somebody with her. It was an older woman. I didn't catch her name, but she looked like she'd had a hard paper round, if you know what I mean.'

'About forty. Haggard. Needs a good wash,' said Sandra Next Door.

'Aye, that's the one. I picked them up again in the afternoon. I dropped the young one back at Bennachie and took the older one to Inverurie. That's all I can tell you.'

'Claire,' murmured Mrs Hubbard.

Sergeant Wilson attempted her friendliest baring of teeth at the taxi driver and asked, 'Have you told this to the police?'

'No. There's nothing to tell. They were whispering all the way, so I don't know what they were saying. I dropped one off at Bennachie and the other off at J.G. Ross, and that was it.'

'Who's J.G. Ross?' asked Mrs Hubbard.

'You haven't been to J.G. Ross? Oh, you're missing out there. Best stovies in Inverurie, although I'm a panini man myself.'

'It's a café?' asked Sandra Next Door.

'And with knobs on. It's a baker's with a restaurant up at the business park. Massive building. You can't miss it. They do ice cream as well, and there's even a post office. I could swing by and show you, if you like.'

'I think you could drop us off there,' said Mrs Hubbard. 'Does anyone fancy a bite to eat?'

There was general agreement that they could probably mainline the entire menu, so hungry were they, followed by a companionable lull in conversation while each of the trio quietly fantasised about food.

Fortunately, they didn't have long to wait. Within minutes, the taxi driver pulled up outside a large, modern building, a sprawling testament to beige harling, and handed the Mrs Hubbard a card.

'If you need picking up later,' he said, 'ask for Eddie and I'll come straight away.'

With a cheery toot of the horn, he drove off, leaving the women to contemplate their next move. The smell of food was almost irresistible, and their lizard brains were compelling them towards the restaurant, but Mrs Hubbard was made of stronger stuff. No lizard was going to tell her what to do.

'I don't know about you, dearies,' she said, 'but I feel a sudden urge to visit a post office.'

CHAPTER 18

The beak-nosed creature fluttering about behind the counter was the sort of person that Mrs Hubbard thought of as "one who always has to be up and doing." Consequently, she was far too busy to stop for polite chit-chat about women who looked like druggies coming into her post office on Monday. There were piles of envelopes to straighten, stamps to arrange and rolls of stickers to put in the sticker printer. Mrs Hubbard's enquiries were a bloomin' nuisance when she had so many important jobs to do.

'I don't recall,' she snapped. 'Now, if you don't mind, I'm busy.'

'I only need a few seconds of your time,' said Mrs Hubbard. 'If you could just stop and listen, dearie.'

The woman did stop, but her objective wasn't to listen. She straightened her cardigan, tugging sharply on the hem, and fixed Mrs Hubbard with a hard stare.

'I'm not your dearie, and you're clearly not here to post anything, so please vacate the premises.'

Mrs Hubbard opened her mouth to apologise and explain that she'd meant no offence, but she found herself firmly moved aside by Sergeant Wilson, who slapped her warrant card hard against the plexiglass and snarled, 'For fuck's sake, it's not hard. Did a druggie-looking, middle-aged woman in a blue hoodie or red anorak post something here on Monday?'

Far from backing down, the woman bridled at this, tugging the hem of her cardigan even harder. Her lips formed a tight, puckered circle and she drew a sharp breath in through her nose.

'I don't know who you think you are, using that sort of language. I shall complain about you.'

Sergeant Wilson's eyes narrowed dangerously, and in a tone worthy of the dirtiest of Harries, she growled, 'I'm a woman with a yeast infection who hasn't had her lunch. A woman who is reduced to two things: food and fanny. Now, I can arrest you for getting between a police officer and her hot panini, or you can just answer the fuckin' question, wifie, and we'll be on our way.'

The woman reluctantly acknowledged defeat. The lips became a hard line, the shoulders dropped, there was a sharp hiss of breath through the nose, then a muttered, 'Fine.'

'Good. Woman with a face rougher than a Fraserburgh off-licence doing two for one on Buckfast. Think back.'

'She was here. She bought a padded envelope, put something in it and posted it recorded delivery.'

'The address?'

'I don't remember.'

'Can you check? If she posted it recorded delivery, there must be something in the computer.'

'I can't,' said the woman. 'I don't have access to that sort of information. You'd have to go through head office.'

Sergeant Wilson clenched her jaw and recalled the counting that the police therapist had suggested she do when she felt angry. The Sergeant had told the therapist that she wasn't sure what good it did to give someone a countdown before you tore them a new arsehole. It was much more fun if they couldn't see it coming. The therapist had sighed and explained that counting silently gave her time to consider not disrupting the integrity of any posteriors at all. Stupid man.

What did he know? But she may as well give it a go. One, two, three...

'Talking about heads going through offices—'

Spotting the danger signs, Sandra Next Door quickly stepped in.

'Do you remember anything at all? What did she put in the envelope?'

'A small black thing,' said the woman. 'It didn't weigh very much. If it helps, I think the address might have been in Kemnay. That's everything I know, so please, all of you leave before I call the...call whoever is in charge of *her*.'

The three women did as they were asked and headed in the direction of the restaurant, the smell of food drawing them in like a big magnet made of mince pies and sausage rolls.

As soon as they were out of sight of the post office counter, Sergeant Wilson declared, 'That went very well. Right, I'm hungry and there's a tube of thrush cream with my name on it. Get yourselves in there and order me a chilli chicken panini while I deal with the growler.'

With that, they parted company, Sergeant Wilson wandering off to find the toilets, and Sandra Next Door and Mrs Hubbard threading their way through the diners, in search of a free table.

The after-school crowd was rapidly displacing the pensioners, their noisy chatter filling the large space as frustrated parents held one-sided conversations with teenagers, groups of young people jostled and berated one another and laughing boys in blazers tried to attract the attention of long-legged girls in obscenely short skirts.

Sandra Next Door spotted an older lady sitting on her own and was about to ask if they could share her table when Mrs Hubbard uttered a cry of joy.

'Dearies!'

She pointed to where Gordon and Jim were sitting in a booth, tucking into bowls of chips.

Delighted to see their friends, the two men scooted over to make room at the table, although their pleasure was somewhat tarnished when Mrs Hubbard fetched an extra chair and informed them that Sergeant Wilson wasn't far behind.

'Martisha's in the loo,' she said. 'Doing ladies' things. We didn't expect to see you here.'

'Aye, well, we were aiming for the restaurant above the chip shop, but we got lost and found this place,' said Jim. 'A restaurant in a baker's is nearly as good. There should be restaurants in all your favourite places.'

'Imagine they put a restaurant above the Country Clothing Emporium,' said Gordon.

Jim smiled and gave a wistful sigh.

'Do you think Penny and Fiona would consider moving to Inverurie?' he asked.

Gordon wasn't sure.

'I think we should leave them and move here ourselves.'

'Okay, but you're not borrowing my boxers every day.'

Gordon offered his hand, and Jim shook it, then he turned to Sandra Next door and asked, 'What brings you here?'

'Long story. It has been a very difficult day,' said Sandra Next Door, patting her stiff helmet of blonde hair, 'and I'm not just saying that because we've had to spend it with you know who.'

While Mrs Hubbard went to order food, she explained what had happened on Bennachie, begrudgingly admitting, 'I suppose I should give credit where it's due. Sergeant Wilson took charge, and if it hadn't been for her, Claire might not be alive.'

'On a scale of nine to ten, how much did it hurt to say that?' asked Sergeant Wilson, approaching from behind. 'Alright there, boys? I was just away to apply some ointment to the old bajingo, when I realised I'd taken Easy's athlete's foot cream by mistake. Mind you, I don't know how long he's had it. All curdled and lumpy, like Stilton in a blender. But I lathered it on anyway. Is that macaroni cheese you have there, Gordon? Where's Mrs Hubbard? I need to change my order.'

Without waiting for a response, Sergeant Wilson marched off towards the counter, leaving a slightly green around the gills Gordon to push aside his plate of macaroni cheese. Wordlessly, Jim slid it towards himself and placed his own sausage roll in front of Gordon. He was a vet. He'd seen far worse than anything Gordon was imagining right now.

By the time Sergeant Wilson and Mrs Hubbard returned, both men had finished their food and were having an in-depth discussion about whether they should have pudding.

'If we have pudding now, Fiona won't let me have pudding tonight,' said Gordon.

'We're on holiday,' opined Jim. 'You can have two puddings when you're on holiday. It's the rules.'

Gordon looked doubtful.

'Aye, I suppose. Maybe if we didn't tell her. Up hands who will keep my secret.'

Only Jim's hand went up. With little nods and pleading eyes, he silently urged the three women to support Gordon, but they were having none of it. Two of them were the most stubborn buggers on the planet and the third was firmly in camp Fiona. He looked on his friend with pity.

'Sorry, pal. You could always say you're leaving her to live beside the dungaree shop with me. Then it wouldn't matter. I think I'd make a far better wife than her anyway.'

Gordon lowered his head and gazed fixedly at the table.

'Aye, but no. There's the bairn to think about.'

'Fair enough,' said Jim. 'We make a good team, though. Does anybody want to hear what team Jordon have been doing today.'

'No, but we'd like to hear about team Gor*dim*,' said Sergeant Wilson.

Ignoring her, Jim said, 'We found a man in a dungaree shop who knows a farmer called François Michelle. We went to see him, and he told us that Layla had visited him. She was

166

looking into the farms being sold so she could write an article about it. Cowrie Robert has been trying to intimidate him into selling, and the other farmers who have sold their farms have signed non-disclosure agreements. That's why they wouldn't talk to us. Frankie's the only one who held out.'

Sergeant Wilson's ears pricked up at this and she barked, 'Frankie? Did you say Frankie?'

'François goes by the name Frankie. Some joke that the locals–'

'Claire's not into eighties pop! She was trying to tell me something before she passed out. She kept saying Frankie, Frankie. I thought she was on about Frankie Goes to Hollywood.'

'Sometimes I wonder how you passed the Sergeant's exam,' said Sandra Next Door.

'Slept with the invigilator like everyone else, obviously,' said Sergeant Wilson. 'Use your noodle, woman. Where do you think I first got the thrush?'

'The taxi driver said he'd taken Claire to the farm with Layla,' Mrs Hubbard reminded them. 'What time did Layla die? Did you manage to get any information from the pathologist's report, Martisha?'

The Sergeant plucked a chip from her plate and chewed it thoughtfully.

'Time of death was about three in the afternoon on Monday, so we can rule Claire out as a suspect because it looks like Layla was killed after the taxi dropped her off at the Visitor Centre. Presumably while she was walking back up to the Colony. Claire wouldn't have had time to post the letter, get a taxi back to the Visitor Centre then catch up with Layla.'

'One other thing,' said Gordon. 'Frankie said she had a laptop. You didn't mention her having one in her bag, Sergeant Wilson.'

'That's because she didn't,' said the Sergeant. 'Whoever killed her must have taken it. I think we have our motive.'

'We certainly do,' said Gordon, nodding vigorously.

'Claire paid someone to kill Layla or...or someone needed a new laptop.'

He caught Sandra Next Door rolling her eyes and asked, 'What?'

Just for good measure, Sandra Next Door rolled her eyes again.

'Claire has nothing to do with the murder. When Claire came here to the post office, she sent something to Kemnay. Anni-Frid lives in Kemnay, remember, and she's a journalist. It's more likely that Claire was helping Layla with the article and posted a floppy disc of whatever they found out to Anni-Frid, who was writing the article with them.'

Sergeant Wilson and Gordon, both almost thirty years younger than Sandra Next Door, looked confused.

'A floppy what now?' asked Sergeant Wilson.

'Whatever it is they use these days,' said Sandra, flustered.

'Memory stick,' said Jim. 'But why wouldn't she just email it?'

Sergeant Wilson, having finished her own chips, helped herself to one of Mrs Hubbard's.

She said, 'Possibly because they were in the taxi when they decided to send the information to Anni-Frid. They probably wouldn't have got a signal on the back roads around Bennachie, so they couldn't hotspot Layla's laptop to her phone. The taxi driver said they were whispering. We should ask him if they were using a laptop as well.'

'Why would you suddenly decide in the taxi that you need to load down everything to a remembering stick?' asked Mrs Hubbard. 'You'd think they'd have done it at Frankie's farm where there's some internet thingies or waited until they got a phone signal.'

'I'm a police officer and a Sandra Next Door certified life-saver, nae a mind reader,' Sergeant Wilson scoffed. 'Maybe they suddenly realised it wasn't safe to take the information back up Bennachie with them, and from what we know now, they were right. When Claire comes round, we can ask her.

Jim, did Frankie mention that Claire was at the farm with Layla?'

Jim helped himself to one of Mrs Hubbard's chips and said, 'No, and I'll ask him why. I'll also ask exactly what he said to them because if you're right and something did occur to them in the taxi, we don't know when Claire will be fit enough to tell us herself.'

'Can anyone think of anything else that we haven't covered,' asked Sandra Next Door.

'No,' said Jim and Gordon in unison.

'Pudding,' said Sergeant Wilson. 'I think I'll have the apple pie.'

'Aw,' said Gordon.

'Stop feeling sorry for yourself. I've just noticed that you're wearing dungarees. Where's my jodhpurs? You better not have ruined my jodhpurs.'

Gordon winced and looked pleadingly at Jim, who said, 'They're in the car and they're fine.'

He made a mental note to remind Gordon to remove the labels from the new jodhpurs and rub a drop of ketchup on the crotch before he handed them over. The Sergeant would never know. Hopefully. Very, very hopefully.

He was about to suggest to Gordon that this would be a good time for them to leave, when his phone buzzed in his pocket. Cursing under his breath, he pulled it out and checked the caller ID. Damn. She'd be wanting to know why his idea of a wee while was so very different from hers.

'Hello. You are through to the Jim Space Agency. Please choose from the following options. If you think he's a sexy bugger, press one. If you think he's a handsome devil, press two. If you think he's a sexy, handsome, bugger-devil, press three. For all other enquiries, please hold.'

'Your idea of a wee while is very different from mine,' said Penny. 'It doesn't matter. Get back to the hotel now, please. We have news. Exciting news.'

CHAPTER 19

Penny, Fiona and Eileen had been busy all morning. Well, most of the morning. There had been a quick head massage in the spa while they'd waited for the hackers to get back to them. But spas were essential to their wellbeing, they reasoned. They needed to heal their hungover brains so that they could think about important stuff.

Eileen had chased the hackers for the remainder of the information on Layla's property and the farms, whatever they'd found on Chauncey Greig and the outcome of their foray into the Kennel Club records. By mid-morning, bodies were relaxed, minds were restored and the results were in.

With the magician's convention in full swing, the three women had the hotel lounge to themselves. Being reduced to three felt quite peaceful, and Penny could have stayed in this cosy room all day. The thick rugs and luxurious swagged curtains made her feel insulated from the world.

It briefly crossed her mind that she'd promised to meet Jim at the swimming pool, but he hadn't seemed too keen on the idea of voluntarily getting wet. She'd spotted him earlier, heading off in the opposite direction, so she figured he'd turn up at some point with a lame excuse. She and Fiona were taking bets on whether that would be the mysterious disappearance of his swimming trunks or the sudden onset of sore ears. She wouldn't put it past him to draw a verruca on himself. She'd already checked – the hotel sold verruca socks and trunks, so he'd be stymied if he tried either of those excuses. That's why sore ears was the current favourite.

She settled herself into one of the wingback chairs, drawing her legs up and cradling a warm coffee cup. On the sofa opposite, Eileen and Fiona were curled up, heads together, poring over Eileen's tablet. Someone had lit the wood stove, and as she listened to her friends discussing farms and wills, Penny began to feel quite drowsy.

She was startled out of her stupor by Eileen's exclamation of, 'Farty fair footer!'

'Va te faire–' Penny automatically began to say, then thought better of it. Eileen's version of French swearing was far more interesting and far less likely to offend the casual bystander.

'The hackers have outdone themselves,' said Eileen, her cheeks pink with excitement or, Penny conceded with a glance at her friends corned beef legs, possibly from sitting too close to the stove.

'What have they found?' she asked, preparing not to be amazed.

This was Eileen, after all. She loved her very much, but her dearest BFF had once told her she'd found a fossilised dinosaur egg on the beach, and it had turned out to be dried dog poo. Penny wasn't getting caught out a second time. It had taken her ages to get the stuff out from under her fingernails after Eileen insisted that she "give the dinosaur egg a quick rinse under the tap. What harm could it do?"

They'd been eleven at the time, but these things leave scars.

'It's proper amazing. Not dinosaur egg amazing,' said Eileen, knowing exactly what Penny was thinking. 'Forget the farm stuff and whether Layla owned property near

Bennachie. It's boring and she didn't. The amazing bit is Chauncey Greig. He's not a person. He's a security company.'

Penny uncurled her legs and leaned forward, putting the cup on the low coffee table that separated her chair from the sofa.

'A security company based in Dyce,' Fiona chipped in. 'It's on the outskirts of Aberdeen.'

'Why would a security company buy drugs?' asked Penny.

Her voice was quiet, almost as if she were talking things through with herself.

'Why would they want to kill Layla? Of course, they wouldn't. We already know that Cowrie Robert is behind this. They're obviously paying someone local to set up Layla's death. But all we have is the video and a loose link to Cowrie Robert through the dog. We need to prove that Cowrie Robert paid the people in the video. How do we do that?'

'We could ask the hackers to go through Chauncey Greig's finances,' Eileen suggested.

'You don't pay killers by bank transfer,' said Fiona. 'Not that I have any experience, of course. It's just that if I was going to have one of you two snuffed out, I'd pay cash. And I wouldn't do it with heroin either. Far too messy. I'd go for a nice clean…'

She let the sentence trail off, the horrified looks on her friends' faces indicating that she'd perhaps put a little too much thought into this.

'No money trail, then,' said Penny. 'Perhaps the company has nothing to do with this at all. Maybe the people are working independently, like they're only loosely connected to Chauncey Greig or simply used the company name to get in the door with the dealer. Bring up the video, please Eileen.'

They watched Ryan Richardson's doorcam footage again, paying particular attention towards the end.

"Man: Chauncey Greig recommended you.

Ryan: Chauncey? Erm…aye. Right you are, come on in."

Penny pressed pause and pointed at the screen.

'You see? Ryan doesn't have a clue who or what Chauncey Greig is. He pretends he does, then lets them in anyway. There's nothing to say that they actually are anything to do with Chauncey Greig.'

'And nothing to say they're not,' Fiona observed. 'They weren't aware that they were on camera, and they wouldn't have expected a drug dealer to be blabbing to anyone, so as far as they knew, there was no risk in mentioning Chauncey Greig. And why Chauncey Greig? They wouldn't have just picked the name of a security company out of thin air. There must be a reason for it.'

Fiona was right, Penny thought. There was a connection there that they couldn't see. Perhaps if they changed tack.

'What does it say about the Chauncey Greig online, Eileen?'

'Their website looks professional. Properly done. They provide security to businesses and bouncers to nightclubs. Guards licensed by the Security Industry Authority. CCTV monitoring. Alarms.' Eileen tapped the screen. 'Five stars and thirty reviews on Google. Sadly, nothing on Trip Advisor.'

'Chauncey Greig of Dyce, Aberdeen's top tourist destination,' Penny teased. 'Are there any details of the directors or the employees? Do the Google reviews mention any names?'

'Give me a minute,' said Eileen.

She tapped, swiped and scrolled, hunching forward in concentration, her tongue between her teeth. Beside her, Fiona provided the narration.

'Photos of people on their website. None of them the man in the video. Reviews mention...scroll down, Eileen. No, nothing in the reviews other than things like Brian did a good job servicing my alarm.'

Eileen did some more tapping, and Fiona clapped her hands, saying, 'Oh, you really have learned a few tricks.'

'Companies House,' said Eileen, a little smugly. 'If a company is registered, you can get information on the directors. Ladies and gentleladies, I present to you Chauncey Greig Limited. Set up two years ago. Director is Amanda Wilkerson. Hold onto your knickers because we're not finished yet. Viola!'

'Voilà!' said Penny.

'That as well!'

'What am I looking at?' asked Penny, as Eileen turned the tablet to face her.

'A photo of Amanda Wilkerson.'

'That's a photo of the popstar Rihanna.'

'Sorry. Wrong tab.'

Eileen clicked on the correct tab and Penny found herself looking at hundreds of images of Amanda Wilkersons.

'There are loads of photos here,' she said. 'It's so frustrating because this is a real lead, yet we're no closer to identifying the people in the video. Was there anything on the dog?'

Eileen laid her tablet on the table and said, 'It's a dead end. The dog was registered by a breeder in Stonehaven, whose last name is Ramsay. Doesn't keep computerised records of sales, at least as far as the hackers can find, so if we want to know more I'd recommend a road trip.'

Penny bent over her phone for a few seconds, then looked up, smiling triumphantly.

'It's only half an hour away.'

'What about Jim and Gordon?' asked Fiona.

Penny flashed her a conspiratorial grin.

'We'll cross that bridge when we come to it. Can we squeeze into your van? Jim has our car keys.'

'And maybe we could go for a little scout around Dyce on the way,' Eileen suggested. 'You lot always get to do the interesting bits and I get stuck on the computery bits.'

'I don't think that's a good idea,' said Penny. 'If they're connected to the people who bought the drugs, then they could be dangerous.'

'What about the farms?' asked Fiona.

Penny rubbed her forehead then ran a hand through her

hair, making it stick out at odd angles. Dammit, in all the excitement of discovering new things, she'd forgotten about the farms. She'd intended to contact all the farms. She ought to do the farms. But now there were puppies. Ickle, wickle, hairy, snuffly puppies. Ooh, farms or puppies? Puppies or farms?

'You're right. We really should make a start on those farms. So, who's coming with me to see the puppies?'

She was pushing against an open door. Thoughts of puppies had a remarkably cheering effect, and they spent the journey to Stonehaven trading cute dog stories. By the time they pulled up at a small farmhouse on the outskirts of the pretty harbour town, they had christened themselves The Three Huskyteers and were engaged in a good-natured debate about which of them was Dogtagnan.

The breeders, Mr and Mrs Ramsay, were used to strangers turning up to ask about dogs. They didn't seem in the least perturbed by three enthusiastic amateur sleuths pleading to see their records.

Mr Ramsay was a jolly, pink-cheeked man with a bushy grey moustache that quivered when he talked. He invited the women in for a cup of tea and proceeded to clatter around the house without removing his wellies. Mrs Ramsay, who was short, stout and fabulously bosomed in a tartan pinafore, let him get on with his hunt for teabags, beaming at him with such love and pride that Penny caught herself sighing and offering the man a tender smile too. She checked her companions and found them equally gooey eyed.

The surface of the table at which they sat was well-scrubbed pine. A dresser on the far wall bore a clutter of plates and ornaments. An ancient stove stood belching warmth, the kettle atop hissing as it prepared to release its triumphant whistle. It is me. I am ready. Look here.

This was a home, not a house, and even had it been devoid of furniture and comforts, these two people would still have made it feel like fresh heather honey on warm toast.

If Disney had created Scotland, it would have started with this couple, this home. Right down to the shortbread that Mrs Ramsay was now taking out of the oven.

Penny had expected outdoor kennels and cages but was instead met by two tiny balls of fur scampering around the kitchen floor, their little claws tapping against the slate tiles as they tumbled over one another in their excitement to greet the visitors. Their mother, a little more wary, sniffed Penny's hand before allowing the patting to begin.

'She's still a touch hormonal, aren't you Betsy?' said Mrs Ramsay, reaching down to stroke the dog's ears. 'They're weaned now and ready to go to good homes, but mum needs a good long rest before she breeds again.'

'Has she had many litters?' Penny asked.

'This is only the second. Betsy's a pet and a farm dog, aren't you, my love? Yes, you are. We have another one, but she's about to give birth any day now, so we're keeping her in the living room where it's quiet.'

'Do you have loads of puppies all the time?' asked Eileen. 'I'd love to have puppies all over the place.'

From his station by the kettle, Mr Ramsay laughed and said, 'Goodness, no. We'd be driven round the twist. We're not big breeders. We don't have a website or advertise. It's all word of mouth. When the puppies arrive, we let folk know, then people turn up and we decide if they're good enough for our dogs.'

'And these little furballs are ready to go,' said Fiona.

'And we've turned up,' said Eileen.

'Absolutely no way,' said Penny. 'We're not here to buy puppies. Just to adore them. And you love being adored, don't you, cutie, wootie pie.'

She had picked up the nearest pup and was kissing its soft little head. Then she felt guilty, so picked up the other pup and kissed it too.

Mr Ramsay delivered five mugs and a teapot on a tray, urging his guests to "help yourselves, there's plenty more where that came from," while Mrs Ramsay fetched plates from the dresser and broke apart five pieces of warm shortbread, serving them with warnings to "blow, lest you burn your mouths."

It was only after they'd eaten and drank their fill that Mr Ramsay fetched a large, hardbacked ledger. He flicked through the pages, stopping at one and running a finger down a column until he came to the entry for Curious Bob.

'I remember him,' he said. 'Dog mad. His last Jack Russell had died a few months before. He still had one left, but he was looking for a pup so that they'd be company to one another. Davey Neish, he was called. An Aberdeen lad, but he'd heard through a friend that we had some puppies. That was Betsy's first litter.'

'Is this him?' asked Penny, scrolling through her phone to find the still she'd taken from the video.

Mr Ramsay searched in his top pocket for his glasses then, not finding them, patted himself down until Mrs Ramsay pointed out that he was already wearing them. He took them off and peered at the photo.

'Aye, that's the boy.' Mr Ramsay ran a finger across the page in his ledger. 'I have an address for him here if you want. I had to send on the pedigree certificate.'

Penny could have hugged the man but made do with a delighted whoop. Finally, they knew who had killed Layla and they knew exactly where to find him. The only thing left to do was identify the woman, then they could hand the whole package over to Dunderheid, all wrapped up with a neat bow. Put your thinking bonnet on, Penny, she told herself. Could our mystery woman be Amanda Wilkerson or is she someone else?

When the women left, Mr and Mrs Ramsay stood at the farmhouse door, waving them off. It was simply all too wonderful. Watching the shrinking figures in the wing mirror, Penny chuckled to herself as she imagined Mr Ramsay going back inside the kitchen, removing his wellies and saying in a cockney accent, 'Thank gawd they've gone. Get us a beer from the fridge, will you love?' Because surely nobody could be that perfect.

The address for Davey Neish was safely stored in Penny's phone, with backups sent to Eileen, Hector and Edith, just in case anything terrible befell her. Naturally, the twins would completely ignore the messages as soon as they saw the sender's name, so Penny felt quite sure that the information was safe with them.

As she'd typed the address into her Notes app, she'd noticed that Jim hadn't called. This was a positive sign, yes? It meant that he hadn't noticed she was missing. Then a thought struck her. Perhaps it was a negative sign. If he hadn't noticed that she was missing, it was quite possibly because he, too, was missing. How very dare he go missing when he'd expressly forbidden her from doing interesting things like hunting down the names of killers.

Penny called Jim and listened impatiently while he pretended to be a sexy vet doing voicemail. He thought that being funny would make her forget to be annoyed that he was missing.

'Where are you?' she demanded.

'Shopping,' said Jim meekly.

'That's a load of old rubbish. You hate shopping.'

'I so am shopping! Look!'

She was so shocked by this manly shopping trip and the sight of Gordon in Jim's boxers that she completely forgot to berate her errant boyfriend. Instead, she arranged to see him in two hours. Which suited her nicely because she had a plan to find the woman in the video. A plan to smoke out everyone. A plan of which Jim would very much disapprove.

CHAPTER 20

"The leadership contest to replace Andrea Forglen is heating up, with Elaine Bear, Cabinet Secretary for Net Zero, Energy and Transport, hotly tipped to win when the votes are counted in less than three weeks' time. Ms Bear has been a strong advocate for–"

Penny leaned across and switched off the radio, ignoring Fiona's protests.

'We have more important things to think about than politics,' she said. 'Elaine Bear can go cartwheeling through Holyrood in a thong for all I care. Listen, I have a plan. We're going to make some noise and draw everyone out into the open. Fiona, can you head for Dyce please?'

Still irritated with Penny for taking liberties with the van radio, Fiona gave her a curt nod and, instead of turning left off the Aberdeen bypass, she went past the airport towards the sprawling mass of industrial estates and office buildings that had sprung up on the outskirts of the city to feed an oil-hungry world.

'This'll do. Pull over here,' said Penny, pointing to a café among the industrial units.

It was a basic roadside diner, set up to service the workers in the units nearby, but it had everything the women desired right now; large mugs of tea, bacon sandwiches and Wi-Fi. Ignoring the curious looks of the men in hard hats and high vis, Penny, Eileen and Fiona found a table at the back and huddled together to discuss Penny's plan.

She explained, 'We need to identify the woman in the video and get a definitive link to Cowrie Robert, yes? I couldn't think how to take this further but then I remembered the farms. We know Cowrie Robert handled the sale of two farms for Thermacorp and probably all the other farms as well. I think we need to turn this on its head and look at the farms that *weren't* sold to Thermacorp.'

'I see where you're going with this,' said Fiona. 'The farmers who didn't sell their farms might talk to us.'

'No, forget the farmers for now and meet Penny Moon, owner of Losers Club and founder of the Losers Spa and Wellness Centre at Bennachie.'

'Eh?' Eileen looked utterly baffled. 'You're expanding the business?'

'No, I'm pretending to buy one of the unsold farms to expand my business. I plan to go into Chauncey Greig and hire them to provide security for the wellness centre that I'll be building on the land I allegedly bought. Don't you see? If Chauncey Greig tell Cowrie Robert that I've bought one of the farms they're interested in, they'll approach me, and I can find out what they're up to. And, bonus, while I'm in Chauncey Greig's office, I can look for the woman in the video.'

Fiona opened a packet of sweetener and tipped the contents into her mug, then seemed to have second thoughts and followed it up with a packet of sugar.

'I don't know about this,' she said, stirring the saccharine brew. 'You're giving them your real name. They could come after you. They went halfway up a hill in the middle of nowhere to get Layla.'

'I'm not a threat,' Penny argued. 'As far as Chauncey Greig's concerned, I'm openly offering a security contract. As far as Cowrie Robert is concerned, I'm not going to expose anyone for dodgy land deals. I'm just a woman buying land that they want. Cowrie Robert phone me, I ask why they want the land, I tell them I'll consider their offer, then later on my purchase mysteriously falls through and nobody is any the wiser.

'Also, bonus number two, if I don't hear from Cowrie Robert, then we know that Chauncey Greig probably has nothing to do with the people who killed Layla and we can scratch them off our suspect list.'

Penny ripped a bite from her bacon sandwich and stared at Fiona as she chewed, her eyes defying the woman to find a flaw in her plan.

Eileen looked back and forth between them, waiting for the winner to be declared.

Her own eyes never leaving Penny's, Fiona calmly took a sip of her tea then said, 'I suppose I'm the one who got us into all of this in the first place. Alright, but I'm going in with you. Call me your assistant or whatever.'

'Yessss,' said Penny. 'Thank you, thank you, thank you. Eileen, do you know which farms didn't sell to Thermacorp?'

Eileen pulled her tablet from her bag and put a finger in the air, signalling to her companions to wait while she compared the list of sold farms against the list of farms along the route.

After some tapping, scrolling and cordon bleus, she said, 'There's only one left, as far as I can tell. Glenmachie. It's owned by a guy called François Michelle. Do you think he's French? Le farmer Frenchaise dans Ecosse. Ooh la la, that's very…what's the French for avant-garde?'

While Penny called Chauncey Greig to make an appointment, Fiona made a trip to the van, then a trip to the toilets, then a trip back to the van. She emerged wearing smart trousers, a buttoned-up cardigan and a pair of black pumps.

'I keep spares in the van. Not everywhere is dungaree-friendly,' she explained. 'I was going to change in the loos, but it's like someone hosed the place down with urine. I don't think they get many women in here.'

'Don't get me started,' said Penny. 'Do men get disgusted by other men for peeing all over the place? Or is it just us women who think it's foul? Oh, it boils my...ha, you know. Anyway, enough of that. The security company. They'll see us now, so are we ready to go, Huskyteers?'

Eileen shoved the last of her sandwich into her mouth, and the women made their way past the men in hard-hats and out into the air-fuel tainted air of the car park, Fiona teeing up Google Maps as they walked.

Chauncey Greig was based in a shabby, three-storey box tacked onto the end of a warehouse off Kirkhill Road. The building's only attractive feature was the free parking outside. Otherwise, it looked like the pebbledashed final will and testament of a depressed 1980s architect.

Penny realised that rocking up in a fruit and veg van was probably not the professional look she was aiming for, so she instructed Fiona to take advantage of someone else's free parking instead, and they walked the short distance to the building, leaving Eileen in charge of being the getaway driver.

The interior of Chauncey Greig's offices was less tired than the exterior, although the carpet tiles, strip lights and panelled ceiling gave Penny flashbacks to her time as an office temp after university. Old Mr Fitzpatrick, known to all as Titsfatprick, had been a very hands-on manager. Penny was fired after a week, when his fingers accidentally squeezed her breast and her foot accidentally collided with his testicles. Although the memory made her shudder, it was also a source of pride. When she had felt so beaten after her divorce, the thought of that kick in the balls reminded her who she was and had helped rebuild her self-esteem. She was Penny Moon, and she was fearless.

'Wait here please and I'll let Mr Blake know you've

arrived,' growled the dragon in reception, pointing to a couple of plastic chairs next to a tall yucca plant.

She was about sixty, with the voice of a forty-a-day smoker. Penny wasn't being rude or judgemental about the smoker's voice. The woman's habit was corroborated by her hair, which was white, except for the fringe; the fringe was stained a deep, nicotine yellow.

They didn't have to wait for long. The receptionist returned after a minute or so with a man wearing the smart-casual uniform of choice for the middle-aged office worker - regulation beige chinos and a blue shirt. He showed them to an overly bright room, where Penny was gratified to see the obligatory dark blazer slung across the back of a chair behind a scuffed wooden desk. Really, no expense had been spared in the office supplies shop Christmas sale, she thought, looking around. Behind the door, four low chairs covered in blue fabric were arranged around a circular, beech laminate coffee table, and it was to these that Blake guided his visitors.

Penny may have been scornful of the Titsfatpricks of the world, but she was not above allowing her skirt to ride a little up her thighs when she lowered herself into the chair. Granted, her bum was the size of two Kardashians stapled together, but the legs beneath were okay, provided you didn't know that under the black tights lurked a lawn that hadn't been mown since Christmas. It's winter, she thought. What sort of person mows their lawn in winter? Beside her, Fiona sat with legs neatly crossed, her trouser leg rising to reveal a smooth ankle. That sort of person, Penny silently harumphed, then made a mental note to google whether it was possible to have alopecia of the legs and how to catch it.

Like a good assistant, Fiona produced a notebook and pen then remained quiet, leaving her manager to take the lead, so with a bright smile, Penny began the performance that she'd been rehearsing in her head on the way here.

'Thanks for seeing us at such short notice, Mr Blake. This is my assistant, Fiona. If we reach an agreement, she'll be your point of contact. I'll be brief. I own a national chain of weight-loss and healthy lifestyle groups and I've been looking to expand. I'm about to complete the purchase of a farm near Bennachie. Do you know Glenmachie farm?'

'I know the area,' said Mr Blake.

'I intend to build a wellness centre there, catering for around a hundred guests. A large portion of the land will also be converted into healing gardens and suchlike. The plans will be submitted as soon as the purchase is completed, and a fair few, erm, charitable donations to Aberdeenshire Council have been made, so I expect them to be passed quickly.'

Penny winked at Blake to emphasise her duplicity. A momentary doubt that she might be over-egging the pudding was put to bed when Blake acknowledged her wink with a knowing wink of his own.

'What I need,' she continued, 'is security for the building site, with a continuing presence once we're up and running. There will also be the installation and monitoring of alarms. If I provide the plans, can you provide a quote for, say, a two-year contract with the option to extend?'

She could practically see the pound signs spinning in Blake's eyes. The carrot had been successfully dangled; now to provide the sense of urgency that any good saleswoman needs to reel in the mark.

'I'm only in town today and tomorrow. You're the first company I've seen, but I do have other appointments. Nevertheless, if you provide me with a reasonable ballpark figure in the next twenty-four hours, I'll be happy to consider it.'

Blake had been scribbling notes and nodding throughout. He could certainly provide a quote, he assured her, just as soon as he'd talked to the big boss.

'I thought you were the boss,' said Penny guilelessly, watching his ego roll over and ask to have its tummy tickled.

Blake's reaction was a deliberately self-conscious dip of the head followed by a confident flash of unfeasibly white Turkey teeth.

'I make the important decisions, but I like to keep Amanda in the loop on the bigger contracts. Amanda Wilkerson, the director. She's working from home today.'

'Tell her she can call me with any questions,' said Penny. 'Or I'm at the Garioch House Hotel if she'd prefer to meet.'

She handed Blake one of her Losers Club business cards, and he tucked it between the pages of his notebook before rising to his feet. Taking their cue from him, Penny and Fiona did the same.

He was just about to proffer a handshake when Penny asked, 'Would you mind if I used your loo before we go? Sorry, sprouts for lunch.'

'No problem,' he said. 'Go to the end of the corridor, through the double doors, then the toilets are on your right.'

Penny gave him a grateful smile and bustled off, leaving Fiona to make awkward small talk about the appalling cost of imaginary guttering for imaginary wellness centres.

There appeared to be two further rooms and toilets on this floor. Across from Blakes office was a large, empty staffroom, complete with kitchen, dining area and sofa. A peek behind door number two revealed a spacious store cupboard containing a photocopier and cleaning equipment. Sandra Next Door would have a severe case of Hoover envy if she saw this, thought Penny, eyeing the industrial sized vacuum cleaner.

The toilets were opposite the fire exit, next to a staircase. So far, Penny could have used the old "looking for the loos and got lost" excuse if caught snooping, even though a blindfolded three-year-old with no sense of direction could have found them. However, the moment she climbed those stairs, she knew that there was no reasonable explanation.

Cautiously, Penny peered around the corner on the first-floor landing. Nobody in sight. Phew. In her head, her father's voice was saying, 'Tread carefully, Pennyfarthing. You shouldn't be doing this.' Beside him, her mother was cheering, 'Fortune favours the bloody minded. Get your fat arse moving,

Chunky.' Above them both was Jim, tutting disapprovingly and reminding her that she had responsibilities. She really had to stop imagining people and get her backside in gear.

There were four offices and more toilets on this floor. Time was of the essence, so Penny skipped straight to the one with the doorplate bearing the name "Amanda Wilkerson." On high alert for any sound, she slowly turned the handle and pushed door.

The office was the mirror image of Blake's downstairs, with the exception of a few accessories which made it feel a little less like the place where Ikea went to die. The desk chair was a red leather boss-throne and there was a studio photograph on the wall. It showed a young blond woman with her arms around an older, dark-haired woman. Both wore identical dresses - long affairs in flowing, green chiffon, with sweeping necklines and tight bodices. Amanda and her daughter, Penny supposed, noting the resemblance. Disappointingly, neither of them were the woman in the doorcam video. She unlocked her phone and took a quick snap of the picture, just in case it ever turned out to be relevant.

Blake's office didn't have a filing cabinet, but Amanda's did, which was unusual in these modern times where everything was stored on computers. Penny could only guess that some clients preferred not to leave a digital trail, although records clearly still had to be kept.

Thankful that she'd spent her Christmas money on sensible things like lockpicks, Penny got to work on the filing cabinet lock. Within a few seconds, she had soundlessly slid open the top drawer and was rifling through the neatly labelled files suspended within.

Most of the contents were invoices and payroll printouts. Penny was no accountant, but she imagined that there was some tax fiddling going on here, or why else keep these? There was no time to go through them all, so she focused on a name she recognised - Cowrie Robert. There were multiple invoices, and with no means of copying them, Penny could only photograph a random sample and set them back in the file.

She was just about to close the drawer when her brain gave her a nudge. She'd seen something in there that might be important. She'd seen it but hadn't recognised it at the time. What was it? Think, Penny, think. Realising that a nudge was not enough, her brain gave her an almighty kick up the backside that resulted in her flicking through the Cowrie Robert folder again.

'Come on, brain,' she whispered. 'I don't have time for this. What did you see that I didn't?'

Her stomach was a tight ball of anxiety, and she felt a prickle of sweat on her top lip as she skimmed through the invoices. With every moment that passed, the likelihood of discovery increased. Anyone could be behind those other office doors, and they might take it into their heads to visit Amanda's office; however, not Blake. Penny had full confidence that Fiona was stalling Blake with a long, embarrassing tale about the effect of sprouts on her manager's digestive system.

She was just about to give up and go, when she saw it – a scribbled note on one of the invoices which read "Cowrie to tell Juniper laptop is extra and will be supplied on receipt of payment."

Juniper? Hmm, Juniper. She'd seen that somewhere before. No time to worry about it now.

Shit, what was that?

Her stomach gave a sickening lurch, and she froze, listening intently as the sound of footsteps came closer. And closer. And closer.

As quietly as possible, she closed the filing cabinet and moved towards the desk, biting down on her lip to stifle a cry as she caught her hip on the corner. She put a hand out to steady herself and once more froze. The sharp creak of the wood must have been heard in the corridor outside because the footsteps stopped. Right outside the door.

Penny dropped onto all fours and crawled behind the desk chair. She flinched as a small stone in the carpet embedded itself in her knee. This was not the moment to worry about damage. This was a moment to hunker down and stop bloody breathing. Her breath was coming in short, sharp rasps through her nose, in time, she supposed, with her beating heart. She was already feeling faint, the oxygen flooding her brain and clouding her thinking. She crawled onto the chair, spinning it to face away from the desk; then, head buzzing, she tucked her legs under her chin and made herself as small as possible. Do not breathe. Do not tremble.

The door opened. Had they seen? Penny clamped her lips shut and tensed her stomach. The slightest wobble would betray her. Head down, she stared at her knees, focusing intently on the tiny hole in her tights. Her forehead felt hot. Her upper lip tingled uncomfortably. Stay. Stay perfectly still.

The door closed. Penny didn't move, every nerve ending on high alert. Had they gone? Were they still here? Shit with egg on it, she was going to have to breathe.

Air hissed out through her nose, then a sharp hiss in again. She waited for a hand to spin the chair, a face to appear in hers and a voice to roar, "What the hell are you doing."

None of those things happened. She spun slowly round to face the empty office and finally opened her mouth to gulp a deep breath. The chair creaked as she lowered her legs and slumped back, giving her racing heart a moment to calm down. She sat like that for a few seconds until, deciding that she was sufficiently in control of her limbs to risk standing up, she tottered to the filing cabinet. There, she took a photograph of the invoice before filing it back with the others; then she closed the drawer and tiptoed from the room.

Fiona was at the bottom of the stairs, her face a picture of barely contained panic.

'You've been ages,' she hissed. 'I was at the stage of telling Blake you can fart Flower of Scotland in your sleep.

Penny winced and said, 'Sorry. I found something important. Let's get out of here and I'll tell you on the way back to the hotel.'

Fiona's eyes widened and she tugged on Penny's arm, urging her to hurry.

'He's waiting for us in reception, and I've had three texts from Eileen saying she needs a wee.'

Blake could barely meet Penny's eyes when they shook hands, causing her to wonder what exactly Fiona had told the man. It didn't matter. No, siree. She had the proof they needed of links between Chauncey Greig and Cowrie Robert. Fiona could tell Blake that she'd produced an accurate rendition of Beethoven's Fifth with her fanny for all Penny cared. She wouldn't be seeing him again.

On the way to the van, she called Jim and once more waited impatiently through his automated answering routine.

'Hello. You are through to the Jim Space Agency. Please choose from the following options. If you think he's a sexy bugger, press one. If you think he's a handsome devil, press two. If you think he's a sexy, handsome, bugger-devil, press three. For all other enquiries, please hold.'

'Your idea of a wee while is very different from mine,' said Penny. 'It doesn't matter. Get back to the hotel now, please. We have news. Exciting news.'

She didn't see the figure in the first storey window, intently watching her retreating back. She didn't notice the security cameras turn to follow her progress to the van.

CHAPTER 21

It was dark by the time Deed and Mac reached Aberdeen. They were relieved to be back on home turf, although Deed didn't have much at home to look forward to. He was renting a flat in Inverurie from an oil worker who had gone to Saudi on a six-month contract. The place had been advertised as fully furnished, and it was, if a sofa and a bed counted as all the furniture one could ever need. It was obviously a place for the guy to lay his head between contracts, there being little evidence that an actual human lived there. Deed was not a man for fussy cushions and ornaments, but even he was tempted to replace the blinds with a decent pair of curtains.

Mac, on the other hand, nested with possibly the most patient woman in the world and their two noisy children in a three-bedroom semi in Westhill, a suburb to the west of the city, only a short hop from the Inverurie road.

As they pulled into the Bucksburn police office car park to collect Mac's car, he told Deed, 'I've texted the wife, and she says you're to have your supper with us. No arguing about it.'

'I'm not arguing,' Deed grinned. 'The alternative is an out-of-date salad and the rest of yesterday's chicken.'

Mac laughed and patted his dad-belly, saying, 'Aye, don't knock it. This is what happens when you live with a cook.'

Privately, Deed thought that the burgers and chips in the police canteen might have more to do with his girth. Mac's wife, Shona, had a small vegan café in the local shopping centre where she created tasty delights for a loyal clientele. For her sake, Mac was vegan at home, but once released into the wild, the man was an untamed carnivore.

Deed was saved from mustering a diplomatic reply by a loud ringing from the glove compartment, where he habitually stashed his phone on long drives to avoid the temptation of answering it. Mac got there first, hoping he could put the caller off before Deed abandoned supper plans in favour of work; however, the moment he heard the voice of the caller, he grimaced, knowing that it would be some hours before either of them saw Shona's roast veg ragù.

'Hello, is that Mr Deed? Sorry, Inspector…Chief Inspector? It's Liam from Cowrie Robert.'

With a heavy sigh, Mac handed the phone to Deed.

'Hello? Hello? It's Liam. Can you hear me, Mr Deed?'

The receptionist sounded jittery.

'I can hear you, Liam. Is everything okay?'

'I thought about what you said. About the girl, yeah? I felt bad, so I went back to the office and had a look at the calendar. Then I had a poke through the files, even though I'm not supposed to.'

'You shouldn't have put yourself at any risk. Tomorrow would have been fine.'

'It's okay. I'm not going back tomorrow. It's a shit job anyway, and I'm sick of Mr Cowrie shouting at me over nothing.'

'Alright then, tell me what you got. Hang on, I'll put you on speakerphone so Mac can hear.'

'Can anyone else hear?'

'No, it's just us. We're in the car in the police car park.'

Deed stabbed at his phone screen, then said, 'Right, fire away.'

'Cheers. The two people in the picture work for a security firm called Chauncey Greig. The woman is Louise Pond and the man's Davey Neish. I was able to check the calendars and invoices, but everything else is in password protected folders.'

'Thanks, Liam,' said Deed. 'Obviously, don't tell anyone you've spoken to us and don't try to find out any more information.'

'Before you go, Mr Deed, look I don't know if this helps but.' Deed could hear a muffled conversation at Liam's end then his voice came back on the line. 'Sorry, I was just telling my mum I want chicken nuggets. Where was I? Aye, some of the invoices from Chauncey Greig had been forwarded on from a charity, which seems weird. Why would a charity be asking solicitors to pay their bills? I've emailed the whole folder to you, so you can see for yourself.'

Deed thanked Liam again and hung up. He turned to Mac, his expression one of regret.

'Sorry, do you think Shona will mind if I...?'

'She probably will, but she's lived with me for long enough to understand. I'll call and tell her we're not coming.'

'You don't need to stay,' said Deed.

'Aye, I do. You and I both know that Davey Neish is Chancer's cousin, and while he's not directly involved in the drugs business, he's still a wee shite. Let's get ourselves into the office and fire up the computer.'

Mac's office was in darkness, his colleagues having long since logged off and gone to their respective homes or pubs. These days, policing was as much about computers as it was about boots on the ground. Twenty years ago, when Mac and Deed were in Constable's training wheels, the emphasis was on getting out there and talking to people. DNA evidence was still a fairly new thing, and the people who trained Mac and Deed had themselves come up in a profession where a blood group, fingerprints and a criminal record was as technical as it got.

Now, it was a different world. Cell site analysis, cyber crime specialists, a DNA database, national intelligence systems, forensic accountants; the digital power of this massive organisation was focused on one thing – catching the baddies. Even a wee fat guy doing two-fingered typing on a keyboard in Aberdeen could create a symphony of search results.

Making full use of modern police technology, Deed accessed Spotify on his work phone and told it to play the 1812 Overture. Then the balding, middle-aged maestro that was Mac flexed his fingers and said, 'Louise Pond, Davey Neish, Chauncey Greig and the dodgy charity. Conductor, baton at the ready.'

Deed flourished an imaginary baton, giving a final tap in Mac's direction, and they were off.

To the sound of clanging church bells, rousing horns and booming cannons, they mined the systems and scoured the internet. Invoices were entered onto a spreadsheet, and a YouTube video was watched on how to sort and filter the information. An hour later, Deed and Mac had done as much as any bobby with access to music streaming services, the Police National Computer and a Google rabbit hole could do.

Technology was all well and good, both men agreed, but sometimes you still needed to do things the old-fashioned way. Mac lifted a sheaf of paper from the printer and, using brightly coloured magnets, attached photographs of their suspects to a whiteboard. With a sly smile, he slid the images of Louise Pond and Davey Neish together under a photograph of Amanda Wilkerson.

'It's quite a romantic story,' he said. 'Louise met Davey Neish a couple of years ago when he was sent by Chancer to beat up her boss. Apparently, it was love at first fight.'

Deed grinned then tapped Amanda's image, his mind moving on to the more important part of their investigation.

'Chauncey Greig, distant outpost of the Neish family empire, delivering sound beatings in the North East since 2021. I didn't find much on Amanda Wilkerson, though.'

'She's a relative of Chancer's oldest pal,' said Mac. 'Remember Greig The Middle Leg?'

'Didn't he get his...?'

'Aye'

'Stuck in a freezer?'

'Aye. When they were teenagers. Thought he could freeze crabs, by all accounts. Got stuck to the middle shelf. Frostbite and a chunk removed. Apparently, his mum was fuming because he ruined the Viennetta she'd been saving for his brother's birthday tea.'

Deed winced, recalling how the story had somehow made it into the newspapers and done the rounds at his primary school, a salutary warning to the next generation of teenagers.

'Ouch. So, we know who the company's named after and that it's loosely linked to the Neishes. Presumably Davey and Pond came up with the idea of buying the heroin from one of Wallace's dealers so that Donald would get the blame if it was traced. Then, being as thick as mince, Davey drops the name Chauncey Greig. Those two are employed by Chauncey Greig and buy the heroin. Cowrie Robert is the middleman. Who ordered the death of Layla Hamdy?'

Mac had printed the invoices spreadsheet then enlarged it using the photocopier, and he now added it to the board. They had filtered the information down to incoming invoices from Chauncey Greig and a charity called The Climate Change Collective, along with outgoing invoices to another company.

Mac used a yellow pen to highlight some of the cells as he explained.

'Cowrie Robert will have kept the invoices for their accountants,' said Mac. 'They're clearly a middleman taking instructions from this client, Thermacorp. You can see that the billing dates correspond. I phoned a friend in intel while you were knee deep in Neishes. She said that Thermacorp has come up before in relation to money laundering, and it traces back to a firm called Juniper Investments. Some sort of hedge fund thing with links to the Middle East and Russia. Anyway, the Met have a big investigation ongoing, so is it worth me giving them a call about Juniper in the morning?'

'I hate it when things grow legs,' said Deed. 'This is going to turn into a right dog's dinner, so for now let's just stick to the basics. Juniper wants Layla dead. Why does Juniper want Layla dead? Why is she a threat to them? Finally, who did the actual killing? Pond and Neish?'

'You're right,' said Mac. 'Find the motive, find the killer.'

Deed recalled the message from Sergeant Wilson. She had talked about Layla being a journalist. He went back to his laptop and checked his emails. Ah, here it was. "Cowrie Robert has also been buying up farmland around Bennachie. No details as yet. Layla is a journalist and possible motive for death is that she found out about the land deals. If so, information is missing. She didn't meet Anni-Frid Mackie."

'I think it's something to do with the land Cowrie Robert bought. We need to find that memory stick. It's the key to everything.'

He grabbed a marker from Mac's desk and wrote on the board:

Things to do

Find Fergus – any leads from bus stations?

Layla – where did she go and how did she get there. Taxi?

Anni-Frid Mackie – what does she know?

Finish checks on the Climate Change Collective

Then, with a chuckle, he added:

Never put your todger in a freezer

'You know we can't leave this stuff on the board, boss?' said Mac. 'If my boss, my real boss, comes in and sees it, she'll ask why the hell the Anti-Corruption Unit is trying to find somebody at a bus station.'

'Fair enough,' said Deed, taking out his phone and snapping a photograph of their handiwork. By now, there was a family tree, with Juniper sitting at the top. 'We've done what we can tonight. I'm bloody starving. Shall we put this lot away and see if Shona's kept the casserole warm?'

Mac, whose stomach was starting to think his throat had been cut, immediately pulled the printouts from the board and got to work with the whiteboard eraser. He scrubbed at the lettering. He scrubbed again. Nothing happened.

'Did you use the marker that was on my desk?' he asked. 'The *permanent* marker?'

They were still scrubbing ten minutes later when Deed's phone rang.

'Hello? Dunderheid? It's Gordon. I think we have an emergency.'

CHAPTER 22

It was late afternoon, nearly teatime, and the car park was almost deserted. The magicians had vanished, leaving Jim with the pick of the spaces and a sense of regret that he hadn't had time to ask one of them to show him a trick or two. Walking into the hushed atmosphere of the hotel felt strange after the buzz and general abracadabra of the past couple of days. As they ordered coffees from the empty bar, Gordon commented on it too. In fact, they were both so preoccupied, it was only when they reached the lounge that they realised something else had vanished.

Gordon stopped dead in his tracks and quickly turned, finding himself almost nose to nose with Jim, who had been walking directly behind him.

'Where's my van?' he asked, his voice rising in panic. 'I didn't see it in the car park. Do you think somebody stole it? What sort of person drives all the way to a posh hotel in the countryside to steal a fruit and veg van? Should I phone the police, Jim?'

'Before you tell them to put out a BOLO for a pink van with a giant broccoli on one side and a tomato on the other, you might want to ask yourself where Fiona, Penny and Eileen are,' said Jim.

'Jesus, you don't think somebody's taken them as well!'

'I'm thinking they took the van. I'm thinking that Penny needs a good, stern talking to.'

'You actually do that?' asked Gordon, sitting down heavily in one of the wingback chairs. 'Give her talkings to?'

Jim took the chair next to Gordon's and they were both quiet for a moment while he gave this some serious thought.

'Aye.'

'How many nights did you spend on the sofa last week?'

'Three.'

'I tell Fiona about my feelings. She likes that.'

'Your feelings? What sort of feelings?'

'Dunno. Whenever I'm hungry, I just google feelings and say whatever comes up. Then she's all happy and makes an apple crumble for tea.'

Jim nodded approvingly and changed the subject to something else that had been bothering him.

'Which dog do you think would make the best First Minister and why?'

'Ah, politics,' said Gordon. 'We're onto the serious stuff now.'

They were interrupted by female voices hailing from the lobby. There appeared to be some argument about one of their number being rude to the taxi driver.

'Martisha Wilson! Telling a man who lost a testicle that he can't go on planes anymore is unacceptable.'

Mrs Hubbard sounded mortified.

'Well, someone *has* interfered with his bags,' came Sergeant Wilson's unrepentant reply. 'Anyway, we only had to walk the last half mile in the dark. It'll have done your varicose veins the world of good. You should be thanking me. I'm starting to think you don't appreciate me.'

Sandra Next Door entered the lounge first, her face the colour and texture of a shrivelled apple.

'Stupid woman,' she said. 'Got us thrown out of the taxi.

It's blowing a gale out there and far too cold for March. I think we might have snow on the way.'

She patted her hair, which had survived entirely intact, and asked, 'Where are Penny, Fiona and Eileen?'

'Good question,' said Jim. 'I was just about to phone them. What did the taxi driver say?'

'Layla was on her computer in the taxi. What did Frankie say?'

'Good question,' said Jim. 'I was just about to phone him.'

'Get on with it then,' snapped Sandra Next Door, throwing her coat onto the arm of the sofa and hovering impatiently over him.

Sergeant Wilson and Mrs Hubbard arrived still bickering, but Sandra Next Door waved them to the sofa and curtly told them to shut up and listen.

Jim placed his phone on the table, selected speaker and dialled Glenmachie farm. Frankie answered on the first ring.

'That was quick,' said Jim. 'It's Gordon and Jim here. We came to see you earlier.'

'I am, how you say, on the loo crushing the candy.'

'Aye, too much Highland toffee will do that to you. When Layla came to see you last time, did she have someone with her?'

Frankie was silent for a moment, then said, 'Oui, but she asked me to keep it under my chapeau. That is where I keep my sandwiches, so of course it is a very safe place.'

There was a rustling sound then Frankie came back on the line, his voice muffled as he chewed.

'You reminded me that I didn't have lunch. Very nice. Liver pâté. Layla had a friend with her. She said her friend will be in danger if anyone knows she is helping Layla. I am telling you this because it was Layla who was in danger, and now I think you must help her friend.'

'Why did they think Claire was in danger?' Gordon asked.

'Claire? Who is Claire? Non, non, Brenda is in danger. She is the one telling Layla about the people who want my land.

She has recordings of people who are making the plots. Brenda and Layla play these recordings to me, but I have never heard these voices. Brenda says they are people in Juniper, where she worked. Do you remember I told you they were the investment company that Cowrie Robert worked for? Do you remember all the bad things that are happening to me? So, I tell Layla to be very careful because my computer was hacked, and I think it is possible that someone has seen Layla's emails to me.'

'Do you have a copy of the article Layla wrote?' asked Jim.

'No, that is why we have the conversation about the hacking. I say please do not send me anything because it is not safe. Layla and Brenda say ha ha bloody paranoid Frankie, they are living on the mountain, and nobody can find them. I tell her bad people can get to you anywhere. And now you must be careful too, Gordon and Jim. Find Brenda and keep her safe.'

'This Brenda,' said Gordon. 'What does she look like?'

'A woman worn down by the cares of the world and life on the run.'

There was a loud plop followed by the deep voice of the Candy Crush man saying, 'Juicy.'

'I must go now,' said Frankie. 'I have completed my level and I have completed my…okay, I think we are done. Take care mes amis. Trust no one.'

He hung up and Jim felt a smack on the back of his head. He turned to look up at Sandra Next Door, who was still standing over him, glaring furiously.

Rubbing his scalp, he exclaimed, 'Ow! What did you do that for?'

'Juniper. We said, "Does anyone have anything else to say," and you two said, "No." Claire, Brenda, whoever she is must have got some information when she worked for Juniper and passed it to Layla. Cowrie Robert is working for Juniper, which is clearly the company behind Thermacorp. Thermacorp paid Layla's dad for some work. Juniper is the connection between them all. I bet they think they're smart taking Layla's laptop. They don't even realise there's a copy of everything on that memory stick.'

'Juniper?' said a voice from the door. 'What have you found out?'

Penny, Fiona and Eileen came into the lounge, shaking snow off their coats. They made a beeline for the stove, where they crouched, shivering and muttering about blizzards, while the others brought them up to speed with their findings.

'I've been sending anything I've got to Eileen, Hector and Edith,' said Penny. 'I wanted to have a backup, just in case. Eileen's been doing the same. Sending it to Kenny, I mean.'

Penny stopped talking, interrupted by Sergeant Wilson's phone, which had beeped to signal an incoming text. The Sergeant stared at the screen and swore quietly under her breath. The others watched her, discomfited by the quiet swearing. They were used to loud and rambunctious swearing, carefully phrased to cause maximum offence, but she looked so stricken that nobody dared mention it. Wordlessly, she held up her phone so that her companions could read the message.

Sad news. Dani died. Tests show thallium poisoning. Claire critical. Searchers found Phoebe and Jake. In a bad way. Search for Kendra called off due to darkness and snow. Doubt we'll find her alive. Snow coming down fast at Bennachie. Inverness road already blocked at the Glens. Don't go out tonight.

'That's my friend at Inverurie cop shop. I knew someone had poisoned the fucking well,' said Sergeant Wilson.

'God, that's awful,' breathed Eileen. 'Why would someone...'

'To kill Brenda Claire? To get the Colonists off Bennachie so they can get on and build their fucking golf course now the road's not going ahead? They wouldn't want that lot kicking up a fuss and spoiling it for the rich folk. I don't know. I keep telling you, I'm not a fucking oracle. One thing's for sure, whoever did it was one of the Colonists because they were the only ones with access to the water.'

'It could be somebody from the charity,' Fiona suggested. 'Fergus said they're often up at the Colony.'

'I asked the hackers to look into the Climate Change Collective,' said Eileen, 'but we decided that it was low priority, so I told them there was no hurry. I'll get them to put a rush on it.'

Looking slightly shamefaced, Penny said, 'That was my fault. Have I been a total bossyboots?'

Eileen gave her a quick hug and assured her, 'You have, but I love you anyway. If it wasn't for you being an old bossyboots, we wouldn't know where to find the man in the video and we wouldn't have definitive proof linking Chauncey Greig to Cowrie Robert.'

Penny gasped then staggered to her feet, saying, 'I almost forgot! Our exciting news is that we have the name and address of the man in the video. And in further developments…drrrrrrr.' She mimed a drumroll. 'I have a photograph of an invoice from Chauncey Greig to Cowrie Roberts with a note on it about Juniper.'

She read out Davey Neish's name and address, explaining that she, Fiona and Eileen had been to visit the dog breeder and had only just made it out of there without buying two of the cutest wee pups in the universe.

Jim stood and dragged his chair away from Sandra Next Door, before sitting down again and saying, 'At the risk of another clap round the back of the head for not mentioning things, I've heard the name Neish before. Chancer Neish is the big drug kingpin that Fergus worked for. It was Chancer's men that Fergus got banged up.'

Penny frowned at her boyfriend. How did he know so much about Fergus and some gangster? Jim clocked her giving him the side-eye and felt his stomach drop. Shit. He only knew about Chancer Neish because Donald Wallace had told him. When he wore a wire. When he bugged gangland central for Dunderheid. When he was told not to mention anything to anyone. Bugger. He ran through about forty excuses in his head. None of them worked.

'How do you know so much about Fergus?' asked Fiona.

Jim did a double take. He hadn't expected trouble from that direction.

'I spoke to Dunderheid earlier, to tell him about Frankie.'

'When did you do that?' asked Gordon. 'You've been with me all day.'

Jim hesitated. He was about to drop a grenade that would explode in his pal's face, but sometimes sacrifices had to be made for the greater good. And he needed to create a distraction.

'It was when you were trying on jodhpurs in Inverurie.'

'I knew it!' roared Sergeant Wilson, her eyes bulging with fury. 'You burst my jodhpurs, you hairy-arsed wee penis dribble. Where's my riding crop? I will flay you alive and nail your skin to the police station door as a warning to others.'

'Martisha, calm down,' warned Mrs Hubbard. 'Gordon, dearie, this might be a good time to make yourself scarce.'

Gordon didn't wait to be offered a second chance. He bolted from the room and headed for the bar, apologising as he almost bowled over another guest in his haste.

'You took that too far,' Fiona told Sergeant Wilson. 'You know full well he'll replace your jodhpurs.'

'He already has,' said Jim, trying to ignore the large, guilty stone that had just settled in the pit of his stomach. 'There's a new pair in the boot of my car. I'm sorry, Fiona. I shouldn't have opened my big mouth.'

Penny regarded Jim with narrowed eyes and mouthed, 'I'll speak to you later.'

She was no fool. She knew he was hiding something.

'Davey Neish, then,' she said, trying to steer the conversation back to the case. 'You think he might be a relative of this Chancer guy? I'm glad we didn't go to visit him.'

'Where did you go?' Jim asked, hoping that she'd done something equally dreadful that he could use as a shield to deflect the barrage that was coming his way later.

'We went to Chauncey Greig,' said Penny. 'And before you get annoyed, Fiona came in with me and we pretended to be inviting them to bid for a security contract. They didn't suspect a thing.'

'How did you see their invoices?' asked Sandra Next Door.

'Told them I needed the loo, searched the boss' office and picked the lock on her filing cabinet, of course. For the head of a security company, Amanda Wilkerson doesn't take her own security very seriously. That lock took me less than thirty seconds to open."

'La, la, la, not listening,' said Sergeant Wilson.

Ignoring her, Penny held up the photograph of the invoice she'd taken earlier then zoomed in on the note.

'It says "Cowrie to tell Juniper laptop is extra and will be supplied on receipt of payment." You were saying something about a laptop when we came in.'

'Layla's laptop is missing,' said Mrs Hubbard. 'She had it in the taxi on the way back to Bennachie, so whoever killed her must have taken the laptop.'

'It must have been someone from Chauncey Greig, then,' said Penny. 'Which means that Davey Neish or the woman killed Layla, and probably poisoned the well while they were up there.'

'They'd have to know about the well and avoid all the Colonists to get to it,' Sergeant Wilson pointed out.

There was a long silence while everyone pondered what this could mean. Whatever theories they threw at this case, there always seemed to be a sticking point – a small fact that nudged everything else out of place, like there was something they were missing.

'Well, if there are no other ideas,' said Sergeant Wilson, 'Weasley, give me your van keys.'

Somewhat taken aback, Fiona said, 'I know Gordon's gone to the bar, and I fully plan on having a few vodkas myself, but none of us will be driving tonight. The snow had just started when we arrived, and we'll be digging ourselves out if this weather keeps up.'

'When God was giving oot brains, did she take one look at you and decide to do something useful like invent the appendix instead? Or did you turn up on the wrong day? Maybe it was Vestigial Tail Wednesday. Have you got a vestigial tail, Fred? Because I've never seen one of them. Get your arse out and show me. And while you're at it, give me your van keys so I can go and ask Anni-Frid Mackie why her dead friend's friend posted her a memory stick, and she didn't tell a single bugger about it.'

Anni-Frid Mackie, thought Penny. Something had been bugging her about that woman. She had seemed so nice, then turned so nasty. Going by the contents of her study, she had a lot to tell. They just needed to somehow get through to her. Get past the defences. They needed leverage. There had to be something…unless…no, surely not…

'I'm coming with you.'

Sergeant Wilson crossed her arms and assumed her best scowl.

'No, you're not, Fanny Features. You stay here with Wank Boy and help him catalogue his semen, or whatever it is he does when he thinks you're not looking.'

Penny was having none of it. She was supposed to have spent the past three days in the spa and going on romantic walks with Wank Boy…erm…Jim. They were going to hand everything over to Dunderheid tomorrow, no choice about that, so she was determined to see this through as far as she could.

'I bloody am coming. I've just remembered where I've seen Juniper before. It was among Anni-Frid's papers. She's clearly up to her neck in whatever's going on here, and if I'm right, we won't just find the memory stick at her house; we'll find something else as well.'

'What?' asked Sergeant Wilson.

'I'm not telling you unless you let me come.'

'Fine, but I'm driving. You're a boring driver.'

'In that case,' said Jim, 'I'm coming too. If you two get stuck in the snow, you'll need a push.'

'Fuck's sake,' Sergeant Wilson grumbled. 'Okay, but nae getting your knob out and trying to trick me into thinking it's the gear stick.'

Half an hour later, they were striding through the car park, heads down against the wind and snow, Sergeant Wilson jabbing the key fob to facilitate their speedy refuge from the hoolie that was snatching at their coats and biting their ears.

So intent were they on reaching the van that they didn't notice the figure slip out of the hotel behind them, a phone clutched to its ear. So harsh was the wind that the words "I know where they're going" were snatched away almost before the figure could utter them. So cold and dark was the night that no ordinary soul could imagine a deeper chill, an inkier blackness.

'But sometimes other people can be devoid of imagination,' whispered the figure as it slid into a sleek Audi and watched the departing van.

CHAPTER 23

Penny found herself mesmerised by the almost impenetrable flurry hurtling towards her. In the warm cocoon of the van, with Jim and Sergeant Wilson silent beside her, it was as if they were in the centre of a storm that was hurling itself relentlessly at an invisible forcefield. This was fanciful, she knew. It was the sort of thought she'd had as a child, when her brain had revelled in finding fresh and wonderful ways to make sense of a world that could be weird and scary yet gloriously magnificent, often all in the same moment.

She wondered at Sergeant Wilson. In the glow of the satnav, the woman's face was fixed in a determined grimace, a dogged gargoyle hunched over the steering wheel, peering into the tumult as though by sheer force of will she could see the road beyond. Utter madness, thought Penny. The five miles or so to Kemnay may as well have been five hundred. Not even the Proclaimers could complete this journey.

'Should we turn back?' she asked hesitantly.

'Wank Boy, check Penny's suitcase tonight,' said Sergeant Wilson without so much as a glance sideways.

'Aye, okay. Eh, what am I looking for?'

'Her big girl pants. I think she must have left them in Vik.'

They drove on in silence, the Sergeant keeping the van at a steady pace as tyres rumbled through slush. The council gritter had been out before the first snowflake fell, scattering a liberal helping of salt and sand in an effort to keep Aberdeenshire moving; however, it would not be long before snow defeated grit and the road became impassable. Penny could only hope that they would finish with Anni-Frid in time to make it back to the hotel because she didn't think the woman was the type to welcome unexpected overnight guests.

Kemnay seemed to suddenly appear, as if someone had parted the curtain of snowflakes to reveal the stage, its set a long line of streetlights guiding the audience past neat rows of squat houses, their lit dormer windows like large glowing eyes glaring disapprovingly at the foolish travellers below. The ability to see the road ahead seemed to lift Sergeant Wilson's spirits and she was soon happily cursing the satnav as she drove up narrow alleys and down dead-end streets.

'I'm starting to think this thing doesn't like me. Penny, what did you do to it? It's like Lord Lucan shagged a deaf bat and this was the result.'

'It would probably help if you followed the instructions instead of thinking you know best,' said Penny. 'Anyway, Lord Lucan didn't get lost, he disappeared–'

She stopped and poked Sergeant Wilson hard in the stab vest.

'Have you been watching conspiracy videos on YouTube again? Because I'm not helping you search the old people's home for Elvis a second time.'

'Och, that was when Doc Harris gave me the wrong painkillers for my back. Although, saying that, I'm starting to think we've more chance of finding him than the Old Manse. Aye, Elvis, nae Doc Harris. I could probably find Doc Harris with a dowsing rod, the amount of beer the bugger puts away. Where are we, Penny? Are we nearly there yet?'

Penny looked around, trying to recognise any landmarks from her first journey, a task made harder by the dark and the snow. Everything looked so different. Quite twee, in fact. Here was Kemnay Chip Shop and the village hall, then to their left the High Street, a name which implied more than a couple of hairdressers and a farm shop, but such was the beating heart of Kemnay.

Eventually the satnav reached a detente with Sergeant Wilson and routed them back to the main road, then out over the bridge towards Fetternear. They were only seconds from civilisation, but already the streetlights were a faint glow behind them, and the snow was once more closing in.

Just beyond the bridge, Penny guided the Sergeant to a cut in the trees, where the Old Manse stood, a solid silhouette behind the harsh halogen glow of the security lights that had activated as soon as they drew near. The sound of their footsteps on the gravel drive was muffled by the layer of snow that blanketed the grounds from house to gate. The escaping heat from the house had melted it into a treacherous slush on the stone steps by the front door, and they approached with caution, pressing the old-fashioned brass doorbell then carefully stepping back to safer ground.

Curtains were pulled back in the bay window to their left and Penny could see Anni-Frid, hands shielding her eyes from the light indoors so that she could view her visitors before she decided whether or not to answer the door. Penny couldn't blame her. It was almost 9pm on a night where only the foolhardy or desperate would venture out. Certainly, neither the time nor the conditions for uninvited guests. Nevertheless, Anni-Frid must have recognised Penny because the curtain was pulled back into place and a few seconds later the door was unlocked.

'What do you want?' Anni-Frid asked, holding the door open just enough for them to see her face.

Ooh, we're not pulling any punches today, thought Penny. All your research and a nice cup of tea please, you rude cow. She held that thought, however, as Sergeant Wilson stepped forward to take them out of the starting gate.

'Is Fergus MacQuoid coming oot to play?' asked the Sergeant, holding up her warrant card. She jerked a thumb in the direction of Penny. 'This one here figured it out. Can we come in or are you just going to stand there all night looking like someone pissed on your polenta? Aye, I'm middle-class too. I know what a quinoa is.'

'Keen-wa,' murmured Jim.

'Never heard it. Back in your box, Wank Boy. I've got this.'

Anni-Frid seemed to sag, her fingers clutching the edge of the door for support; then, heaving a deep sigh, she stood back and gestured for the trio to come in.

'He's in the living room,' she said, waving a hand towards the room where she, Fiona and Penny had taken their coffee the day before.

Fergus was standing by the fireplace, arms crossed defiantly and feet planted firmly apart on the tasteful, hand-woven hearth rug. Yet his eyes darted nervously about the room, as though escape was still an option. It really wasn't, thought Penny. Sergeant Wilson had sat on far larger men than him, gleefully bouncing up and down until they pleaded to be led to the safety of a police cell.

She was about to offer some words of reassurance, but the Sergeant was once more on top of the situation, her people skills testing the boundaries of effective communication.

'Sit down, Bigfoot. We haven't come out in this weather to report a sighting of you. We just want to talk. Aye, you talk, we listen. You can start by explaining what the fuck you're doing here.'

'How did you know?' asked Fergus.

'Fanny Features here reckons you were hiding in the downstairs toilet yesterday, when she and Fred visited.'

'Fred?'

'Aye. Fred Weasley. Married to George. Do you not know your own family, man?'

'Fiona,' said Fergus. 'Is she okay?'

'Other than fretting about her brother who ran away like a

big cowardy yeti? She's fine. Now, enough havering and answer the question.'

'I thought I was going to be arrested, so I came here,' said Fergus.

'And?' prompted Sergeant Wilson.

'That's it. Annie put me up until things calmed down.'

'And gave ye a good bath too. See whatshisface here?' The Sergeant pointed at Jim. 'Imagine he was full of beans, and I punched him, right in the belly, and the beans went everywhere. Because that would be good fun, aye?'

Jim gulped and said, 'No!'

'Aye, it would!'

'No, it wouldn't because I'd punch you back, and God knows what would come out of you. Stingin' jellyfish, black treacle, people who write could of instead of could have, Satan's minions.'

The Sergeant held up a warning finger and said, 'Those last two are the same thing. You're not allowed repeats.'

'Shut up, both of you,' snapped Penny.

'I was only going for a spill the beans scenario,' Sergeant Wilson huffed.

Penny turned to Fergus and put her hands together in supplication.

'For goodness' sake, will you please just tell us everything, before Anni-Frid kicks us out again.'

'Call me Annie,' said Anni-Frid, shuffling her feet uncomfortably. 'I'm sorry about before. When you mentioned Fergus, I got nervous and just wanted you out. Everybody, please sit down and I'll make us all some tea.'

'It's not that herbal shite is it?' asked Sergeant Wilson.

'Normal tea,' said Annie, as she headed towards the door. 'If you manage to keep a civil tongue in your head, I might even give you a biscuit.'

'Chocolate ones?'

'KitKats.'

'You won't even know I'm here.'

Fergus slumped into one of the armchairs and Penny, Jim and Sergeant Wilson took the sofa opposite. He ran a hand through his hair, now clean and brushed, and began his story.

'I met Layla like I said, and she introduced me to Annie and her wife. Cheryl's down in Glasgow showing some paintings at the moment, so she doesn't know about any of this. Layla and Annie studied journalism together and they were looking into firms hired to run social media disinformation campaigns and the like to change public opinion. Cybertroops, they're called.

'An outfit called Team Kastor was hired by a British company called Juniper. Layla wondered why an investment company would want such a service, so she started digging. She dug too hard and stirred things up. The company also had some shady people to do land deals around Bennachie. We joined the road protestors in the Colony so she could be close to the story yet stay out of sight. When she was killed, I realised they must have found her and I might be next, or I might be arrested as chief suspect, so I came here.'

'You missed a bit,' said Sergeant Wilson, then in answer to Fergus' questioning glance, she added, 'Brenda Claire.'

'Ah, you know about Brenda. She worked at Juniper and, after Layla approached her, she put a recording device in the boss' office. What she got was pure gold, but it made Layla worried for Brenda's safety. There was a lot of talking in code, and Layla and Brenda were fairly sure two of the bosses were planning to bump people off. In fact, Layla was convinced they already had. She thought one of their victims might have been her own father. He was a geologist at the university doing a lot of work for private companies.

'Anyway, we hid Brenda at the Colony. I tried to get her to come here with me, but she was convinced that she'd be safer staying where she was. She said that even if somebody knew about Layla, there was no way they'd make the connection to her. Is she okay?'

'No,' said Penny. 'She was poisoned. They all were. It

looks like somebody tainted their water. Claire…Brenda's critical in hospital.'

Fergus frowned and rubbed a hand through his hair again, asking, 'Do you think they were after her?'

'Don't know,' said Sergeant Wilson. 'It seems like overkill. Not a pun, by the way. I suppose if they tried to make the first death look like an overdose, they might try to cover up a second one by poisoning everybody, but you couldn't be sure of killing the right person. It would be easier to go after Brenda on her own. I think Brenda was right when she said nobody connected her to whatever Layla was doing. I also don't think anyone knew she'd gone off to visit the farm with Layla. The killer must have been lying in wait for Layla coming back, but they wouldn't have been expecting two people. You can make one death look like an accident, but two bodies is just cluttering up the place.'

'How did they even know Layla was at the Colony?' asked Fergus.

'Aye, we'd all like an answer to that,' said Jim. 'I think I might have it.'

Penny turned to look at him, surprised.

'I can figure stuff out, you know,' he said. 'What's the one thing all the Colonists had in common?'

'Oh, oh, I know this one,' said Sergeant Wilson. 'Foreskins. Or was it the smell? Or the tents? No, I'll go with the foreskins. Final answer and nae takesie backsies.'

'Aye, well,' Jim chuckled, 'I wasn't going to say that, but you're on the right track. The charity gave them clothes and food, but they also gave them mobile phones, remember?'

'Good thinking,' said Penny. 'If you want to find out what somebody is up to, check their mobile phone. The charity would have received all the bills and seen Layla's calls to the farm. They could even have put a tracker on her phone. But surely they'd have done the same with Brenda's.'

'Brenda didn't have a phone,' said Fergus. 'She was so

spooked by what she'd heard at Juniper that she went almost completely off the grid.'

Penny considered this for a moment, then said, 'What about Annie? They'd have seen Layla's calls to Annie.'

Fergus was on a roll. He smiled and clapped his hands, as if struck by a thought.

'She never mentioned Annie to the Colonists. She called her a friend from near Inverurie, and the only time she contacted Annie was to meet up for coffee, at which point she'd pass on information in person.'

'And another thing,' said Penny. 'I wonder if, when the farmer told her he was hacked, Layla realised how easily her phone and computer could be compromised, and that's why she didn't hotspot to it from the taxi. If Brenda didn't have a phone, she couldn't be traced and that's why she volunteered to go to Inverurie to post the memory stick. Talk about overkill. What a stramash for the sake of a golf course.'

'Memory stick?'

Fergus' expression was one of innocent puzzlement.

'What memory stick?'

'Ah, there's something I should tell you,' came Annie's voice from the doorway. 'The memory stick arrived this morning, and if I'm right, this whole thing goes way beyond a golf course.'

CHAPTER 24

Annie laid the tray she was carrying on a side table. All eyes were on her as she passed around steaming mugs of tea. Sugar and milk came next, with chocolate biscuits last. Her guests had left her chair by the fire free, and before she sat, she threw another log on top of the embers, causing sparks to flash and drift upwards. Penny eyed the expensive rug and wondered if she would have dared place such a thing so close to those sparks. Annie caught her looking.

'Better a burnt rug than a burnt carpet,' she said.

A loud rumble from outside forestalled any further discussion. Within seconds, it was followed by a flash that, even through trees and curtains, briefly filled the room with a stark, white light that elicited startled oohs from Penny and Jim.

'Thundersnow,' said Fergus. 'They said on the news that we'd have it tonight. It's quite rare, apparently.'

'Somebody go out there and tell the weather it's fucking March,' grumbled Sergeant Wilson, seemingly unmoved by the phenomenon.

She was carefully gnawing the chocolate off a KitKat

finger, attempting to leave only the strip of wafer. It put Penny in mind of a bad-tempered squirrel.

'The memory stick, Annie,' Jim prompted.

Annie nodded and reached beneath her chair, dragging a laptop across the carpet and placing it on the coffee table that separated her from her visitors. With a knowing smile, she went to the fireplace and ran a hand behind the monstrous mantel clock, producing a small, black object.

Deftly slotting the memory stick into the laptop, she said, 'The key to it all. I figured nobody would find it by accident if I hid it there. The cleaner refuses to dust the horrible clock. She says it's an abomination.'

Crouching down, she pressed a button and the screen came to life, asking for a password. Some typing, a few clicks, and she spun the device around to face Penny, Jim and Sergeant Wilson. Fergus stirred from his chair and came to kneel by them. Four faces moved forward, illuminated by the LCD glow like children in Christmas adverts, anticipating something wondrous and magical.

Layla's legacy was a patchwork of folders, each labelled with different facets of her investigation.

'These are the transcripts of the conversations Brenda recorded,' said Annie. 'It's quicker to read them than to listen. We agreed that Rupert is Elaine Bear, the energy minister and the woman tipped to be Scotland's First Minister. I have some emails upstairs where it's clear that there's contact between her and the head of Juniper, Sir John Gatenby. Cassian Abery's his right-hand man. Just read. Hopefully it'll make sense.'

RECORDED AT JUNIPER HQ, LONDON, 13th JANUARY

Sir John Gatenby: Ah, Cassie. Come in. How was Chamonix?

Cassian Abery: Not bad. We got off lightly. Some of the other

French resorts haven't had enough snow this year. Where are we on Project Tartarus?

Sir John Gatenby: Good news. This isn't public yet, so keep it under your hat. They're going to drop the plans for the dual carriageway at Benaitchee..Benakey..how do you say it? I can never remember.

Cassian Abery: Ben-a-hee. We've had the place in our sights for years, Johnny. It should be burned into your synapses by now. Although good news, indeed. And the Minister for Transport?

Sir John Gatenby: Taken care of. Rupert's having him moved to Employment and his replacement is some womble with green credentials who'll go along with building the road somewhere less…sensitive.

Cassian Abery: Despite the cost?

Sir John Gatenby: Let's not forget that the cost is to the taxpayer. Whereas we are in a position to provide more *personal* incentives. Walls have ears and all that jazz, so least said the better.

Cassian Abery: Agreed. Where are we with phase two?

Sir John Gatenby: There have been a few delays. Our visitors are likely to be reluctant to move. We may have to incentivise there too. There has also been a small hiccup in the geology department, but I'm taking care of it.

Cassian Abery: Taking care of it?

Sir John Gatenby: Again, least said etcetera. Rupert will be speaking with the First Minister this week. We may have to use leverage there, but let's try diplomacy first.

Cassian Abery: The wheels are fully lubricated and in motion, then. Too soon for a celebratory snifter?

Sir John Gatenby: You read my mind, old chap.

RECORDED AT JUNIPER HQ, LONDON, 27th JANUARY

Cassian Abery: What the hell, Johnny? Uluru? Please tell me this isn't going to link back to us.

Sir John Gatenby: Untangle your knickers, my friend. A mere bump in the road.

Cassian Abery: Nothing outsourced to Burke and Hare?

Sir John Gatenby: There may have been some pressure to swing the report in our favour. A few unsavoury photographs, that sort of thing. But it really was suicide. Seems the man couldn't live with his lies, not that his family will ever know, of course. I had Auld Jock ensure everything was cleaned up, including the suicide note.

Cassian Abery: We have the report, so that's something. I've had one of our people speak to the others. They've heard about Uluru's death, and it's brown underpants time. They'll support his report. How's Rupert getting on?

Sir John Gatenby: Things are looking up there. The First Minister was somewhat reluctant to rock the boat, but the consequences of continuing with current government policy have been explained. Something to do with her shady dealings with the Russians. We pay handsomely to know where the skeletons are hidden, so I've left it with Rupert.

Cassian Abery: The media side is coming along nicely. Influence-peddling, they call it. A few articles have fed through to the mainstream and some of the social media posts are gaining traction.

Sir John Gatenby: Did you go with the Israeli company?

Cassian Abery: Yes, Team Kastor. Hired them before Christmas. Their ethics are more flexible than the British company and they can create thousands of social media profiles at the click of a few buttons, which is quite impressive. All we need to do is keep drip feeding the public, and we should see things move in our favour. Patience, I'm told, is the name of the game.

Sir John Gatenby: Good. Hearts and minds being captured on all fronts, and the science will be sorted. Fancy a few at the club?

Cassian Abery: You read my mind, old chap.

RECORDED AT JUNIPER HQ, LONDON, 6th FEBRUARY

Sir John Gatenby: Do you have a moment?

Cassian Abery: Come in. I was just about to tidy up and go home. Have to spend some time with the wife and kids occasionally. You look worried, Johnny. What's up?

Sir John Gatenby: There's a journo sniffing around. Some pinko from the left-wing press asking awkward questions.

Cassian Abery: What? How on earth? They're digging about us? How would they know?

Sir John Gatenby: Someone might have blabbed, I'm afraid.

Cassian Abery: Damn. Who?

Sir John Gatenby: They approached the Finance woman. Whatshername. Brenda something. Asking about suspicious payments to that Israeli bunch we hired.

Cassian Abery: Team Kastor. The journalist must have been digging into them and found out that we're a client. How much do you think they know?

Sir John Gatenby: Can't be certain, but hopefully not much beyond us being the client.

Cassian Abery: How did you find out? Did you speak to Brenda?

Sir John Gatenby: Not yet. I wanted to discuss it with you first. Saira in Press Office has a cousin who works for the newspaper. The cousin got a bit loose lipped after a few drinks and let something slip. Saira came to me.

Cassian Abery: How much could Brenda have told them?

Sir John Gatenby: She's not exactly in the loop, is she? Probably seen a few unusual payments but knows better than to ask. Which is why I doubt the journalist knows anything other than that we hired Team Kastor. And we can probably explain that away, or at least do some damage limitation on it. It's not illegal, after all, so it's a non-story on its own.

Cassian Abery: Still, if she got suspicious, Brenda could have poked around. The money trail is buried deep, but it is rather a large amount to make untraceable.

Sir John Gatenby: I think we need to consider our options. Do we talk to Brenda or…

Cassian Abery: Burke and Hare?

Sir John Gatenby: Burke and Hare. And the journalist?

Cassian Abery: Let's take this discussion out for dinner. I fancy a steak. Rare. I'll call the wife on the way

'I know it's a lot to take in,' said Annie. She scrolled back and pointed to the screen. 'This bit, where they say "Our visitors are likely to be reluctant to move. We may have to incentivise there too. There has also been a small hiccup in the geology department, but I'm taking care of it." Layla and I thought the visitors might be the Colonists. We wondered if they were planning something to make them move on once the news about the road became public.'

'Oh, they've done that,' said Sergeant Wilson. She explained about the poisoning of the water and how Brenda was critically ill, concluding, 'That confirms our thinking. For whatever reason, it was no longer convenient to keep the foreskin-ninjas around. What about the taking care of the geologist. Layla's dad?'

Annie nodded. 'We think so. We think he's Uluru – the big rock in Australia. It looks like they pressured him into writing a geological report and he must have left a note explaining. Except this Auld Jock got rid of it. Maybe a corrupt police officer?'

Jim thought back to the name and telephone number that Donald Wallace had given him and quietly whistled.

'Bugger me with a badge and truncheon. Aye, he's a corrupt cop. And no, Penny, don't ask me how I know. I just do, okay.'

'I can sort you out there,' said Sergeant Wilson.

'You know how Jim knows about Auld Jock?' asked Penny.

'No, I was offering the services of my truncheon. What about this Burke and Hare? Cowrie Robert? Chauncey Greig?'

'Whoever they are, it doesn't sound like good news for Brenda,' said Fergus. 'Is somebody guarding her at the hospital, Sergeant Wilson? If she's in there under her real name, she might be in danger.'

Sergeant Wilson produced her phone from under her protective vest, stared at the screen and twisted her mouth into a snarl. She noticed the others staring.

'I was in a bad mood the day I set up the facial recognition. Does anybody have Dunderheid's number?'

'You work for him,' said Penny, a note of disbelief in her voice. 'You must have his number.'

'Aye, but I deleted it. Every time I scrolled past his name, I got this weird feeling in my fanny and stomach. Like something was melting and trying to batter its way out at the same time. Easy came up with a load of nonsense about me fancying the boss, but I told him it's just the thrush reacting to stress. I deleted the man's number, and it hasn't happened again. Until I saw him on Tuesday. That's why I've been ladling on Easy's old athlete's foot cream. It's like chopped liver and mashed tatties down there.'

Jim had heard enough. He could stick a hand up a cow's backside as easily as the next guy, but even he had limits. He reeled off Deed's number, returning Penny's curious look with a short shake of the head. Don't ask, it said.

There was another low rumble outside, louder than before. Penny could almost feel it in her belly and, despite the messages from her brain that all was well, her heart quickened instinctively. While the Sergeant dialled, they all counted Mississippis, waiting for the flash. It came on the fourth Mississippi, the bright flicker coinciding with an expletive from Sergeant Wilson.

'No service,' she said. 'I'm telling you, there's something not right about this weather.'

Annie, Jim and Penny checked their phones. No service.

Not to be defeated, the Sergeant asked, 'Can I borrow your computer, Annie? I can phone him or email him on that.'

She was, nevertheless, trounced, trumped and soundly thrashed by technology.

'No Wi-Fi either. This is your fault, Penny. It's like

Christmas all over again. You don't have any secret passageways and diamonds, do you Annie?'

Penny shuddered at the memory of Sergeant Wilson being shot and her own close shave with death.

'Don't say that,' she said.

There was another clap of thunder, followed by a flash. Only two Mississippis this time. The storm was coming closer.

Fergus looked uneasily at Annie.

'All we need now is for the electricity–'

There was a click then a sudden, eerie stillness as the background hum of daily life stopped, and the lights went out.

Nobody moved. Beyond the pool of firelight, the room was cast into deep shadows. The clock ticked. The log crackled. The wind whipped through the trees outside, rushing and tearing at them, thrashing leaves and branches into a roaring frenzy, the absence of electricity serving to amplify those sounds that sat just within the conscious mind.

The log settled in the fire. Crash, thump, whoosh. Penny squealed and clutched Jim's hand.

'Power cut,' said Jim, stating the obvious.

There was a collective release of breath, an easing of tension and Sergeant Wilson muttered, 'I don't know how we'd have coped without you to keep us right.'

Ignoring her, he said, 'I'll walk down to the end of the drive and see whether the streetlights are still on in the village. If the power's on there, we could knock on a door and ask for help.'

'I'll go with you,' Fergus offered. 'It's wild out. Branches will be coming down. Better that there's two of us.'

'Aye, away you go and just leave us little women to cope on our own,' said Sergeant Wilson as the men went off in search of a torch. 'Shall I put your pipe and slippers in the fire?'

A few minutes later, the front door slammed, caught by the wind, and Penny watched from the window as a flash of lightning illuminated two tall figures, hunched against the wind, striding through the snow.

It felt strange, thought Penny, being down to three. Less safe, even though her rational mind knew there was nothing to worry about. Annie must have felt it too because she stirred into action, rooting through cupboards and drawers in search of candles, even though firelight would do. Lordy, the fire. We don't want to let that go down.

'Do you have enough wood for the fire?' Penny asked.

'Not in the house,' said Annie, handing her the torch she had just unearthed from behind a bottle of gin in the tall cabinet. 'There's some outside, just by the back door. Watch your feet, though. The step will be slippy.'

Penny couldn't dispel a sense of deep foreboding as she slowly walked through the hallway towards the kitchen. Her hackles were up. The back of her neck tingled as if from the gentle brush of a stranger's hand. An evil stranger. The thought came unbidden, even as she tried to throw her rational brain into gear. Another boom reverberated outside. Her heart fluttered in her throat. Dark, old house, she told herself. You're spooking yourself out.

She crept on, focusing on the beam of light from the torch, ignoring the strange shadows. Her hand touched something soft, and she moaned, the sound coming involuntarily from deep within her throat. A tensing of the stomach and a low, hard exhalation of air. Bloody hell, calm down. It's a coat. Everyone keeps a coat by the back door.

The door was locked. Of course it was. The old-fashioned, iron key was cold, the lock stiff and unyielding. Penny clasped the torch between her teeth, using two hands to turn the key while the light bounced off walls, the door, the sink. With a clunk, the lock gave, and she struggled outside, her hair blown flat against her scalp by the howling gale, the snowflakes clinging to the strands then quickly turning to slush against her skin.

It was black out here, blacker than a coal cellar full of

serial killers. Stop it, Penny. There's snow. You can just about make out the snow. She flicked the torch back and forth, searching for the woodpile. It was there, right next to her. Even through the wind, she could smell the earthy tang of chopped logs. Bugger, there was no basket. She would have to do this by hand, a few at a time. Already her fingers were frozen, almost welded to the torch in an icy grip. Icy grip? Stop it, Penny.

Anxiety gnawed at her, driving a sense of urgency. With the torch once more between her teeth, she lifted armfuls of logs, throwing them through the door and into the warm house, where they lay on the doormat in a puddle of icy slop.

Again and again, she tossed logs, two, three, four at a time, until she was exhausted. The others must be wondering why she was taking so long. She shivered and pictured the cosy fireside, five friends drinking tea while they waited for the storm to clear, discussing theories about the case and eating KitKats softened by the heat from these very logs. Penny smiled and straightened, relieved that her task was done. The return trip was always quicker, and hopefully less creepy, than the way there.

Careful to avoid the slippy step, she placed a foot on the threshold, and that was when she felt it, the gentle brush of a stranger's hand against her neck.

'Shh. Don't make a sound. Careful. We wouldn't want any accidents, would we?'

CHAPTER 25

Gordon switched off the television, threw another log in the stove then sat back, beer in hand. Ah, this was the life. Fiona wasn't mad at him, Mrs Hubbard was having her post-happy hour snooze on the sofa and Sandra Next Door was flitting happily around the lounge, having borrowed a cloth from the bar so that she could "dust properly."

Beside him, Eileen said, 'Sedlay moyu loshad. Saddle my horse. Ya idu v sportzal. I am going to the gym.'

'You must be getting good by now, if you're saddling horses,' said Gordon.

Eileen removed her earphones and tapped her tablet.

'Ya khoroshiy lyubovnik. I am a good learner. Ya oblizyvayu drugiye yazyki. I like other languages.' She beamed at him, adding, 'Thanks to Old School Russian Online, I can do all the manly sports and tell the hackers to plough the fields. Do you want to try it?'

'Nah, I'm fine with holding back Fiona's hair after she's had a few too many vodkas. I've been thinking about the case. Have you heard back about the charity yet?'

Eileen quickly checked her emails and shook her head.

'No. I don't think there's much more we can do for now. Poor Layla.'

Fiona, who had taken full advantage of the hotel's free newspaper service, laid down the crossword that had caused her so much angst for the past hour and shuffled her armchair closer to the pair.

'It might be worth going through what we have again,' she suggested. 'Maybe, now we know more, we'll have a different take on some of the earlier stuff.'

Eileen opened the folder where she'd stored the emails, screenshots, search results and ephemera they'd collected over the past few days. She opened the various items and slowly scrolled through them, giving her friends time to read the long messages from the hackers and the land records.

Sandra Next Door watched her friends, heads together over Eileen's tablet. Having rendered the lounge dust-free, she was considering a raid on the housekeeping cupboard. Her goal was the big vacuum cleaner. She briefly wondered whether Mrs Hubbard would be annoyed that she'd visited the mecca of free teacakes and shampoo without taking the older woman with her, but quickly dismissed the idea. Mrs Hubbard was taking up a whole sofa. Sandra Next Door hadn't been able to dust said sofa, and this irked her. Mrs Hubbard didn't deserve teacakes and shampoo. Anyway, the housekeeping cupboard would also be packed with more interesting things, like cleaning fluids and a vast choice of cloths, so Mrs Hubbard and her teacake thieving fingers would only be a distraction.

'I'm going to the housekeeping cupboard,' said Sandra Next Door, keeping her voice low so as not to wake the old lush on the sofa. 'Does anybody want anything?'

There was no reply. Her fellow Losers were engrossed in whatever was on the screen.

'What are you lot doing?' she asked, prodding Eileen with a bony finger.

Eileen rubbed her arm and looked up, pouting.

'I thought you'd agreed – no poking. We're looking through the stuff we've gathered on Layla.'

'What's that?' asked Sandra, jabbing a knuckle into Fiona this time.

Three vodkas had numbed Fiona to both the woman's intractable nature and her armour-plated fingers.

'Eileen took a photo of the photo of Layla and Anni-Frid getting their journalism award. The one Penny stole... borrowed from Anni-Frid's house. It's not perfect, but you can zoom in now.'

They had enlarged the certificate but had learned nothing more. Eileen used a finger to move the photograph around, focusing first on Layla's face, then Anni-Frid's. Despite the slight blur, their joy was evident, radiating from lips, eyes, the flush in their cheeks.

'Hold on a minute,' said Sandra Next Door. 'Move up. Left a bit. Zoom out a touch. Stop there.'

She was looking intently at a face in the background of the photograph. Something about it...no, she'd have to go and clean things while she gave it some more thought.

Fiona took the tablet from Eileen and peered closely at the screen. She zoomed out, then in again. Something about the face in the background. Something familiar...

She gasped and closed the application, going back to the main folder.

'Here,' she said, opening an item and jabbing the tablet so hard that Eileen grabbed it from her. 'That's the photo Penny took earlier.'

They looked at the screen in silence for a moment, putting the pieces of the puzzle together, before Gordon said, 'Remember when Sergeant Wilson was horrible?'

'Which time?' asked Fiona.

'Ooh, ooh. Was it the time she told me that if I didn't give her some of my chocolate, I'd be sentenced to a year of police raspberries?' asked Eileen.

For a moment, they all thought back to Eileen lying on the

pub floor, Sergeant Wilson on top of her, joyfully threatening to blow raspberries on her belly until she handed over a milk chocolate caramel delight.

'Was it the time she confiscated my good sweeping brush on the grounds that it was a lethal weapon?' asked Sandra Next Door.

'Well, you were threatening to wrap it round her head at the time,' Fiona pointed out.

'She told Easy to cut down my tree to rescue Mary and Len's cat. A cat that came down of its own accord and proceeded to shit in my begonias. Again.'

Sandra Next Door's expression was quite murderous.

'No,' said Gordon. 'When she was horrible to me earlier and I went to the bar. I swear that's the person I bumped into just outside the lounge door.'

'Shit,' said Fiona. 'If that's the case, Penny, Jim and Sergeant Wilson are in real trouble.'

Gordon was no longer listening. He already had his phone to his ear. He dialled, waited, swore, dialled again.

'Hello? Dunderheid? It's Gordon. I think we have an emergency.'

CHAPTER 26

Penny felt hard metal press into her side and froze.

'What do you want?' she babbled. 'I don't have any money. I'm just a visitor here. I have a nice pair of earrings that Jim gave me for Christmas. You can have those, if you like. Although, I don't know if they're real gold and the stones are just cubic zirconia.'

'What I'd like,' said the woman behind her, 'is for you to shut up. We're going inside the house, where we'll find all your little friends. You'll tell me what you know, and I'll decide what to do with you. Simple as that. Now, move.'

Penny didn't argue. She assumed that whatever the woman had pressed into her was a gun, and self-defence classes aside, she didn't fancy her chances against a bullet. There was also the matter of the little bit of wee that had escaped when she'd felt the hand on her neck. And her trembling legs. And the fact that any minute now her heart was going to explode out of her mouth.

She instructed her legs to co-operate with her brain and slowly moved through the doorway, kicking the pile of logs on the floor to one side. It was only once they were in the kitchen that she realised there was more than one person behind her. The heavy tread put her in mind of a man...two men. She started to turn, but a sharp jab in her side made her stumble, and she faced front again, trying to keep the wavering torch beam steady as she placed one tentative foot in front of the other, all the while thoughts of Jim racing through her mind. Was he back yet? Would he know this woman? He seemed to know all sorts of other things he hadn't told her about. Who were the people behind her? Why were they here? What would they do if she just stopped? Refused to go any further?

Penny came to a sudden halt in the hallway.

'Move,' the woman instructed.

Penny didn't move.

'I said get moving.'

Penny stayed perfectly still, save for the uncontrollable tremor that refused to listen to any pleas from her brain to leave, vacate, desist.

She heard the heavy tread behind her, and the gun was removed from her side. For an instant, she felt relief. For an instant. Before she was forced forward by a blow to the kidney. It came hard and fast, like a cattle prod. A sharp jab that pitched her into the wall, face first. Her nose collided with a picture frame, and she felt liquid, hot and thick, rush into her open mouth. The pain in her back was radiating outwards now and her legs gave way. She vomited before she hit the floor, her mouth filled with a sour mix of tea and blood. There in the dark, she lay on the floor in a pool of her own liquid, writhing and gasping for air through a burning throat and a nose choked with the very stuff of life, while she watched the torch skitter across the floorboards towards the living room door.

A muffled voice.

'Is that you, Penny? Are you okay?'

Anni-Frid. Penny's chest heaved as she tried to suck in enough air to shout, to warn her friends. But there was no time. The man, the beast, whoever he was, stepped forward and grabbed her hair, dragging her through the stinking mess towards the door. He didn't hesitate. He lifted her head and pulled her behind him as easily as one might drag a small, reluctant dog on a leash. Penny's feet scrabbled on the floor, slipping and sliding through the ooze, vainly seeking purchase on layers and layers of smooth varnish. She could hear the door now. Click. A faint orange light from the fire finding its way through the gap, throwing the stairs into relief.

'Penny? Oh my God.'

Anni-Frid's scream was a piercing wail, slicing through the gloom, tearing into the darkness beyond.

The man was relentless. He didn't falter or lessen his grip. He took the final few steps and shouldered open the door, hauling Penny onto the carpet and dropping her unceremoniously in front of the coffee table. Penny rolled over and lay looking up at him, this behemoth. She could see that with his other hand, he had taken tiny, doll-like Annie by the throat and was lifting her, up, up and away, tossing her towards the window. She hit the table in front of the curtains, sending pot plants tumbling hither and thither, soil erupting and clay shattering around broken stems.

Penny watched, coughing and heaving in lungfuls of air, as Annie slid to the ground, where she lay still and unmoving. Where was Fergus? Where was Jim? Through stinging tears, she could see figures moving into the room behind the giant. The woman and the other man. He was shorter. She blinked, trying to clear her sight, squinting in the firelight to make out her adversaries. The other man and the woman looked familiar. Holy cannelloni, it was Blake, the guy from Chauncey Greig. And the woman…she had seen her in the photograph, with her long blonde hair, next to the older woman. This meant that the younger one must be…his boss, Amanda bloody Wilkerson.

Wilkerson and Blake stood in the threshold, letting the big boy take care of business. And business it was. He hadn't uttered a word and his face was cold and impassive. He had dealt with Penny and Annie expediently, throwing them aside as if they were mere obstacles in his path. However, for all coolness, his calculated violence, he had failed to spot one thing – the angry woman clutching the packet of KitKats, poised behind the living room door.

Sergeant Wilson didn't move. She didn't catch his eye, merely biding her time until she could pounce. Penny shook her head then nodded to the door, the tiniest of movements to indicate that a bigger threat was coming. By her side, she formed two fingers into the shape of a gun, hoping that the Sergeant would understand the significance. The woman gave nothing away, not so much as a a twitch of the eye or a blink to indicate that she'd seen Penny's signals. She stayed in that semi-crouch in the shadows, sweat glistening on her brow, reflected firelight glittering in her eyes.

'Amanda Wilkerson,' Penny croaked, trying to ignore the ache in her back and belly.

The least she could do was distract everyone. She didn't know if Sergeant Wilson was going to spring into action, but perhaps Jim and Fergus would return to make this an even fight. Except the gun would never make for an even fight. She had to get Wilkerson to put the gun away.

'I don't understand,' she said. 'Why are you here?'

Wilkerson moved into the pool of light from the fire and pointed the gun directly at her. The woman was dressed in an expensive dark ski jacket and a pair of boots that Penny, even through the fug of pain, recognised as Jimmy Choo Timberlands. Wilkerson looked down the barrel, her smug smirk never reaching her eyes.

'Because you know too much, you and your friends, Penny Moon. All that talk of memory sticks and Anni-Frid Mackie. It only took a little google to find out who she was and where she lived. I thought we had everything we needed with the laptop, but no. Turns out Layla wasn't the only journalist in town. Then there's poor little Brenda, all sick and poisoned in hospital. I might even get a bonus when we finish *her* off. I'll do you for free, of course. The same for the man and the three women at the hotel. But we seem to be missing two. Where are the man and the ugly woman who came with you?'

'If you stop pointing that thing at me, I'll tell you,' said Penny.

Wilkerson smiled and raised the gun a little, her finger tightening on the trigger.

'Wait.' Penny's voice cracked as she shouted the single word. She drew in what she supposed would be one of her last breaths and asked, 'How did you know to look for us here? How did you even know we were a threat?'

Blake stepped up beside Wilkerson. He withdrew the Losers Club card she had given him earlier and said, 'You told me where you were staying. It was just a matter of getting to the hotel before you and doing some surveillance, which wasn't hard. Amanda blends in very well with the posh crowd.'

Penny shook her head, trying to make sense of how they could have even known that she was investigating in the first place. How had they connected her with Layla's murder?'

'I don't understand. I said I was looking for security. How did you know I was looking into Layla?'

Blake waggled the card, saying simply, 'Losers Club.'

'You and your friends have been all over Bennachie asking questions,' said Wilkerson. 'I killed Layla to keep things quiet, not make more noise.'

'You killed Layla,' Penny muttered. 'Cowrie Robert paid you to kill Layla.'

'They were just the middlemen. Juniper paid me.'

'But why? What about a few farms is worth killing over?'

'Oh, I can think of a few hundred million reasons. Fracking. There's gas under there worth a bloody fortune. Whatever they're paying us to kill you, Layla and her dad, it's peanuts compared to what the hedge fund will make.'

Penny's mind was buzzing, questions tumbling over each

other. If she was going to die, there was a chance that Sergeant Wilson would live. Whatever she asked, it had to be the most important questions, the ones that the Sergeant could use to put these bastards in a fucking hole forever. She still didn't understand how Wilkerson knew about the Losers being on Bennachie, but there was bigger fish to fry here - the ones at the top.

'But fracking's banned in Scotland,' she said.

'Not if you have the First Minister in your pocket,' Wilkerson crowed. 'A little nudge to Andrea Forglen to move on, a few generous donations to pave the way for her successor and a disinformation campaign to make fracking more palatable to the public. But I seem to have become distracted. Where are the man and the ugly woman?'

'Call me fucking ugly again, and I will rip off your head and shit down your neck,' came a growl from behind her.

Wilkerson, Blake and the giant turned, but it was too late. Sergeant Wilson had already launched herself at Wilkerson and made a grab for the gun. She landed on the woman with the full weight of her body armour, a backside that no longer fit police trousers and a packet of KitKats. Wilkerson, with her skinny jeans and preening narcissism, stood no chance against the woman who single-handedly broke up bar fights in Bertie's pub every weekend. This woman who, through sheer force of will and a pair of handcuffs with Stevie Mains' name on them, kept an island in a state of quiet obeisance. She was human nature at its most terrifying. A no holds barred, self-declared bitch with a badge.

Before either Blake or the giant could react, Wilkerson was on the ground and the two women were engaged in a struggle for the gun. With her free hand, Wilkerson scratched and clawed at the Sergeant's face. The police officer ignored her, keeping her full weight on the woman while she tried to grab her arm, which was waving in the air, the gun swinging this way and that, keeping Blake and the giant at bay as they ducked to avoid it.

Wilkerson must have realised that help couldn't come because she allowed her arm to be pulled down. At the same time, she pushed the gun away from her, trying to slide it along the carpet to Blake. He made as if to rush forward but backed off in the face of a flying plant pot. Penny looked to her right, beyond the fighting women, and gave a small cheer for Annie, who had regained consciousness and was now in charge of a pottery arsenal.

The giant looked too and seemed about to charge towards her when a heavy metal urn hit him on the bridge of the nose.

'Sorry mum,' shouted Annie, staring after the object she had just thrown.

It split and a cloud of ash burst into the air, covering the giant's face. He howled, momentarily blinded, and stumbled backwards, colliding with Blake, who had taken advantage of the brief pot throwing reprieve to once more make a play for the gun.

He wouldn't have made it. Ignoring the pain and the urge to vomit again, Penny rolled onto her knees and lunged at the weapon, her fingertip hooking around the trigger just as Blake reached for it. She snatched it away, watching the two men come crashing to the ground in a haze of ash.

Wilkerson was now using two hands, hissing and spitting as her nails raked the prone woman on top of her. Sergeant Wilson had clearly had enough. She levered herself up and punched the woman hard in the mouth, then shuffled forward, grabbed Wilkerson's arms and planted her knees on her shoulders. The woman's lower body was thrashing and kicking as she tried to buck the Sergeant off, but it was to no avail. Sergeant Wilson leaned forward, pinning Wilkerson's arms to the ground and let her wriggle.

Penny had barely ever seen a real gun, much less shot one, but she had watched enough cop shows to instinctively hold it two handed. The giant was untangling himself from Blake now and his eyes were on her. Penny felt another bit of wee warm and then cool in her knickers. If he got to her, he would break her in two. She reared backwards, coming to land on her bottom, her legs splayed out in front of her. A quick glance to her right told her that Annie was out of pots, her mother's urn seemingly having been the last. The giant stumbled to his feet and staggered towards her, his hands out like every movie of Frankenstein's monster ever. Come on, Penny. Stop thinking of movies. You can't let this guy get near you.

Then everything slowed, caught in a single pivotal moment. To Penny, it felt like she was watching the scene from a few steps away. She heard the whish-whoosh of her own breath, in and out, the screams of Annie as she picked up the plant table to throw at an oncoming Blake, the muffled yowls of Wilkerson from somewhere beneath Sergeant Wilson's crotch. The trembling left Penny's body, and the pain receded, leaving only her, the gun and the monster. In that millisecond, that blink of an eye, she shifted the barrel and pulled the trigger. Then watched the bastard drop.

Time speeded up again. It was almost too fast as everything happened at once. The giant lay clutching his kneecap, blood pooling under his leg, the table crashed into Blake's head and two figures appeared in the living room doorway.

'What the actual…,' said Fergus. 'Was that a gunshot?'

'Aye, just leave the little women to fight off the bad guys, you pair of twisted cockrings.' Sergeant Wilson looked down at the face between her legs. 'And you can shut the fuck up as well.'

Blake was struggling to his feet, blood pouring from a large gash on his forehead. Fergus didn't pause to ask any further questions. He strode over and punched Blake hard on the side of the head, sending the man straight back down. This time, Blake didn't get up, and Fergus walked away without a backward glance. Job done. The man could be dead, but job done.

Jim had rushed straight to Penny's side and wrapped his arms around her.

'Are you okay? The lights were on in the village, so we're

not cut off. We're going to be fine. Penny, can you hear me? Penny? Fuck, we need an ambulance.'

Penny couldn't answer. She was in shock, quivering uncontrollably, her breath coming deep and fast. Too deep and fast. At the edges of her vision, a darkness was coming. It wavered and wobbled as Jim gently took the gun from her hands, and she welcomed it, this escape from pain. The last thing she heard before she passed out was Fergus.

'Sergeant Wilson, why are you sitting on Kendra Lawson's face?'

CHAPTER 27

Deed pressed his finger on the doorbell and kept it there, ringing and ringing. No reply. He glanced at the man beside him, watching as the officer raised the heavy, metal battering ram they called "the big red key," readying himself to swing it at the thick oak door. Just before he did so, the door swung open, and Deed nearly fell into the hallway.

'This is a welcome surprise,' said Fergus, 'and, believe me, I never thought I'd say *that* to a policeman.'

'Is everyone alright?' asked Deed. 'Are you safe?'

'Safe, aye. Alright, that's debatable. Nobody's dead, if that's what you mean, but it would be awful handy if you could call an ambulance or six. Come in and see for yourself.'

Deed gave the thumbs up to the armed response vehicle, then watched as it turned on the lawn and sped away, its thick tyres leaving deep tracks in the snow.

The front drive was bathed in the blue lights of half a dozen police cars, multiple officers in yellow high vis coats awaiting orders. Deed signalled to the three closest to accompany him, shouting at the others to get on the radio and call an ambulance.

The scene which met him in the living room was one of

carnage. A man appeared to be bleeding out on the carpet and another lay unconscious, while a young woman with a head wound stood guard over him, wielding a very large, very ugly clock. Jim was there, cradling Penny in his arms, and she too appeared to be unconscious. In the centre of it all was Sergeant Wilson, her bottom tilted towards him as she leaned forward, restraining a squirming blonde woman.

'Sergeant, why are you sitting on that woman's face?' Deed barked.

'If you're worried about her biting my fanny, sir, there's no need. I knocked her teeth out before I got on. It's okay, though. I lift every few seconds to let her breathe.'

As if to emphasise the point, the Sergeant leaned forward and raised her bottom a little, letting a small fart escape as she did so.

'Sorry, sir. Unintentional consequences of too many KitKats.'

Deed signalled to the uniformed officers to take over and Sergeant Wilson reluctantly got to her feet.

'Kendra Lawson, boss, otherwise known as Amanda Wilkerson, head of Chauncey Greig and admitted killer of Layla Hamdy, Ahmed Hamdy and whoever else. I suspect she also poisoned the well at the Colony, so you can add Dani to the list. She was up there posing as a Colonist, probably to get close to Layla or maybe it was just coincidence.'

'I think it was coincidence,' said Deed. 'One of my colleagues did some checks on the charity that's been funding the Colonists. It was set up by Cowrie Robert, although the people behind it were probably–'

'Juniper. Aye, I know them, boss. They've been bribing and blackmailing politicians and swaying the leadership election so they can get the fracking ban lifted. Cowrie Robert handled everything for them. Apparently, there's a lot of gas under those farms they bought and now the road isn't going anywhere near Bennachie, they want rid of the Colonists.'

Deed nodded. 'Yes, and it looks like Wilkerson must have

been posing as one of the Colonists to do just that, but she got a surprise. Somebody she went to university with was there. Someone who told her all about the story she was investigating.

'Your pals back at the hotel recognised her in the background of a photo, then they compared it with a photo Penny took at Chauncey Greig and realised that Amanda Wilkerson and Kendra Lawson were one and the same. Gordon remembered spotting her lurking outside the lounge at the hotel and called me. Good thing the ploughs have cleared the main roads. I came as quickly as I could.'

'You came faster than an incel wi' an invitation to the Playboy mansion…sir,' said Sergeant Wilson.

'Erm, thanks, I think.'

There was little more to be said. Deed sent officers upstairs to check for any more intruders. Unlikely as it seemed, should one come out of the woodwork after they'd left, he would see the sharp side of Superintendent Gilani. Downstairs had already been checked, but he took a torch and walked through the house to the open back door.

Nearly going backside over breast on the back step was one of his less dignified moments, but he survived to make a quick tour of the garden. The faint imprints of police boots, already filling with snow, reassured him that he was not the first to check the grounds. To the left of the front door was a woodpile, presumably the source of logs on the floor by the back door. Someone must have been out here fetching logs when the intruders forced their way in. Beyond the woodpile was a pair of storm cellar-style doors set low, at an angle to the ground. A padlock dangled from one of the handles and footsteps told him that this, too, had been checked. Nevertheless, Deed donned his gloves, opened the doors and, clasping the torch between his teeth, made his way down a ladder to the basement.

His predecessors had been checking for people. Deed was checking for something else. Sweeping his torch over the walls, he soon found it. The fusebox was modern, presumably updated when the fancy kitchen that he'd passed through a few minutes ago was installed. The lid was hanging open and he could see immediately that a large, red switch was down. The label beneath read "Main." Deed pushed it back up and was gratified to hear a small cheer above him as the lights went back on. Smiling to himself, he once more swept his torch along the wall until he found the basement light switch.

Now for phase two, he thought, standing in the centre of the room and turning slowly. He doubted that Wilkerson and her cronies would have bothered to hide it, but the thing would be hard to spot in this clutter. Deed doubted that Anni-Frid and her wife used the attic. All their unwanted worldly goods appeared to be stacked in this basement. Piles of boxes and stacks of old paint cans nestled against broken furniture, like a giant game of junk Jenga. Deed stepped carefully around the items, aware that one knock could bring the whole lot down, burying the item he was hunting. He reached a container labelled "Christmas" and breathed a little easier. On the lid sat a small, black box with an array of antennas protruding from the top. Beside it lay some discarded instructions titled, "Setting Up Your Signal Jammer."

He left the device untouched. Forensics may thank him for switching the lights back on, but they wouldn't thank him for messing with the evidence.

Deed walked up the steps and tried the basement door that led into the house. Locked. This must be why the intruders had lain in wait by the back door. With the fire being the only likely source of heat or light, eventually someone would come out for wood.

With a sigh, he climbed the ladder and made his way back to the house, just in time to hear the wail of ambulances making their way through the village.

CHAPTER 28

Garioch House Hotel was putting its best foot forward for the Police Scotland Bravery Awards. The red carpet was out, the press photographers were in place and a small surprise awaited some very special guests at the back entrance.

Deed stood at the rear of the hotel kitchen with Penny, Jim, Eileen, Mrs Hubbard, Gordon, Fiona, Sandra Next Door and Sergeant Wilson. The women glittered and sparkled in long dresses, and the men had dialled up the sex appeal several notches by donning kilts and full regalia. Earlier, Gordon had loftily informed his friends that, for once, going commando was not a problem.

He and Fiona had been in high spirits all day, following the arrival at the hotel of Fergus. Fiona was overjoyed because her brother had agreed to come back to Vik with them, for a while at least. Gordon was overjoyed because Fergus growled menacingly at Sergeant Wilson whenever she said something rude about people who ruin nice police officers' jodhpurs. The group had instantly adopted Fergus, welcoming him into the fold as one of their own. He in turn had told them how grateful and proud he was to call them his friends. He had, however, balked at attending the awards ceremony, joking that too many police officers in one room brought him out in a rash. Which was why he wasn't with them now, all dolled up in a busy kitchen.

The smell of venison in red wine sauce drifted from the cooking area, drawn by the cool draught from the back door. Pans bubbled and spat fat as cooks in white coats and hairnets clattered and shouted orders. Hardly the place for glitz and glamour, but this is where Deed had asked them to meet, so this is where they obediently came, half-anticipating a reprimand for their meddling antics. Instead, they had found champagne on ice and nine glasses.

'I don't know how we'll ever thank you,' said Deed, raising his glass to the group. 'A bravery award doesn't seem enough. Here's to you all. Slàinte.'

'Slàinte,' his companions echoed, raising their own glasses.

Deed smiled, glancing at Mrs Hubbard, who he suspected would appreciate his treat the most.

'Now, the even better bit. Thanks for bearing with me and slumming it down here. I know you're staying at the hotel, so you'll miss out on the full red-carpet treatment. That's why I've hired this for you.'

He opened the door to reveal a long, silver limousine glistening in the late afternoon sun.

'This is so you can arrive in style,' said Deed. 'Drive around for a bit, enjoy the ride, then roll up for your red-carpet moment.'

'Oh, dearie, dearie, dearie,' said Mrs Hubbard, so overwhelmed she was almost speechless. Almost. 'I can't wait to tell Al Cuppachino and Huge Ackman that I've been in a limo like a real Hollywood star. They'll be so jealous.'

'You didn't need to do this,' said Penny. 'It's awesome, but we're just pleased to have helped.'

'I needed to do something,' said Deed. 'Somehow you all managed to get further than I could, with the might of Police Scotland behind me, so as soon as the roads cleared this morning, I phoned Timmo's Limos.'

The roads were, indeed, completely clear. As quickly as it had arrived the night before, the snow had melted that morning. All day, Aberdeenshire basked in the glorious North East sunshine that around this time of day, turned its fields into a patchwork of deep greens and yellows. At breakfast, Sergeant Wilson had been heard quietly singing, 'Happy days are here again, the sky above is clear again.' Around the table, the other Losers had looked at one another, wondering if they should join in, before coming to an unspoken agreement that highlighting the Sergeant's good mood would only put her in a bad mood for the rest of the day.

Later, Jim had trundled Penny around the hotel gardens in a wheelchair. They stuck to the paths, the lawns being too sodden to support wheels. Not quite the romantic stroll Penny had envisioned, but it was good to be outside in the fresh air, spending time together.

'I can walk, you know,' she'd told him.

Jim had tutted disapprovingly.

'Only short distances, and until you stop peeing blood, the hospital says you're to stick to this thing.'

The doctors had reset her nose and scanned her kidneys, declaring no lasting damage beyond a lot of bruising, external and internal. Painkillers and makeup were getting her through tonight. She was also under strict instructions not to drink alcohol, but surely a few glasses of champagne didn't count.

Eschewing the wheelchair, Penny hobbled to the limo and carefully climbed in. Mrs Hubbard was already inside, cocktail menu in hand.

'They've got wee cans of sweetie juice, dearie. Shall I pour one for you?'

'Not right now, Mrs H. I'm not supposed to have any alcohol, so I'm pacing myself.'

'Oh, that's very sensible. In that case, I'll pace myself too. I'll just stick to the pornstar martini, the zombie and the Long

Island iced tea. That's tea, dearie. Are you sure you don't want one?'

Penny chuckled and strapped herself in. She leaned her head back against the cool leather and closed her eyes, thinking how lucky she was to have times like this with friends like these. The sound of happy voices drifted around her like a warm bath. She felt the weight of a body settling next to her and a cool hand squeezed hers. Jim. From the front of the vehicle, she could hear the faint drone of a radio presenter's voice.

"Shocking news today with the announcement from Elaine Bear's office that she is stepping down from the race to be First Minister and will be leaving politics. Ms Bear had been predicted to win and the reasons for her sudden change of heart are unclear. This leaves the way free for the three other candidates to..."

Penny opened her eyes and smiled lazily at Jim.

'What do you think will happen to her? Elaine Bear.'

'Dunderheid thinks it will all be swept under the carpet,' he replied. 'Says there are forces at play here beyond a single corrupt minister.'

'Another thing I've been wondering. If Wilkerson and Layla were old pals together, how did she not know that Lawson was Wilkerson?'

'Dunderheid said everything the woman told us was a lie. There was nobody left to contradict her. She knew *of* Layla and recognised her from uni, but they were never friends. Layla never knew her at all.'

Penny closed her eyes again and murmured, 'You still haven't told me how you knew so much stuff and why you knew Dunderheid's number off by heart.'

'I'll tell you tomorrow. You'll only get annoyed with me, so why ruin tonight. Anyway, I was hoping that after the ceremony, you and me could have a special wee get-together of our own.'

Jim turned to her, the twinkle in his eye quickly turning to a soft glow of pure love. She was sound asleep on a cocktail of champagne and painkillers. He didn't care about any awards or being hit over the head or running up and down secret passageways or people with guns. He cared about this woman here – this quick-tempered, fiery, bossy, courageous, warm, funny, caring, beautiful woman, who wore pyjamas with daft slogans, solved crosswords in a minute and knew all the lyrics to every Spice Girl song. They could pin a bloody gold bar on him, and it wouldn't come close to how proud he was that she was his and he was hers. She refused to marry him, but he was patient. He would get her up that aisle.

Penny stirred and whispered, 'Are we nearly there yet.'

'Aye, soon, darlin'. Soon.'

EPILOGUE

A stiff breeze blowing in from the North Sea chased Deed and Mac inside the Inversnecky café. Indoors it was warm, the diners cocooned behind steamy windows in a hubbub of conversation and clinking cutlery. The Thursday afternoon crowd was an eclectic mix of pensioners, students and rampaging toddlers, the latter being ignored by groups of chattering mothers.

Trippy lip waitress was back on duty, although she seemed happier today. Deed noticed that the nose piercing looked a little less inflamed, her eyes a little less sunken, her shoulders a little less bowed. He hadn't given her much thought the other day, so focused had he been on the case, and he felt a little guilty for dismissing her as merely the miserable waitress. Yet, whatever the reason for her misery, he was glad that her mojo had returned.

'I'm going to order the soup,' said Mac, passing the menu to Deed. 'The odds of her not spitting in it have improved.'

Deed didn't bother to look at the menu.

'Cheese and onion toastie. I need some comfort food after the morning I've had. Cowrie's been on to the Superintendent, complaining about me barging in and harassing his staff.'

'He's got a cheek,' said Mac. 'I suppose it's deflection, but the high heidyins will be wary of him, what with his reputation.'

'Gilani's got me writing it up. I'm surprised she hasn't come to you yet.'

Mac stretched and yawned, his shirt buttons straining apart to show a glimpse of hairy belly.

'Yet being the operative word. I'm knackered. When are you going back to Tayside? All these late nights are killing me.'

'I've got some news on that front,' said Deed. 'I'm not going back to Tayside. The DI in the Major Investigations Team is taking early retirement.'

'For that, read jumped before pushed,' said Mac.

'Aye. His Super's raging about them turning down what she calls "the case of the century," so the DCI is getting shuffled sideways to man in charge of ticking boxes and the DI has turned down a post in outer Mongolia.'

'Shetland,' said Mac. 'Although it's not as bad as it's made out to be. The place is louping wi' drugs and every year they set some poor lad on fire.'

'You're thinking of the film, the Wicker Man,' Deed chuckled. 'Shetland has Up Helly Aa, where they burn a boat. But you're right, it's a brilliant place. Just a bit far to come when your mother's in a care home in Huntly.'

'They've offered you the DI post?' asked Mac.

'My reputation precedes me, apparently,' Deed replied. 'But there's something else they want. They think the DI and the DCI were taking orders from someone else. I'm to be a regular part of the team, and at the same time, I have to find the rotten apple. Which is where you come in.'

'Me? I'm a lowly DS. What could the likes of Gilani and Detective Superintendent…'

'Galbraith.'

'Galbraith. What could they want with me?'

Deed glanced down to where his long, thin fingers cradled

the thick, heavy coffee cup. He hated these cups. The handles were always too small, the balance imperfect. Why did everywhere these days have these large cups with stupidly tiny handles? And don't get him started on places that served coffee in glasses. Because those things, those things…Deed could feel himself becoming quite curmudgeonly on the subject and wondered whether he should mention it to Mac, yet he knew he'd be deflecting. He felt guilty because what he was about to say would put Mac in a difficult position.

'You work for the Anti-Corruption Unit. I used to be ACU, although nobody knows that. I'm fairly sure you can put two and two together. We need someone who can discreetly support me. It will be business as usual on the front end, but we'll be looking for that bad apple behind the scenes. Only four of us will know – You, me, Gilani and Galbraith. It means extra work, though. We'd be going above and beyond.'

'Will I get a big, shiny sheriff's badge?' asked Mac.

'You'll get a shit ton of overtime once we're done,' said Deed.

He knew that Mac and Shona had been saving to build their own house. He also knew why and felt guilty about dangling this particular carrot.

A spinal injury had left Mac's wife struggling to walk. Shona managed well in their current home, with its lowered kitchen and the dining room transformed into a bedroom, but they were both hankering for a place where she didn't have to rely on a stairlift to get upstairs to the shower.

'It's not about the money, Mac,' Deed said. 'Damn, I shouldn't have said anything, knowing what you and Shona are going through. It will be a lot of extra work, probably for nothing but the satisfaction of getting the bad guy, and it will mean less time with your family. We can find another way to do this, so don't just say yes for the overtime. Think about it.'

'Watching you tie yourself in knots is almost worth saying I need another day to decide,' laughed Mac. Then he leaned forward, his expression suddenly deadly serious. 'I'm not daft enough to think that the overtime fairy is going to solve my problems, but aye, the extra will come in handy. Look at the state of the Met right now. There will be very good police officers feeling under the cosh because of some very bad police officers. I don't want Police Scotland to be like that. I don't want to feel ashamed to work here. Aye, not the Inversnecky. I haven't suddenly accepted a position as a bad-tempered waitress wi' a bogey collecting ring in my nose. I mean the bobbies.'

'Is that a yes?' asked Deed.

'Why do you think I took the job with ACU in the first place? Who are we looking for?'

'Auld Jock. We're to take him down, no matter how high he is.'

'Then bring it on, boss,' said Mac. 'Bring it on'

AFTERWORD

Thank you for reading my wee book. If you enjoyed The Juniper Key, please leave a review on Amazon and tell your friends. Losers Club book 6 will be out this summer and keep an eye out for the first DI Hunter Deed book. Auld Jock must pay.

You can hear more about my books and special offers by subscribing to my newsletter at www.theweehairyboys.co.uk and by following me on Facebook at Yvonne Vincent – Author. For a daily giggle, you can follow my Facebook blog, Growing Old Disgracefully. I'm the chatty one in the dressing gown who posts pictures of her dogs.

If you would like to know more about the original Colony on Bennachie, courtesy of Google and the Internet Archive, I have reproduced some text from 'Bennachie' by Alex. Inkson McConnochie, published in 1890. You can find it on my website - blog post The Colony on Bennachie.

Printed in Great Britain
by Amazon